Christie Barlow is the bestselling author of *A Year in the Life of a Playground Mother*, *The Misadventures of a Playground Mother*, *Kitty's Countryside Dream*, *Lizzie's Christmas Escape*, *Evie's Year of Taking Chances*, *The Cosy Canal Boat Dream*, *A Home at Honeysuckle Farm*, *Love Heart Lane* and *Foxglove Farm*. She lives in Staffordshire with her four kids, labradoodle and mad cocker spaniel.

Her writing career came as somewhat of a surprise when she decided to write a book to teach her children a valuable life lesson and show them that they are capable of achieving their dreams. The book she wrote to prove a point went on to become a #1 bestseller in the UK, USA and Australia.

Christie is an ambassador for the @ZuriProject alongside Patron of the charity, *Emmerdale's* Bhasker Patel. They raise money and awareness for communities in Uganda.

Christie loves to hear from her readers and you can get in touch via her website, Twitter and Facebook page.

🐦 @ChristieJBarlow
📘 Christie Barlow author
www.christiebarlow.com

Also by Christie Barlow

Foxglove Farm

Christie Barlow

O

OneMoreChapter

One More Chapter an imprint of
HarperCollins*Publishers*
The News Building
1 London Bridge Street
London SE1 9GF

www.harpercollins.co.uk

This paperback edition 2019

First published in Great Britain in ebook format by
HarperCollins*Publishers* 2019

A catalogue record for this book
is available from the British Library

ISBN: 9780008319724

Set in Birka by Palimpsest Book Production Ltd, Falkirk
Stirlingshire

Printed and bound in Great Britain by
CPI Group (UK) Ltd, Croydon CR0 4YY

For the four most awesome people in the world,
My gang, Emily, Jack, Ruby and Tilly.
I love you more xx

Chapter 1

Isla felt the tension bubbling away in the room the second she walked into the kitchen. She hovered by the table and watched her husband Drew slamming every drawer and cupboard door.

'Have you lost something?' she asked cautiously, wondering what the hell had gotten into him.

Drew spun round and held her gaze. His face was mottled crimson, the tendons in his neck bulging. Isla knew that look. Drew was spoiling for a fight, but she had no clue to why. It wasn't very often he reached boiling point but when he did there was little time to duck and take cover.

'It's always down to me, isn't it?'

Trying her best to keep composed against the sudden onslaught – after all, she wasn't a mind reader – Isla kept her voice calm, 'What's always down to you?'

Drew ran his hand through his hair numerous times in quick succession, a trait he had when he was agitated.

'Everything!' He threw his arms up into the air. There was an irritation to his anger, a sort of impetuousness.

His words packed a powerful punch. 'Everything?' she repeated.

'Yes, everything. Who's up milking the cows at ridiculous o'clock?'

Isla narrowed her eyes; this conversation had come out of the blue and wasn't one she was expecting at all. She didn't understand the point Drew was trying to make, and for a second she thought about reacting with a flippant comment about the fact that he chose to be a farmer. But instead she replied with a calm voice, hoping not to fuel whatever was burning inside him: 'And who's been up three times in the night feeding our son while I let you sleep? I'm shattered too, Drew, as well you know.'

'That's not in dispute, but then you go back to sleep whenever you can while I single-handedly keep the farm afloat.'

'The last time I checked, it was a joint effort.' Drew was beginning to agitate Isla now. How dare he?

'You've got it easy, Isla.'

Isla absorbed what he was saying, feeling shocked to the core. 'Are you serious?' The anger was now rising up inside her. How dare he accuse her of having it easy? Isla couldn't remember the last time she'd had a decent night's sleep.

'You swan around without a care in the world, breakfast at the teashop, lunch at the pub ... I'm not here to bankroll your social life.'

'My social life?' Isla's voice rose an octave.

'While I'm working every hour, you're frittering it away before it's even reached the bank.'

'So now I'm not allowed to see my friends?' she protested.

'That's not what I'm saying.'

'Goodness knows what you're trying to say.'

They held each other's gaze and Drew exhaled.

'I mean it Isla, I'm sick to the back teeth of bringing in the cash. If you carry on spending it faster than I am making it, then we might have to think about you getting a job.'

His words had an air of finality to them but there was no way on earth she was prepared to just go back to work yet, especially with the baby being so young. And they'd talked about her staying at home while the kids were little. He'd never mentioned this before ... What had gotten into Drew?

'If you want to talk about what's really going on here, without attacking me the second I walk into the room, I'm all ears.' Isla's voice was firm.

Drew stared at her, then yanked his coat from the back of the chair with anger before flouncing out of the door with a slam.

'Damn you, Drew Allaway,' she bellowed after him, close to tears.

Chapter 2

Perplexed, Isla stood in the window and watched Drew stamp across the yard. Of course, she knew the pair of them could squabble from time to time, just like any other married couple, but recently things seemed different between them. This argument seemed different. Drew seemed more distant, his sleep restless. Isla knew having a new baby in the house had changed the dynamics of their normal routine completely, and she knew Drew wasn't a huge fan of the baby stage – he preferred when he could chase them up the stairs, give piggybacks and hold a conversation with them. Maybe, he just felt he wasn't getting enough attention from her? But then, neither was she and surely that was what family life was all about?

'Who does the cooking, the cleaning, the washing ... takes Finn to school etc. etc.?' she mumbled under her breath, picking up her phone from the table and texting Felicity.

'Ask Rona to throw me in a Full Scottish. I'll be over in ten minutes.'

Almost immediately her phone pinged, 'You got it! Reserved your favourite table too.'

Isla knew she could always rely on Felicity. She was her best friend and Isla would be able to vent her frustration about this morning's argument without it going any further, even though her partner Fergus was Drew's right-hand man on the farm.

She was maddened by Drew's behaviour, even more so after she'd woken up feeling quite chirpy. Baby Angus had only woken once in the night for a feed, leaving her feeling refreshed, even though she longed for the time when he'd sleep straight through. Isla knew she would have to tackle Drew's mood again later and wasn't looking forward to that. As soon as she picked up Finn from school, the hours were hectic until bedtime. Every night was the same routine: preparing the tea, bathing Finn and Angus, followed by making the sandwiches for the following day, putting the children to bed ... the list was endless.

The more she thought about it, the more Isla became even madder with Drew. Who did he think looked after the day-to-day running of the farmhouse? Did he think the food miraculously appeared on the table in front of him the second he stepped through the door after a hard day's work on the farm?

'Get a job ... get a job,' she puffed to herself, reaching for the money pot on the shelf and tugging off the lid. She stared inside, shook it, then turned it upside down in bewilderment, but nothing fell out, it was completely empty.

'That's strange,' she muttered, knowing that's where Drew kept the cash. At the beginning of the week there had been over a hundred pounds stuffed inside.

Hearing Angus cry from his cot, she hurried upstairs and found the baby lying on his back kicking his legs. She reached inside and nestled him into her shoulder. 'You are all that matters,' Isla said softly. 'You and Finn ... us ... our family. We need to get to the bottom of what's up with your daddy and put it right.' Isla kissed his head lightly.

'Come on, let's go and see Auntie Flick at the teashop.'

Five minutes later, with Angus bundled up tightly in his blue woven blanket and strapped inside his pram, Isla began to stroll towards the teashop with her argument with Drew still very much on her mind. She spotted him and Fergus thudding their mallets into the new wooden fence panels they were erecting in the bottom field. 'Let's hope daddy comes home in a better mood,' she said hopefully, smiling down at Angus.

As Isla walked along, hearing the woodpeckers drumming against the trunks of the trees and the birds twittering away in the line of blush-pink-blossomed trees that adorned the pavement of Love Heart Lane, she hovered for a second, her nose pointing skyward, eyes closed as she inhaled the earthy spring smell, a perfume of rain, grass and soil. Isla immediately began to feel calmer. Spring had definitely begun to arrive in the small village of Heartcross.

There wasn't another soul in sight on Love Heart Lane, which Isla was thankful for, as after the argument with Drew she didn't feel much like exchanging pleasantries with anyone.

As she approached Bonnie's teashop, she saw Felicity and her mum Rona beavering away behind the counter. Rona

7

swiped Felicity with a tea towel as she pinched a cup cake and shovelled it into her mouth. They both burst into laughter.

Watching them, Isla felt a tiny pang of jealousy. They were both having so much fun and that's what she missed ... fun. The more she thought about Drew, the more she couldn't pinpoint the last time that they'd spent any quality time together or the last time they'd laughed, and she meant proper belly laughing when the tears rolled down your cheeks and your stomach ached that much, you could barely breathe or move ... which made her sad. She missed those times.

Isla manoeuvred the pram through the teashop door, the tinkle of the bell above alerting Felicity and Rona to her arrival.

'Rescue me, Isla,' Rona beamed. 'I've been up since the crack of dawn ... baking cakes ... savouries,' she swung her hand towards the delicious array of food displayed in the glass cabinets. 'Not to mention,' she continued, 'the homemade carrot-and-leek soup simmering in the pot, rounds of cheese-and-pickle, beef-and-mustard, and tuna-and-cucumber sandwiches stacked away in the fridge, ready for lunch time. Jacket potatoes prepped, and this one ... this one,' she wagged her finger at Felicity in jest, 'decides she's already eating the profits before we begin our day!'

Felicity allowed her lips to twitch into a smile and patted her stomach. 'When life hands you lemon cake ... and it was just looking at me! And never mind the profits,' she added. 'It's my waistline I'm more worried about. Since re-opening this place, it's expanding by the day.'

'So, stop eating the cake!' said Rona, laughing.

'Never mind you pair, I need rescuing myself this morning.' As a wave of emotion washed over Isla, her voice faltered and she suddenly felt like she was going to burst into tears.

Felicity and Rona exchanged a glance before Felicity quickly pulled out a chair and ushered her friend towards it.

'I'll get the tea ... always good in a crisis,' offered Rona, swiping her hands on her apron, leaving Felicity to take care of her friend.

'I need gin ... in fact a double ... no, a triple wouldn't go a miss,' said Isla, wiping an escaping frustrated tear away with the back of her hand.

Felicity parked the pram next to the table and gently ruffled Angus's soft hair before sitting down next to Isla.

Isla's eyes trailed after Rona as she disappeared back behind the counter, before she turned back towards Felicity. 'You've got a good life, haven't you?'

'I can't complain.'

Isla took a breath. 'Just now, I saw you both laughing through the window, having fun.'

'I have to admit,' said Felicity, 'I do like this time in the morning, the calm before the storm.'

Felicity took a swift look around the teashop that had once been her gran's life. Bonnie Stewart had converted the front room of her cottage into a tearoom for passing ramblers and had enjoyed every minute of it.

Since she'd passed away Felicity had taken over the running of the family business with her mum, Rona, and felt proud keeping her grandmother's business and name very much alive in the heart of the village. Being back in Heartcross was where Felicity belonged, and she couldn't ever imagine leaving it again.

'But what's this got to do with why you're upset?'

Isla blinked away more tears.

'Come on, Isla, it can't be that bad?'

'Drew and I had an argument,' shared Isla, feeling a tiny bit disloyal to him even mentioning it to Flick. Pouring herself a cup of tea from the pot and cupping her hands around the mug, she added, 'And I wouldn't mind, but I'd woken up in a good mood, until he decided to ruin my day.'

'What were you arguing about?'

'I'm not entirely sure. Out of the blue he suggested ... no, actually he didn't suggest, he insisted I was sponging off him, wasn't pulling my weight and that ... wait for it ... I need to get a job ... Can you believe it?' Isla rolled her eyes.

Before Finn was born Isla had worked at a nursery over in the town of Glensheil and Isla could remember quite clearly Drew suggesting that she should become a stay-at-home mum. They'd discussed it at great length. The children were only young once and neither of them wanted to put them in full-time child care or after-school clubs.

'He actually said that you were sponging off him?'

'Well, not in so many words,' admitted Isla. 'But basically, that I wasn't financially pulling my weight ...' Isla whispered, feeling the anger beginning to rise again. 'And how the hell am I going to fit a job in, as well as taking Finn to school, washing, ironing, shopping etc. etc., and wouldn't I just be working to pay child-care costs? It all seems ridiculous to me.'

'But it might be good for you to have a little independence, something just for you,' Rona said, overhearing a small snippet of the conversation. 'Maybe a little extra pocket money,' added Rona, sliding a Full Scottish breakfast towards Isla.

'Mum!'

'Sorry ... sorry, I was only saying,' she said, flinging her hands up into the air and quickly scurrying back into the kitchen.

'Oh, and then, he's decided I can't see my friends.'

'What?!'

'He said I spend too much time in the teashop and in the pub seeing my friends and wasting his hard-earned cash. What does he expect me to do? Sit in the farmhouse all day, staring at four walls and talking to no-one?'

'And you have no idea what's prompted this outburst?'

Isla shook her head, 'None at all.'

'And what do you feel about going back to work?'

Isla stabbed the sausage on her plate and poised the fork near her mouth. 'It's too soon ... look at him.'

All eyes turned towards Angus, who was making sucking noises with his mouth while fast asleep. 'I'm not handing him over to anyone, and we agreed I didn't need to work when I had the children. Financially it wasn't worth it, which is what makes this all so confusing.'

Felicity shrugged, knowing Isla's frame of mind was justified. 'And let's face it, in this small village there isn't much opportunity for work unless you travel.'

Isla looked horrified at the thought. 'Has Fergus said anything to you about Drew's moods?'

'Only that he didn't seem himself at the moment ... moody

... a bit short-tempered, but he just put it down to interrupted sleep, with a new baby in the house.'

'Believe me, his sleep is far from interrupted.'

Isla knew that they usually managed to communicate without conversations escalating into rows, but recently she did feel like she was treading on eggshells around her husband.

'I'm sure there's nothing to worry about, we all have off days and with a new baby in the house, however adorable, it must put a strain on things,' said Felicity reassuringly, as she reached over and squeezed her friend's hand. 'Now go and give your face a quick wipe and I'll get you a fresh pot of tea.'

'Thanks Flick, for listening to me.'

'Don't be daft, what are friends for.'

As Isla disappeared into the bathroom, Felicity stood behind her mum, who seemed deep in thought.

'Penny for them,' said Felicity tentatively, watching her mum closely.

'I was just thinking about this place, how many people have passed through that door over the years, how many cups of tea have been served and how many cakes have been devoured since Mum opened up all those years ago.' She smiled, 'I'm so glad you came home, and we are here ... together.'

'Me too,' replied Felicity, grabbing the tea towel and drying the plates on the draining board. 'It must have been thousands of cups of tea,' she said and smiled at her mum.

'And you best turn that sign around, otherwise we'll have no customers today.' Rona nodded towards the door. 'Is Isla okay?'

'She will be,' answered Felicity, walking towards the door.

As soon as she flicked the sign over to 'Open' and returned to the kitchen, the old-fashioned bell chimed to signal a customer. Rona was expecting an influx of customers today, as Julia who ran the village's B&B had informed her she was already full to the brim this week with a rambling club all the way from Staffordshire. As soon as the weather became warmer the teashop was always busy with hikers grabbing a packed lunch before setting off on their trek over the Scottish Highlands.

'I could murder a cuppa and a slice of toast.'

Immediately on hearing the voice, Rona screwed up her eyes and stared, 'No way! It can't be ...'

'Yes, way!' There in the doorway stood an elderly woman, wearing a shabby green coat that hung from her tiny frame, thick black tights that were laddered at the knee and a pair of chunky Doc Martens shoes. She looked around seventy, short and plump with her grey wispy hair wound up in a bun, and she had a huge beam on her face.

Immediately Rona stood up and flung her arms open wide and hugged the woman. 'Martha Gray! Where the hell have you been? How lovely to see you! It must be at least ...'

'Too long to remember,' interrupted Martha.

Felicity was scrutinising her mum's face for clues to who this woman was, as Rona turned towards Felicity.

'Martha ... it's Martha ... Isla's grandmother, your Grandmother Bonnie's best friend,' said Rona. But by the time Rona had jogged Felicity's memory, Martha was already kissing her on both cheeks.

'Oh my, so it is!' Felicity hadn't seen Martha since she'd moved away to London eight years ago. She'd lost a lot of weight and seemed shorter than Felicity recalled. She remembered her working in the teashop alongside her grandmother years ago.

'Well ... where is she?' said Martha, straining her neck and casting a glance over the teashop. For a second Felicity thought she meant Isla until she added, 'My old partner in crime, surely she hasn't taken the day off ... I've never known Bonnie Stewart to take a day off before.'

Rona felt puzzled and looked towards Felicity as the penny dropped. Rona swallowed a lump in her throat and took a deep breath. 'She's gone, Martha ... she's gone.'

'What, to the shops? ... Over to Glensheil for the day?'

Rona shook her head, 'No, Martha ... there's no easy way to say this ... Mum passed away.'

As the words registered, Martha slumped into a chair and unbuttoned her coat. 'I can't take this in ... when did this happen?' She gulped back a sob, dabbing her face with a tissue from her pocket.

'Christmas time,' replied Rona, taking her coat and hanging it on the stand in the corner of the teashop.

'I'm so sorry for your loss. I know I've not been around for a while, but she was always my best friend, you know. I had visions of us running riot over in Glensheil on my return. Surely the nightlife is still the same over the bridge ... gin nights and late-night parties are all the rage nowadays, knit and natter is so last year and way too tame these days.'

'I'm sure if she was still here, she wouldn't have hesitated to join you.' Rona couldn't help but smile. Martha had always had a zest for life and lived every day like it was her last. It didn't matter how long Martha was away from Heartcross, she always slotted straight back in, like she'd never been away.

Many years ago, Bonnie and Martha had been inseparable, thick as thieves, and for a short time Martha had worked in the old teashop alongside Bonnie when the rambling trade was soaring. The teashop was the last stop on Love Heart Lane before the stile that led the ramblers over the heather-wreathed glens, beautiful waterfalls and majestic mountains. The climb was one of spectacular scenery.

Martha had last been seen in the village last spring. It had been a fresh, crisp morning when a gang of ramblers had fallen into the teashop before a five-hour hike. And that's when Martha had met Walt, in the teashop over eggs benedict. Later that evening he'd changed his walking trousers and boots to an outfit of brown tweed jacket, checked shirt and navy corduroys ... and that had been that. After their very first date she'd stepped down as chair for the Women's Institute, had removed herself from the parish council and had done a moonlight flit with Walter, leaving Isla to report her as a missing person until a postcard had landed on her doormat all the way from a Caribbean cruise.

'Taken too soon,' Martha was muttering over and over again.

'Let me get you a coffee?'

'I need something stronger, I'm in shock.'

'Nothing changes,' Rona mouthed to Felicity.

'Sherry,' said Martha, 'or whisky?'

'Go and pour a whisky from the decanter on the sideboard,' Rona whispered.

Felicity nodded and soon returned with the amber-looking liquid in a crystal glass.

'Rest in peace, dear Bonnie,' Martha said, swirling the whisky around in the glass before necking it in one gulp.

Felicity winced at the very thought of the burn in the back of the throat.

'Does Isla know you are coming?' asked Felicity, taking a swift glance towards the bathroom door, thinking that Isla hadn't mentioned her grandmother's return.

'I thought I'd surprise her,' answered Martha.

They were both in no doubt that Isla would be in complete surprise, especially after Martha had upped and left the village to live life to the max.

Martha had been Isla's only real family left in Heartcross. Years ago, Isla's parents had emigrated to New Zealand, but Isla hadn't wanted to leave the village or Drew and had moved into the farmhouse with his family.

'You do know you have two great-grandchildren now, don't you?'

'What ... two ... When did that happen?'

Rona nodded her head towards the sleeping baby in the pram. 'When you were travelling around the world ...' said Rona, raising her eyebrows. 'Or doing whatever you've been doing all this time.'

'Two boys,' chipped in Felicity. 'Finn has a brother, Angus.'

Martha peered inside the pram, 'And this is him?' she said, overwhelmed.

'It sure is.'

'Well I never,' she exclaimed, reaching for his tiny hand.

As Isla stepped back into the teashop, she stopped dead in her tracks. Immediately Isla recognised the shabby coat, the Doc Martens boots. 'Gran, is that you?'

Martha spun round and flung her arms open to a rather flabbergasted Isla, whose jaw had dropped somewhere below her knees.

'It most definitely is!'

'Granny ... what the ...' She stopped to catch her breath. 'What are you doing here? And where's Walter, is he with you?' she asked, quickly scanning the teashop.

'Always asking questions!' Martha kissed her granddaughter on both cheeks. 'What do you mean, what am I doing here? I've come to stay. I knew you'd be so happy to see me.'

'Stay? How long for?'

'You know what, dear granddaughter, I think this time I'm back for good.'

Martha enveloped Isla in the tightest hug ever, and as Isla struggled to breathe she locked eyes with Felicity. Over her gran's shoulder she mouthed wearily, 'Back for good? Forget the tea, I'm in need of that gin.'

Chapter 3

Finally releasing her granddaughter from her tight grip, Martha swooped straight into the pram and planted a noisy, sloppy kiss on to Angus's head. His warm body wriggled in her arms as she inhaled his baby smell.

'Isn't he just the best? Angus ... what a good Scottish name. Me and you are going to be the best of friends.'

Isla felt perplexed. Angus was now three months old and there had been no interest from Martha for all that time, and suddenly they were going to be the best of friends? And never mind Finn, who was six years old and hadn't seen his great-gran in the last twelve months! And now she was acting like the doting granny. Of course, Isla had thought about trying to contact her when Angus was born, but she hadn't a clue where to begin. Martha wasn't one for staying in one place for a long time. From experience Isla knew her granny was of a flighty nature and goodness knows where she was or what was ever going on in her life. But one thing she knew for sure was that eventually she'd turn up again.

'I can't take my eyes off him,' Martha was still gazing adoringly at Angus.

Christie Barlow

'Gran ... are you serious ... are you back for good?' Isla had to ask, as the realisation of her words had well and truly sunken in after the initial shock.

Martha jerked her head towards Rona, 'You'd think my granddaughter wasn't happy to see me.'

'It's not that,' Isla added quickly, but the look on her face said it all. 'A bit more notice wouldn't go amiss. Have you booked into the B&B? Julia never mentioned it.'

Martha threw back her head and laughed. 'The B&B? Why would I want to stay there when I can stay with my beautiful granddaughter?'

The words hit Isla like a high-speed train. She wasn't sure if she could muster up enough energy to wait on another house guest, and what was Drew going to say? Not that he had anything against Martha, but his mood was a little unpredictable lately.

'I'll have to make up the spare room.'

'I can help with that,' said Martha, gently rocking Angus in her arms before safely placing him back inside the pram.

'And where's Walter? Will he be joining you?' asked Isla, suddenly panicking that there were going to be two unexpected house guests.

Martha shook her head. 'Walter ... He's long gone ... I've seen the last of him. One minute he was contentedly reading the *Daily Mail* like he did every morning with his cup of tea, and next he was on a train to Brighton, with that floozy Jennifer from the corner shop, and that was that.'

'What do you mean, that was that?'

'They ran off together ... and I took myself off on holiday

with Fred with the cash he'd forgotten to take from the kitchen drawer.'

'Fred ... who's Fred?'

'No-one important ... After Fred, I hooked up with Greg for a while, but he was old before his time and then ...'

'I think I get the picture,' cut in Isla in amazement.

'It doesn't matter how old you get, Isla ... love isn't guaranteed to run smoothly and that's why I'm here ...'

After this morning Isla knew that only too well. 'To mend your broken heart?'

'Far from it ... I'm back because I miss my family ... it's been too long ... and I can't keep gallivanting all over the world ... it's time I settled back down, and where else is home?'

Isla's eyes widened and she swallowed hard. It was tough enough looking after two small children, never mind a whirlwind of a granny who had more energy than all of them put together.

'I knew you'd be happy and welcome me back with open arms. Just think of me as a babysitter on tap, isn't that every new mum's dream? ... You won't even know I'm here.'

Isla had her doubts and swung a glance towards Felicity, who gave her a forced sympathetic smile.

'I've brought a few bits and pieces with me ... they are in the car.'

Everyone took a swift glance towards the Union Jack-roofed mini parked outside. It was bursting at the seams with Martha's belongings and it looked like her whole life was packed into the small car.

'Gran, that looks more than a few bits and pieces.' Isla felt herself physically slump. She'd already had quite a morning of it, and after the row with Drew she felt this was yet more pressure. Life was hard enough with two young children, a husband and a farm to run, and now there was another person thrown into the mix.

'And I can't wait to see Drew and Finn,' said Martha, quickly swerving the conversation.

'They will be pleased to see you, too,' said Isla, stumbling over her words while taking a gurgling Angus back out of the pram. She gave him a cuddle while she mixed the milk powder with water in his baby bottle and fastened his bib around his neck.

'He is just adorable,' Martha gave her granddaughter such a huge smile and Isla felt a little guilty for not sounding more welcoming, but things were tough at the moment and the argument with Drew was still fresh in her mind.

'Would you like one of these,' asked Martha, rustling in her pocket, whipping out a Werther's Original and waving it in front of Angus.

'Gran! He can't eat one of those ... what are you thinking?'

Martha chuckled, 'Relax! I was joking. As if I'd offer a tiny baby such a thing.'

Isla exhaled with relief.

'I think strong coffee is needed all round,' suggested Felicity. 'And you've not finished your breakfast,' she added, looking at Isla.

In the last few minutes Isla had completely lost her appetite. This wasn't the start to her day she'd anticipated, but as there was no such thing as a time machine, she would have to get through the best she could.

'You need to keep up your strength,' Martha's bony fingers wrapped around Isla's arm, 'there's no meat on those bones, and what's with the hair?'

Isla's hair was scraped back into a simple, easy-to-manage ponytail and she hadn't applied any make-up for weeks. Isla knew that since Angus was born she'd let herself go a little but she didn't need anyone reminding her of it, especially in public. But what was the point of having a full face of make-up and immaculate hair? Who was she trying to impress? As Isla thought about what her grandmother had just said, a slight niggle loomed inside her. Might this be the real cause of Drew's anger? Maybe he didn't find her attractive anymore. But immediately she knew she was being ridiculous; Drew had seen her at her worst and it wasn't as though he was dolled up to the nines every day in his dung-stained overalls.

'Any more compliments you fancy dishing out, Gran?'

Martha ignored her sarcastic tone.

'It's a good job I arrived back when I did.'

Isla wasn't one hundred percent convinced.

Chapter 4

Polly Cook huffed and puffed her way up Love Heart Lane towards the teashop, welcoming the light breeze sweeping through her hair. There hadn't been many hills to climb in London, and the only exercise she ever got there had been walking down the stairs to the cellar to change a barrel in the Chatty Banker, the pub she'd managed up until a week ago before she'd descended on Felicity. Or the 193 steps at Covent Garden tube station.

Everyone looked up as Polly pushed open the door to the teashop.

'That walk looks like it's done you the world of good,' said Felicity, knowing that Polly had tossed and turned all night.

'It did, it's so peaceful down by the river,' she said, slipping off her coat and draping it around the back of the chair.

'And who is this?' asked Martha, narrowing her eyes. 'I've not seen you around these parts before.'

Polly met the gaze of the elderly woman, but before anyone could answer, a loud squelchy noise erupted from inside the pram.

'Eww ... I can smell that from here,' said Felicity, looking into the pram and wrinkling her nose.

'Polly Cook, meet my gran, Martha Gray, who didn't make that squelchy noise, by the way.'

Polly grinned, 'Please to meet you.'

Martha gave her a smile and a nod of the head. 'Bad timing! I think this little fellow could do with a nappy change.'

Polly quickly took a step back, 'I'm not used to such little people.'

'Give him to me, I'll do it,' said Martha, stretching out her arms, much to Polly and Felicity's relief.

Isla looked alarmed, 'Gran, do you know how to change a nappy?'

'It's like riding a bike.'

Isla narrowed her eyes, 'I can't ever remember you actually riding a bike.'

'Fair point, neither can I,' grinned Martha, immediately retracting her hands.

'Give the wee fellow here,' offered Rona.

'I can do it,' said Isla.

'You take advantage of my offer,' insisted Rona, slinging the nappy bag over her shoulder and holding Angus at arm's length before disappearing towards the bathroom.

'And tell me more about you, Polly. What brings you to Heartcross?' asked Martha, turning her attentions back to Polly.

'Polly's my friend from London, she's staying with us for a while,' Felicity replied.

'I'm at a loose end, a very loose end. I've been made redundant and lost my home at the same time. I lived above the pub I managed, but it was sold to a new owner and they moved their family in and didn't need extra staff. That's why I'm here, a change of scenery, a break from the rat-race of the city, and I'm loving this beautiful village.'

'This is the best village, I've travelled in my time but always come home and ...' Martha turned back towards Isla, 'I can't wait to get settled in the farmhouse. Am I in my normal room?' she asked. 'You know, the gorgeous English rose room with the triangular floral bunting draped across of the wall. I do love good bunting ... and the view ... the view from that room is spectacular. Earth to Isla ... are you listening, you're in a world of your own.'

Isla's thoughts were tumbling over each other in her mind. A wave of worry ricocheted through her body at the very thought of going home with her gran in tow. The room was jam-packed full with baby paraphernalia. Anything and everything was stuffed in that room while the nursery was being decorated, which had been an on-going project for the last six months. Where were they going to put everything that her gran had packed into her car? She could visualise the disgruntled look on Drew's face if things needed to be piled up in their bedroom for a while, but hopefully his day had turned around and whatever bee he'd had in his bonnet had well and truly flown away. She didn't feel like getting stung by another argument today.

Rona came back into the room juggling a clean Angus, before passing him to Martha, who made a series of sniffing sounds towards him.

'Yes, he smells acceptable again,' joked Martha, cradling him in her arms.

'So, what's changed in this old village since I was last here?' asked Martha, now rocking a droopy-eyed Angus in his pram.

'Apart from being cut off from civilisation for a while when the bridge collapsed, everything else is just the same old, same old,' chipped in Rona, who was polishing the glass cabinets for the umpteenth time so far this morning.

'Ooo, I saw your video on Facebook,' trilled Martha.

'You're on Facebook?' Rona exclaimed, who struggled with any type of technology.

'Of course! You have to move with the times. It's all about social media these days, but I'm still getting to grips with Tinder ... I keep swiping the wrong way and having numerous undesirables match with me ... I mean, they must know they are punching above their weight.'

'Gran ... you are never on Tinder?' Isla couldn't hide her disbelief.

Both Felicity and Polly stifled their laughter, not knowing whether Martha was being serious.

'Tinder ... what's Tinder?' asked Rona, trying to keep up with the conversation.

'A dating app,' chorused the girls.

'You're on a dating app?' Rona's expression was now one of dismay.

'How else am I going to meet someone at my age? You should give it a go, Rona.'

'Me?' Rona's eyes widened and she brought her hand up

to her chest in horror. 'I can't think of anything worse,' she said, looking appalled.

'Don't knock it until you've tried it.' Martha raised her eyebrows and gave Rona a knowing look.

'I'm perfectly happy on my own and that's the way it's staying.'

'Not for you then, Mum?' teased Felicity.

Rona made a series of huffing and tutting sounds, 'It most certainly is not.'

'What about you? Have you ever tried dating on line?' Felicity turned towards Polly, who shook her head.

'But it would be nice to be rescued by someone ... in fact anyone,' she answered, all dreamy-eyed. She was still single after eighteen months.

'And what about your love life?' asked Martha, looking at Felicity. 'Who's the lucky man?'

'Fergus.'

Martha let out a low whistle, 'That's a turn-up for the books after everything that happened, and you running off like that all those years ago.'

Isla gave her Gran an impromptu shake of her head, knowing a random switch of conversation was very much needed.

'We've sorted everything out,' said Felicity, with a slight feeling of agitation rising inside.

'Didn't his wife die?' Martha wasn't for letting go of the conversation.

'They weren't married. Lorna passed away, leaving Fergus to bring up their daughter Esme.'

29

'Right ... come on now ...' said Rona, fidgeting from one foot to the other while looking out of the window, 'those ramblers will be on their way from the B&B, ready for their packed lunches, and you lot are under my feet.'

'Are you kicking us out?' asked Martha in disbelief.

'I am, unless you want to order anything else?'

'Well, I've been kicked out of some places in my time, but never a teashop!'

'First time for everything, Gran.'

'And are we still on for tomorrow night?' asked Felicity, looking between Isla and Polly. 'Girly night?'

'Absolutely,' they both chorused in unison.

Rona moved towards Martha and kissed her on her cheek, 'It is good to have you back.'

'And I'll see you tomorrow night too,' Martha snagged Felicity's eye as she walked towards the door. 'Girly night.'

Knowing Felicity would just want it to be the girls, Rona thankfully came to the rescue: 'How about you join me at the pub tomorrow night? I'll ask Aggie and Meredith will be behind the bar. We can catch up properly.'

'Good plan, and I'll show you how to use that app.' Martha winked at Rona who let out a chuckle.

'Behave,' she said, waving Martha and Isla on their way. 'I've no intention of joining the minefield that is social media. I'm quite happy with the way things are ...'

'We'll see,' Martha shouted over her shoulder with a wicked twinkle in her eye as the door closed behind them.

'She's a character and a half,' added Polly, with a grin.

'There is no doubt that one has lived life to the full and

is still doing so, by the sounds of it,' answered Rona. 'Isla has definitely got her hands full there.'

'Maybe you should have a think about that dating app. I can always sit here and set you up a profile over a couple of mugs of tea,' teased Polly, as Rona playfully rolled her eyes.

Felicity was still chuckling. 'Martha is right though, Mum, maybe you should put yourself out there, you have so much to offer and deserve to be happy.'

Shaking her head in despair, Rona coaxed her daughter towards the sink. 'Don't be daft, my life is perfect just the way it is, unlike Isla's, by the state she was in when she arrived today.' Rona gave Felicity an inquisitive stare, but Felicity brushed it off, not wanting to break her friend's trust.

'New babies, change of routine, tiredness, I'm crying just thinking about it.'

'It's an exhausting time for any woman, and you feel like you don't know if you are coming or going, you're someone's mother, wife, daughter, sister, grandmother ... you lose all perspective of who you are. Everyone wants a piece of you. I can remember screaming and crying *What about me?* Thank God for your grandmother's support, that's all I can say. Just be there for Isla. She'll be in need of a good friend. It's really not that easy.'

Her mum's words rang in Flick's ears. Maybe Isla was feeling the pressure a little? She didn't have any hands-on support; with Drew running the farm, looking after the children was left solely down to her. Felicity didn't elaborate on the conversation with Isla, but she was worried about her friend. Isla wasn't a moaner, she worked hard and saw the good in everyone and every situation and didn't like any sort of confrontation. Felicity knew she would have felt disloyal talking to her about the argument with Drew, which meant it must have really bothered her.

Hopefully a night with the girls tomorrow would pep her up a bit, but Felicity knew she was going to keep a closer eye on her.

Chapter 5

Through the kitchen window, Isla could see Drew and Fergus loitering in the yard in front of the stable block. Fergus was tapping on his phone with a goofy grin on his face. Isla felt an *aww* moment, followed by a tiny pang of jealously. Still in the first flourish of love, Felicity and Fergus texted each other at every opportunity. Isla missed that closeness with Drew. Those butterflies-dancing-in-the-pit-of-your-stomach-type moments seemed to have disappeared recently for them. Maybe once you had kids that's what happened, life just became life that didn't knock your socks off you anymore.

Isla scrutinised Drew's stony face. He didn't look like his mood had improved as he shovelled the muck into the wheelbarrow. Any second now he'd be taking a tea break and she was surprised he hadn't already popped his head around the door to ask who the Mini belonged to.

Martha had taken a stroll to the corner shop to catch up with Hamish, while Isla did her very best to make up the spare room as best she could. It felt like Martha had brought everything except the kitchen sink, and after the umpteenth trip to the car the Mini was finally empty, much to Isla's relief.

She switched on the kettle and placed two mugs on the table. Already she was feeling apprehensive about telling Drew that Martha was here to stay ... indefinitely.

The door swung open. 'No Fergus with you?' Isla asked, noticing him walking off towards the driveway.

'No, he's nipped to the teashop to see Flick. She's all he ever talks about just lately, Flick this, Flick that,' he said, slinging his phone on to the table and pulling out a chair.

'I think it's lovely that they are so in love, don't you?'

Drew looked up and rolled his eyes, 'Not if you have to listen to him going on about it twenty-four/seven.'

Isla felt saddened by Drew's reaction. In the past her friends had been jealous of Drew's romantic ways, snatching every moment he could with her, texting her from the fields at every opportunity, leaving presents and flowers on the doorstep. He made her feel like she was the only girl in the world. Isla poured him a mug of tea then began to unload the dishwasher, whilst wondering how and why things had changed so quickly between them.

'Where's Angus?' asked Drew. 'And no biscuits?'

Isla sighed and slid the biscuit barrel over in his direction. 'Angus is taking a nap and I see your mood hasn't improved much.' She turned her back on him and carried on putting the clean dishes away.

'What do you expect? A morning at market with hardly any produce sold.'

'What do you mean, hardly any produce sold?'

'Exactly what I said, and I noticed you did your usual trick of disappearing to the teashop to spend money, no doubt on a cooked breakfast.' His tone was accusing. 'When we have more eggs on the farm than we can actually sell, oh and thinking about it, you're paying to eat our own eggs, as we supply the teashop. It's ludicrous!'

Isla began to feel her hackles rise again. After the argument he'd instigated this morning she'd needed to let off steam to her friend. He worked alongside his best mate day in and day out, and unless she left the house she had no-one to speak to.

'You know what Drew, I woke up in a good mood this morning until you decided to throw your toys out of the cot about ... Actually, I have no idea what the argument was about.'

Unlike Isla, she was now spoiling for a fight, she could feel the hot flush rising up her neck and stood there, rooted to the spot with one hand on her hip.

Drew was staring straight at her before he snapped his ginger biscuit in half with dramatic effect and dunked it into his tea.

'I'm just sick to the back teeth of being the cash cow. I think it's time you thought about getting a job.'

There was that word again ... job. Isla just didn't understand where all this animosity was coming from.

'A cash cow?' Isla was astonished by his choice of words. 'So, let's just throw this out there, if I go to work who do you think is going to take Finn to school ... look after Angus, wash, iron, cook, run the house? Are you going to do all that? Or are we going to use the money from this job I'm meant to be getting to pay someone else to do the job I'm already doing at home?' She flung her arms up in the air, prompting Drew to answer, but before he had a chance she continued, 'And where's all the money gone from the jar? The emergency money?'

'Having breakfast at Bonnie's teashop is not an emergency.' His voice was firm. 'I've hidden it.'

If Isla had been a cartoon character, she would have had steam bursting from her ears with rage, 'You've done what?' she shouted angrily. Drew had well and truly overstepped the mark now.

'If you need any cash for an emergency, just ask.'

Isla shook her head in total disbelief. 'Are you for real, what do you think this is, the 1950s? This is ridiculous. What the hell has gotten into you?' Isla's eyes threatened tears, frustration building inside her. She didn't really have the faintest clue why they were arguing like this. It was so out of character for Drew. 'You put that money back in the jar. You couldn't do the job you do if it wasn't for me supporting you, looking after the house and *our* children. I thought this was a partnership ... obviously I'm very much mistaken.' Isla was at boiling point. 'I don't get it Drew, why are you hell bent on sending me back to work all of a sudden?' Trembling with rage inside, Isla wanted to shake him.

Drew cowardly cast his eyes downwards, he knew he was pushing Isla to the limit, but he couldn't help himself. 'And whose is that awful-looking Union Jack Mini parked outside? I thought you had company.'

Isla swallowed, she'd been dreading this moment with the mood Drew was in, but maybe she was worrying too much.

Drew had always seemed to like Martha. Maybe, just maybe her arrival would be a blessing in disguise.

Feeling apprehensive, she said, 'This is going to make your day ... you'll never guess who's back in town?' Isla painted a smile on her face and crossed her fingers behind her back.

'Huh,' came Drew's reply.

'Gran ... Gran's back in Heartcross! Walked into the teashop ... no-one could believe it, but she had no clue Bonnie had passed away. Isn't that sad?'

'No clue about her new great-grandson either,' Drew huffed.

Isla didn't rise to his comment. 'She looks so well ... single again. I've cleared some of the stuff from her room, just piled it up in our bedroom for now.'

Drew bristled, 'What do you mean, cleared her room?'

Seeing the black thunderous look on Drew's face, Isla tried with all her might to sound positive. 'Gran is staying with us here ... obviously,' she said.

'Another mouth to feed?'

'Considering she looks like a size six, I'm sure she hasn't got the largest of appetites, and you know what ...' Isla took a breath. 'If it bothers you that much and we've got more eggs than we can sell, we'll just feed her on eggs. Scrambled, boiled, poached ...'

Drew stood up, 'I'm going back to work.'

'I'll just wash your cup then, shall I? Or shall I leave it for the maid? You know what Drew, just don't bother coming in later unless you're in a better mood.'

He growled as he slammed the door behind him and Isla stood there bewildered, shaking her head in disbelief as she watched him once more stomp across the yard. It worried Isla, she'd never seen Drew like this before and was unsure what to do or say to him. Things were bad between them. In all the years they'd been together she could barely remember them ever having a cross word. Of course, they'd had the normal disagreements any married couple had but they'd never ever gone to bed on an argument. And this felt different, was on a different scale altogether and somehow things seemed to be escalating fast. For whatever reason, it felt like Drew couldn't stand to be anywhere near her, but one thing Isla knew for certain was if he carried on talking to her in this manner, he was in for a rude awakening.

Chapter 6

Isla waved Martha off to the pub to meet Rona and walked up Love Heart Lane towards Heartwood Cottage clutching a bottle of wine. The last twenty-four hours in the farmhouse had been tense, but luckily Martha seemed oblivious to the strain between Isla and Drew. Thankfully Drew hadn't taken whatever frustrations he had out on Martha and was pleasant enough with her, even though he'd disappeared off to bed earlier than normal without kissing Isla on the top of her head like he'd done every night of their married life without fail, leaving her feeling dejected.

After a hectic teatime Isla was relieved to be escaping from the farmhouse for a couple of hours this evening. As usual Angus had screamed through the whole of the meal and the second Isla had put down her knife and fork had been the time Angus had decided to fall asleep in his bouncy chair.

Drew had been late returning to the farmhouse, and she'd left him eating his tea from a tray in front of the TV while gently rocking Angus in his chair with his foot and instructing Finn how to build his Lego house.

Isla spotted Fergus racing along the road jiggling Esme on

Christie Barlow

his back, who let out a rapturous giggle. They were on their way up to the farm to keep Drew company. Isla smiled at them both and waved her hand above her head as they both grinned back.

Swinging open the garden gate to Heartwood Cottage, Isla could see her friends Allie, Jessica and Polly gathered in the living room already sipping wine. Their laughter filtered out through the open window which immediately lifted Isla's mood. She needed this, a night with her friends, where she could just be herself and not feel like she was walking on eggshells.

'Flick ... I'm here,' shouted Isla, opening the front door and kicking off her shoes in the hallway.

Felicity appeared with a beam on her face, 'And you've brought wine! You can come again ... but you shouldn't have!'

Isla laughed, 'I'd be the talk of the village if I didn't turn up with supplies!'

'Too right,' shouted Allie from the living room.

Isla walked into the living room to a group of smiley girls. There were already at least four bottles of wine on the coffee table alongside bowls of nibbles and leftover pastries from the teashop.

Felicity welcomed Isla like a long-lost friend, pulling her in for a hug and squeezing her hard before whipping the coat off her back and handing her a glass of wine.

The mood was jovial, and Isla settled on the settee next to Polly.

'What have I missed?' asked Isla, grabbing a handful of nuts from the bowl on the table.

'Well I'm unemployable,' said Polly, exhaling.

'I've had a row with Rory,' claimed Allie.

'And I've got a pile of marking to do when I get home,' Jessica rolled her eyes.

'And it looks like I've got a bunch of miserable friends that need cheering up,' grinned Felicity.

'So, we can conclude we are all living our best lives! And it's just the same old same old,' laughed Isla, putting her arguments with Drew to the back of her mind while she enjoyed time with her friends.

'But in other news, mum mentioned Martha was back in the village?' said Allie, looking towards Isla. 'Who's the latest squeeze?'

Everyone laughed.

'She drove into the village early yesterday morning with her Mini jam-packed to the rafters. Apparently she kicked Walter into touch a long time ago ... or maybe it was the other way around.'

'Were you expecting her?' asked Allie.

'No ... but we all know what Gran's like ... lives every day like it's her last ... and disappears for long periods of time.'

'But always turns up in the end ... I hope I grow up to be like her,' added Allie, topping up her wine. 'I'm quite envious of her carefree lifestyle.'

'She does amaze me, her energy ... she'll outlive us all, that one, but no doubt she'll hook up with another man soon.'

'Off Tinder,' added Felicity with a chuckle, 'then she'll be off on her next adventure.'

'Tinder?' Allie queried. 'Stop winding me up ... are you telling us Martha is on Tinder?'

'I'm absolutely telling you my seventy-year-old gran is on Tinder and probably has a more active sex life than all of us put together ... eww ...' Isla scrunched up her face. 'In fact, I don't even want to think about it.'

'I'm actually quite jealous,' laughed Jessica, 'this single lark is getting a bit boring.'

'I'll second that,' chipped in Polly.

'You can borrow Rory anytime ... the way I feel at the moment, I was thinking of putting him on eBay ... free to a good home.'

'I can't actually tell whether you are joking,' said Jessica, her laughter evaporating.

All eyes were on Allie.

'Ignore me, I'm just having a moan.'

'That's what we are here for,' said Felicity, tucking her feet underneath and getting comfy on the old battered armchair. 'Spill.'

Allie's tone was sulky, 'It's the job.'

'Rory's job? He's got a brilliant job,' said Isla.

Allie pulled an unimpressed face, 'That's not in dispute ... you'd think he'd be happy, wouldn't you?'

'And he's not?' asked Jessica.

Allie rolled her eyes, 'We all know he's a partner in the family veterinary business. A business that has been built up from scratch by his parents ... a steady solid income ...'

'So, what's the problem?' interrupted Felicity.

'Hmm,' said Allie, 'I think he kind of feels stifled by his dad's ways.'

'I kind of get that ...' said Felicity. 'A young vet with new ideas, and a dad who's run the business successfully for years and probably doesn't see any sort of need for change ... it's a generation thing.'

'That's exactly it. Rory just gets a little frustrated and wants to expand ... open a second practice, increase the staff ... he's enthusiastic, whereas ...'

'His dad is set in his ways and probably ready for retirement,' chipped in Jessica.

'Exactly,' agreed Allie, 'I'm just a little cheesed off with having the same conversations and frustrations over and over again. I think he should bide his time and not rock the boat, and as soon as his dad decides to retire he can do whatever he likes.'

'There's the old saying: don't try and fix something that isn't broken,' said Polly, topping up everyone's glass. 'But if there are any jobs going that might be an excuse to stick around ... going back to London is becoming less appealing by the day.'

'That's the problem with living in a small village, it's a beautiful place but most of the businesses are family run, so there are few employment opportunities. I've fallen on my feet with the teashop and working alongside Mum, but if it wasn't for my grandma and her good ideas, goodness knows what career path I'd have ventured down.'

'So, you fancy sticking around then, Polly?' said Jessica.

'I wish, but it's not that easy, is it? There's nothing keeping me in London and I'm finding it so difficult to even get an interview ... it's disheartening.'

'And I didn't know you were looking for a job, Isla?' Jessica said, turning the conversation towards Isla, whose eyes widened and locked with Felicity's.

Felicity shrugged discreetly, she hadn't told a soul about the conversation between them. Everyone was now looking at Isla.

'Sorry, have I said something I shouldn't?' asked Jessica, clocking the look between them both.

'What's going on?' asked Allie, sitting up straight. 'Why are you looking for a job?'

Suddenly, Isla was overcome with emotion, all the tension between her and Drew she had been bottling up snapped. She felt enveloped with anguish and it churned her stomach up.

'It's just Drew asked me whether there were any jobs going at the school ...'

'He did what?' Isla stared open-mouthed.

'The other day, he caught me outside school and asked me,' elaborated Jessica.

'How bloody dare he go behind my back like this?' Isla shook her head in disbelief, she was fuming.

At a loss for words, she gulped back her wine. This behaviour was so out of character for Drew. He would never normally go behind her back like this, but at the minute it was like she didn't know him at all.

'Why the need to get a job?' asked Polly.

'Your guess is as good as mine. Drew's got a bee in his bonnet about me wasting money on breakfast and lunches while he's out working on the farm.'

'Maybe he's just panicking with a new baby in the house and doesn't want to struggle financially,' added Allie, noticing Isla's eyes welling with tears.

'That's all good and well, but if I do get a job, all I'll be doing is earning money to pay someone else to look after Angus, and what's the point in that?' Isla knew leaving baby Angus with anyone would definitely pull at her heartstrings.

'I watched a programme recently about a secretive gambler, it all spiralled out of control and his wife hadn't got a clue about his debts, until the bailiffs turned up,' said Jessica dramatically.

Isla sat up straight, 'You don't think Drew's gambling, do you?' she asked alarmed, feeling all panicky inside.

Everyone laughed.

'Of course not,' reassured Felicity.

'He's on his phone more and more though. You can get those gambling apps, can't you?'

'Isla, don't be daft. Drew isn't the type to risk everything he has or put his family in any sort of jeopardy.'

In spite of everything, Isla knew that Felicity was right, Drew would never risk his business or their family home. He had been working every hour possible and more than likely this was the reason he'd been so difficult to talk to recently. And with the new baby, he was probably just tired.

'Maybe Martha is your fairy godmother, turning up when she did,' smiled Felicity softly. 'Having her around might help to defuse any tensions.'

'Let's hope so,' answered Isla despondently, but attempting a smile.

'Anyway, let's put all this doom and gloom behind us and talk christenings,' suggested Allie, lightening the mood.

Felicity clapped her hands together joyfully, 'Have we got a date yet?'

It had been on Isla's list nearly every week to visit the minister to confirm a date for the christening, but she just hadn't gotten round to it. 'Not yet, but I'm on it,' she said, and her worried expression began to change into a smile. Feeling more joyful, the thought of an afternoon celebrating with all her friends and family lifted her mood. And maybe it was just what Drew needed too, to let his hair down and enjoy himself for a change.

'We can take care of the catering between us,' Allie flapped her hand between herself and Felicity, 'obviously we can have the party at the pub.'

'And I'll bake the cake,' added Felicity.

'And I can ask the children at school to make some decorations,' added Jessica.

'And I'm on hand to help with anything too,' smiled Polly. This was just what Isla needed, all her friends rallying around her. They had a way of making her feel better about things.

'And try not to worry about Drew, it'll be something and nothing. We are all entitled to off days,' said Felicity, her gaze drifting towards the second empty bottle of wine.

'Hopefully ... and anyway ...' said Isla, shifting the conversation into a different direction, 'when are you moving in with Fergus?'

Felicity blushed, 'Hmm ... not just yet.'

'Why, is there something wrong between you pair?' said Jessica, leaning forward and grabbing a handful of peanuts from the bowl on the table.

'No, it's not that.'

Felicity had mixed feelings about her situation with Fergus. Of course, she wanted to move into Fox Hollow Cottage with Fergus and Esme, she'd fallen in love with them both, but the thought of leaving her mum on her own in the cottage since the death of her grandmother just didn't sit right with her at the moment. She was torn between her own happiness and that of her mum.

'It's too soon for my mum, but I'll know when the time is right. It's just ... I'm not even sure about moving into Fox Hollow Cottage.'

'Why? It's a beautiful place,' queried Isla.

Felicity pinched the bridge of her nose, 'I know, but, as much as I love Aggie, I want our own place, just for the three of us.'

'It's a difficult one,' Allie said softly.

Fergus had lived at Fox Hollow Cottage for all of his life and when Esme's mum had passed away he'd stayed living with his mother, Aggie, who'd supported him through his grief and was very much a hands-on grandmother.

'Do you think that sounds selfish of me?'

'No, not at all, you need your own family space,' answered Polly.

'Maybe in time you could do a house swap?' said Jessica in all seriousness. 'Aggie could move in here, or Rona could move in with her.'

The thought crossed Felicity's mind for a fleeting moment, but she knew her mum would never move out of Heartwood Cottage. This place was her life and no doubt Aggie felt the same about Fox Hollow Cottage.

'Do you think there will be room for my gran too?' giggled Isla, now feeling a little tipsy on wine and forgetting her own troubles for a brief moment. 'Even though I'm not sure how long she's going to stay around for this time ... your guess is as good as mine, but can you imagine their Friday nights ... nights of gin, poker and Tinder.'

Everyone laughed.

'Living the dream!' chuckled Allie. 'I'd actually be quite jealous.'

'Shh, what's that noise?' asked Polly.

'That'll be Mum back,' answered Felicity, amazed at how quickly the time had flown. They heard the sound of the garden gate being opened, followed by the cackle of laughter.

'Sounds like Gran is with her ... and tipsier than us,' said Isla in a whisper, while straining to hear.

Felicity had not witnessed her mum drunk for as long as she could remember. She often enjoyed a gin and tonic at the pub but was never one for excessive drinking. But it was about time she let her hair down and had some fun with her friends.

The girls heard Rona, Martha and Aggie fall into the hallway still giggling.

'I've got a match,' squealed Rona. 'Oh my ... he's got no teeth and looks like he would be better fitted in a police line-up ... look!'

'I told you, you were swiping the wrong way ... let's have a look,' chuckled Martha. 'He's not too bad, maybe a little overweight, bald and probably has his own teeth – well, the ones he has ... well worth a date, I say.'

Rona looked horrified as all three of them appeared in the living-room doorway. 'There's not a cat-in-hell's chance.'

'I'm with Rona,' laughed Aggie, who sounded relatively sober compared to the other two women.

'You can't judge by a photograph. What if he has an amazing personality or is a millionaire in disguise?' Martha gave Rona a serious look.

'Mmm,' said Rona, far from convinced, 'I don't mind missing out this time and I really can't see why any millionaires would need to be on a dating app. Is this what my life has become ... is this all I'm destined for?'

The girls supressed their giggles.

'Sorry, it appears my gran is leading your mum astray,' Isla said, grinning, while shaking her head in disbelief as Martha stumbled into the living room clutching her phone.

'We've set your mum up on a dating app,' she informed everyone proudly. 'And I'll have you know she already has a match.' Martha gave a goofy grin and seemed rather pleased with herself.

'Even though she's been swiping the wrong way, apparently,' joined in Aggie, who'd eyed the remaining bottle of wine on the table.

'I really didn't have much choice, Martha wouldn't take no for an answer.' Rona rolled her eyes in jest.

'I can believe that,' laughed Isla.

'Martha is very persuasive,' Rona replied, before trying to walk in a straight line towards the kitchen. 'One for the road,' she said, returning holding three wine glasses.

'And I'll have you know,' hiccupped Rona, 'I don't want a man or need a man. I'm perfectly happy on my own.' She began to pour the wine while Martha and Aggie squeezed on to the settee.

'So, what have we missed ... anything interesting?' asked Aggie, looking between the girls.

Isla snagged Felicity's eye, a look that meant, *Don't mention anything about my argument with Drew.*

'Just general stuff,' answered Jessica.

'So how long are you staying for, Polly?' asked Aggie.

'However long Felicity and Rona will put up with me for. I've nothing to rush back for but I don't want to outstay my welcome either.'

Felicity gave Polly a warm smile, 'You're welcome to stay as long as you want.'

Everyone's attention was suddenly drawn to Martha's phone which pinged with a notification.

'It's another match!' she squealed in a drunken stupor. She narrowed her eyes and then they sprang back open. She scrutinised the screen. 'Not bad ... not bad at all,' she said, twisting the phone to Rona. 'Let's message him.'

'Let's not,' replied Rona, making a series of huffing and puffing noises and taking the phone from Martha's hand.

'You're no fun,' Martha claimed, a little disgruntled.

'Can you see what I've had to put up with all night?' grinned Aggie. 'It's like refereeing children.'

To everyone's surprise, Rona was quiet, then the corners of her mouth lifted. 'Oh ...' she exclaimed.

'Told you,' exclaimed Martha, in a smug tone. 'He's quite dishy.'

Everyone waited in anticipation to hear Rona's verdict.

'Come on ...' urged Allie. 'The suspense is killing us.'

'He's actually, not bad ... Prince Charming, indeed.'

Martha gave Aggie a knowing look, 'See, just call me Cupid.'

All attention was on Rona.

'This is exciting! Maybe I do need to get myself on Tinder after all,' joked Polly.

'He's called Bill, and lives ten kilometres away ...'

'He must be somewhere over in Glensheil then,' interrupted Isla.

'And he's retired and loves hiking. He does have a kind face,' said Rona, thinking out loud.

'It can't hurt to drop him a message,' said Felicity, beginning to clear away the empty bowls from the table.

But Rona wasn't listening. 'As much as I've had fun tonight ... there ... the profile is deleted.'

'Spoilsport!' the disappointment was written all over Martha's face as Rona handed her back the phone.

'If I'm going to meet a man, and call me old fashioned, but I want to meet him because he's walked into my life, not through some sort of ... what do you call them ... apps?'

'Unfortunately, it's the way of the world these days,' chipped in Polly. 'But I know what you mean, I want someone to walk into my life and knock me dead.'

'You're no good to anyone dead,' grinned Allie.

'You know what I mean! I want to feel the first flush of love, feel the butterflies flutter in my stomach and be swept off my feet by someone in person. I want the whole fairy tale.'

'So, you won't be joining Tinder then, Pol,' said Isla, draining the last of her wine from her glass.

'Not any day soon!'

They all chatted and listened to Martha's stories for the next ten minutes, then Isla felt herself beginning to physically tire. She knew she'd be up during the night with Angus for his night feeds. 'It's time for me to be making a move,' Isla said, knowing she should make a move yet dreading going home to Drew, but as her gaze drifted towards her watch, she felt relieved knowing he'd be fast asleep due to his early morning start.

'And me,' admitted Jessica. 'I'm up early for school.'

Everyone began to gather their belongings and they all thanked Felicity for a great evening. As the front door shut behind them, Felicity slouched into the chair and smiled to herself, hearing Martha singing down the road. 'I hope I have that amount of energy at that age,' she said.

'Don't we all. I'm exhausted just watching her,' laughed Polly, pressing a swift kiss to Felicity and Rona's cheeks. 'See you in the morning ... night.'

As Rona and Felicity began to load the dishwasher, Felicity noticed her mum deep in thought.

'What is it, Mum? You seem like you've suddenly got the weight of the world on your shoulders,' added Felicity tentatively.

Rona straightened and exhaled slightly. 'Don't mind me,

I'm a little tipsy.' Rona took a breath and leant over to wipe the worktops. 'But for the first time in a long time I actually laughed tonight, and I mean *laughed*.'

'So why the sigh?' asked Felicity, perplexed.

'Because as much as Martha is a loveable old eccentric, she knows how to have fun.'

'You know how to have fun.'

Rona leant against the worktop. 'When do I ever have any fun? Don't get me wrong, I'm not saying I'm unhappy, far from it ...'

'But?' interrupted Felicity.

'Even though I'm surrounded by people every day and I have you ... sometimes I actually feel lonely.'

Felicity felt saddened, she'd never even considered that her mum felt this way.

'I do the same thing, day in and day out ... and I love my life ... and I love our teashop and you are my world, but tonight ... it made me think about the past ... and all those special times I'd spent with your father. Nothing will ever replace the love we had, but sometimes ...' She took a breath. 'Sometimes I wish to be cuddled or even have the opportunity to make more of myself ... dress up, maybe be wined and dined.'

Felicity was unable to hide her amazement at her mum's words but was quick to reassure her. 'Dad died many years ago and you are very much alive. It's natural you should feel this way. As much as we laughed and joked tonight, maybe it's about time you looked for that special someone in your life,' she said, knowing it was only a matter of time before she and Fergus would talk about setting up home together, leaving her mum rattling around in Heartwood Cottage all by herself.

'Maybe it's the drink talking,' admitted Rona, pouring herself a glass of water. 'But look at Martha, she's still living life to the max even at her age. The stories she told us tonight ...'

'No-one can deny Martha lives every day like it's her last,' Felicity touched her mum's arm tentatively. 'But you have to do what's right for you, and who knows who'll walk through that teashop door when you least expect it.'

Rona gave a short smile, 'I look at you youngsters, all flourishing in life, starting out and I still feel young inside, but I know I'm not ... my knees remind me of that every morning when I climb out of bed. What I'm trying to say is, my life is trundling along so fast. One minute you are here and the next you are gone.'

'Mum, don't talk like this,' said Felicity, feeling the tears well up in her eyes.

'It's true ... one minute I'm a little girl pinching my mother's baking whilst she wasn't looking and now, she's gone. In a blink of an eye everything changes.' Rona took a breath. 'I do know you'll want to set up home with Fergus and Esme.' She took her daughter's hand and squeezed it gently. 'I don't want you to worry about me.' Her voice faltered and a tiny tear slid down her cheek. 'Don't put your life on hold for me. You deserve your happiness ... your happy ever after, and it'll make me happy to see you happy, but there's just one thing I ask.'

Felicity swallowed down the lump in her throat, she'd never

heard her mum talk this way before. 'This place, Bonnie's teashop, keep it alive for Mum, me and you.'

'Always, Mum ... always. I'll never let you down.'

Rona pulled her daughter in for a hug. 'I don't say it often enough, but I love you.'

Felicity nodded, 'I love you too.'

Chapter 7

The 5 a.m. alarm sounded, and Isla woke feeling exhausted. It only felt like she'd closed her eyes five minutes ago. As usual, Drew was lying next to her in a deep sleep which she was extremely jealous of. As she shook him lightly, he began to stir. 'Drew, it's time to get up, the alarm went off.'

'Already,' he murmured, half-asleep, before gingerly pulling back the covers and slowly swinging his legs to the floor. Isla shivered as a blast of cool air hit her, she quickly pulled the duvet back up around her neck.

Drew reluctantly wandered down the stairs and Isla turned over as she heard the kitchen light switch on, followed by the sound of running water. Her head felt fuzzy, the wine hadn't helped last night but she'd barely slept in between Angus waking up and worrying about Drew's mood.

At 2 a.m. she'd found herself drinking a mug of tea in the kitchen while staring at Drew's phone charging on the side. Jessica's comment was firmly on her mind. What if Drew did have a gambling problem? What if there was something wrong with his health and he was too scared to tell her? Or could he even be having an affair? Isla couldn't settle with all these thoughts whirling around in her mind.

Part of her was itching to check his phone, but the other part of her knew it was dishonest. But before she could stop herself, she reached over, unplugged the phone and stood at the bottom stairs and listened.

Silence.

Thankfully, she hadn't disturbed anyone by coming down-stairs.

She rolled the phone over and over in her hands. Drew's screensaver was a photo of them all, a picture taken at the hospital when Angus was born. Isla took a deep breath and pressed the home button. She was relieved when the phone didn't have a passcode, which she thought was a good sign. Surely if Drew had anything to hide, he would ensure his phone was locked at all times. Firstly, she scrolled through his messages, but they were just the usual texts from suppliers, and the usual banter about footie from Fergus and Rory. There was no-one in his contact list that she didn't know and his photo albums were jam-packed with pictures of her and the boys, and she took a moment to appreciate the wonderful family they had. It made Drew's moods even more worrying.

'Apps ... what apps does he have?' said Isla, quickly scrolling. Her hands were sweating and her heart was thumping, but again there was nothing unusual and certainly no gambling apps.

'What are you doing, Isla?' she mumbled to herself.

She hadn't got a clue what she was hoping to find but she certainly hadn't found anything incriminating on Drew's phone. And now she just felt bad for even looking. Riddled with guilt for thinking the worst, she plugged the phone back into the charger and took herself back off to bed.

A couple of hours after Drew had left Isla decided to make herself a strong coffee before waking Finn up for school. Thankfully Angus was still fast asleep in his cot.

She sat with her hands cupped around the mug, feeling disappointed in herself, and exhaled heavily.

'Now that's a sigh and a half.'

Isla looked up to see Martha ambling into the kitchen. 'Headache tablets, I need headache tablets … you'd think I would have got the hang of this drinking lark at my age,' she gave a small chuckle and pulled out the chair next to Isla.

'Water?' Isla asked as she stood up.

Martha managed a nod and gratefully accepted the glass and tablets from Isla as she swallowed down the pills.

'Did you sleep well?' asked Martha, picking up the paper that Isla had left on the table.

Isla hugged her mug of coffee and after a second noticed the drops of water on the table. She was crying.

'What is it, dear? It can't be that bad.' Martha squeezed her hand, 'What's this all about?'

Isla tried to blink away her tears, but it was no use, her emotions bubbled to the surface and came spilling out. 'Gran … I've done something terrible.'

Martha straightened herself up, her eyes widened.

'Terrible … what sort of terrible?'

Isla told her gran about checking Drew's phone, and about how awful she felt.

'Don't beat yourself up over it. His change in behaviour has caused you to question him. You're just reacting to how he's treating you. First things first, let's get Finn ready for school. I'll stay here with Angus and make us breakfast, you need to eat to keep your strength up, and then we'll have a chat about what's going on or what you think is going on.'

Isla broke eye contact and wiped her eyes with the back of her sleeve. 'Thanks, Gran.'

Martha tilted her head, 'Sometimes things happen for a reason and come to try us ... but one thing I've learnt in my life so far, there's no point wasting energy on worrying. You need to ask Drew outright what's bothering him. Otherwise it will eat away at you both. Maybe he's just exhausted, and we can't be happy-go-lucky all the time, can we?'

Isla attempted to hitch a smile on her face, even though she was still feeling awful. 'You are a wise old woman ...'

'I've had a lot of practice,' said Martha, giving Isla's hand a quick squeeze.

An hour later Finn was ready for school and kissed his great-grandma on the cheek before slipping on his coat.

'Remember your promise,' he said, attempting to wink at Martha, but he didn't quite get it right and over-exaggerated a blink instead.

She tapped her nose and winked back. 'I won't forget.'

'What's going on here?' asked Isla, feeling a little out the loop as she ushered Finn towards the front door.

'Great-Gran has promised me one of those sticky buns from Bonnie's teashop after school,' he said with a huge grin.

'That sounds like a very nice treat.' Isla cupped her hand around Finn's as they began to walk down the path towards school. She could see Drew and Fergus shepherding the cows towards the bottom field.

'Do you think Daddy will let me help him out on the farm when I'm bigger?' asked Finn, noticing his dad too.

'Of course, but it's very hard work. Early starts, late finishes and you don't smell very nice most of the time,' teased Isla, taking another glance towards Drew. Finn's question had prompted her to think. Drew was so hard-working, the hours he put in at the farm left him exhausted. Maybe he was overworked recently and was lashing out at her because she was the closest one to him? Feeling sombre, she was suddenly sorry for arguing with him lately. Maybe he just needed to vent his frustrations?

'I think you'll make an excellent farmer,' said Isla, smiling down at Finn. 'Your daddy would love it if you followed in his footsteps.'

Finn screwed up his face. 'Followed in his footsteps ... my feet would need to grow very big.'

Isla laughed, 'You're a funny little boy.'

Foxglove Farm had been in Drew's family for generations and Isla knew Drew hoped his boys would become farmers too one day. She felt privileged to live in this beautiful corner of the Scottish Highlands and waking up to the spectacular scenery was just magical, and if it wasn't for Drew following in his father's footsteps Isla had no clue where she would have ended up.

Isla spotted Felicity at the corner of Love Heart Lane. Esme was next to her, swinging her bag and chatting away. In the past Aggie had always walked Esme to school, but since she had suffered with pneumonia at the beginning of the year Fergus wanted to take the pressure off her and now he dropped Esme off at the teashop every morning on his way to work. Isla knew that Felicity cherished the extra time with Esme.

Isla called out to Flick and waved at her as she turned round to greet them. They waited for Isla and Finn to catch up and immediately Finn and Esme were joined at the hip and skipped off up the pavement in front of them both.

'Finn, mind that puddle,' but it was too late – his foot landed in the puddle and muddy water splashed up his leg. 'One day we will get to school without any dramas,' Isla smiled at him and shook her head jokingly. 'You can change into your socks from your PE kit.'

'How's your head?' smiled Felicity, stepping towards Isla and linking her arm through hers as they began walking.

'Another night of not much sleep and it wasn't down to the alcohol ... between feeding Angus and my boomerang of a brain keeping me awake with its to-ing and fro-ing and constant worrying about what is worrying Drew.' Isla's voice wobbled. 'And ...'

'And what?' interrupted Felicity.

'I checked his phone.'

'Isla!'

'I know, I know it was wrong, but wouldn't you do the same if Fergus's behaviour suddenly changed?'

'I suppose,' admitted Felicity. 'And did you find anything?'

Isla shook her head, 'Absolutely nothing.'

'Well, that's something, at least your mind should be at rest now.'

'But there's still something bothering him. I know him.'

'I did question Fergus.'

'You didn't say I wanted to know, did you?' asked Isla, feeling panicky.

'Of course not! I just said you were feeling tired with the new baby and he said Drew is exhausted too.'

'And that was it? Nothing else?'

'Nothing else.'

As they reached the school gates, they ushered Finn and Esme towards their line in the playground. The bell sounded and Jessica appeared and waved over towards Felicity and Isla before escorting the children into the classroom.

'Life is so simple at that age,' sighed Isla, blowing Finn a kiss as he disappeared through the door.

'Isla! Isla, wait!' a voice called out.

Isla spun round to see Julia from the local B&B hurrying towards them. Her cheeks were flushed and she had a look of panic on her face, 'I'm glad I've caught up with you.'

'Since when have you been frequenting school playgrounds?' asked Isla, knowing Julia didn't have any children.

'I'm looking for you, I tried your mobile, but it went straight to voicemail.'

'That's the joys of living in the sticks ... no signal.' Isla was intrigued, 'What's up?'

'Let's walk and talk,' said Julia, who attempted to get her breathing under control. 'I've jogged from the B&B and I'm out of breath.'

'I'm all ears,' said Isla, fascinated about what was troubling Julia as all three of them headed out of the school playground.

'I've messed up,' spluttered Julia. 'And I'm hoping you are the woman to help me out.' Julia exhaled, 'And I know it's a big ask and I don't like letting anyone down ... but ...'

Isla stopped walking, 'Spit it out.'

Julia took a breath, 'I've made a blunder with my bookings, and I've double-booked a week on Friday. One of the parties is a rambling group trekking the mountain to raise money for charity and the other one is a booking for a sixtieth birthday ... I don't want to let any of them down.'

'And how can I help?'

'I didn't want to cancel either of them, if word got around it's not good for business, and I was thinking ... who do I know who has enough room to accommodate one of the parties?'

The penny dropped and Isla laughed until she realised Julia was serious, then her expression turned to one of bewilderment before smiling nervously, 'You are joking, right?'

Julia eyed Isla warily, 'I wasn't, to be honest.'

'Julia, I've got a new baby and my gran's just turned up unannounced to stay. And I'm not sure Drew would want a bunch of strangers traipsing through the farmhouse, and then there's Finn too, and what about their meals?'

'You could direct them to the teashop for breakfast or fry up a bit of bacon,' said Julia with hope in her voice.

As much as Isla didn't want to let anyone down, she knew that at this moment in time she couldn't face strangers in the house even though there was ample space and vacant bedrooms.

'They'd pay the going rate,' urged Julia, hoping to sway Isla. 'Sorry ... sorry ... I shouldn't have mentioned it ... I know you have enough on your plate.'

'If I could help you out, you know I would. What's plan B?'

'I haven't got one,' admitted Julia, taking a breath.

'I'm so sorry Julia, I just can't help you at the minute.'

'No worries, if you don't ask you never know.'

Julia touched Isla on her arm tentatively before sadly walking away.

'Can you imagine strangers traipsing through my house ... no thank you,' said Isla, knowing that she wouldn't even feel comfortable mentioning it to Drew after his reaction to Martha turning up.

'I can see your point, you've got way too much going on at the moment with the baby to think about, not to mention you and Drew. Oh, by the way, I forgot to mention, a guy came into the teashop yesterday and I pointed him in your direction, Rory's too. Did he come by the farmhouse?'

'What guy?'

'If I remember rightly, he went by the name David O'Sullivan.'

Isla shook her head, 'Never heard of him. What did he want?'

'He had a herd of alpacas that needed re-homing. Prize-winning, apparently. He was looking for a nearby farm to home them.'

'Oh, Drew never mentioned it, I'm sure I would have known if he'd visited the farm. Alpacas, you say?'

'Yep, those funny-looking creatures with a tuft of hair bouncing on top of their heads.'

'Farmed for the fleeces.' Isla began to turn the information over in her mind. 'Did he say how much he wanted for them?'

Felicity shook her head, 'No, but I think he gave Mum a card?'

As they turned on to Love Heart Lane Isla stopped for a second. 'Come with me,' she said, quickly striding towards the farm with Felicity struggling to keep up.

As they approached the driveway, Isla traipsed Felicity around the edge of the field, over the small wooden bridge and through the orchard. In the far field there were Shetland ponies grazing alongside sheep and the mountainous terrain in the background. Even when the visibility wasn't good the view was spectacular.

They stopped to get their breath back as Isla swung her arms open.

'I don't get it,' said Felicity in wonderment.

'We have acres of space! Can you imagine seeing alpacas grazing here? The children would love it!'

'It's not as though you haven't got the land ...' Flick replied.

'Isn't it all the rage these days ... alpaca farms? You never know, it might even cheer up my miserable husband looking at the comical creatures each morning. And you know it's his birthday next week, and what do you get a man who has everything?' said Isla, mulling it over.

'A herd of alpacas?' grinned Felicity.

'They can't take that much looking after and I've read somewhere they are fabulous with children. You said he gave your mum a business card?'

Felicity nodded as her phone buzzed into life, 'Talk of the devil.'

'I'll walk back to the teashop with you.'

'Here it is,' said Rona, pulling the card from the till. 'David O'Sullivan. I'm not sure where he was from, I've never seen him around these parts before.'

Isla turned the card over in her hand. 'You know what, I'm going to give him a call,' she said, taking herself to the quiet sofa area in the corner of the teashop. 'I'm intrigued to know the cost of a herd of alpacas.'

Rona and Felicity watched as she chatted away and hung up the call with a huge grin on her face.

'Oh my,' she said, with excitement fizzing inside her.

'The call went well then?' asked Felicity, leaning against the counter.

'Apparently, he's the son of a farmer over in Glensheil. His father has passed away and has left a herd of prize alpacas that need re-homing. He's over from Wales tying up the legalities of the farm ... Anyway, cutting a long story short, I'm buying them!'

'Woah, really?'

'Yes really! He assured me they are self-sufficient, easy to look after, so ... I'm going to surprise Drew! As much as he's moody at the minute, he loves his animals and what a birthday present this is going to be! I can't wait to see his face.'

Isla had made the decision there and then. Talking to David on the phone, they'd negotiated a price for the herd, and he would deliver them on the morning of Drew's birthday.

'Some things are just meant to be,' exclaimed Isla, pleased with her purchase and feeling impressed with herself. She knew Drew would be over the moon and that this extraordinary gift would definitely bring a smile to his face. Isla was elated, this was just meant to be and farming the fleeces would bring in a hefty sum. The alpacas would pay for themselves in no time at all.

'But I want to keep this amongst ourselves ... no telling Fergus or Drew. I want this birthday present to be a complete surprise!' said Isla excitedly.

Chapter 8

One week later …

Isla's eyes opened slowly as she focused on her surroundings. A quick glance at the clock told her she'd slept for a full eight hours. Throwing back the duvet, she saw that Angus was still fast asleep, the second night he'd slept through. Things were definitely brighter after a good night's sleep.

Drew had already left for market with Fergus, and Isla and Martha's plan was to decorate the kitchen with banners and balloons for his birthday. Once Drew had fallen asleep last night Isla had left his birthday card on the kitchen table along with a note asking him to be back at the farm by noon. She planned to cook him birthday lunch before the alpacas arrived at one o'clock.

Over the last few days Drew had seemed to be back on an even keel. Yes, he had still seemed tired, but he hadn't snapped at Isla. Maybe he had just been having an off day. Isla couldn't wait to see his face when he arrived home, she knew he was just going to love the alpacas.

Quietly, she padded past the cot and pulled back the curtains. Her mood dampened a little when she noticed there wasn't a chink of sunshine to be seen, only dark clouds looming in the sky. The cows were already shielding themselves from the rainfall that was about to teem down at any minute. She had pictured the alpacas arriving in gleaming sunshine, their mops of hair bobbing on top of their heads as they were unleashed, running across the meadows. Torrential rain was not what she needed today.

Leaving Angus to sleep, she grabbed her dressing gown and wandered downstairs where Martha was busy in the kitchen.

'You've made a start,' chirped Isla, staring around the kitchen. Martha had already hung up the birthday banners and the colourful paperchains that Finn had secretly made draped the window and the spaces between the picture frames. Even at Drew's age he was always like a kid on his birthday. Usually they cooked the best steak, followed by birthday cake, always chocolate, and would open a decent bottle of wine to toast another year together.

'I caught Drew before he went, he seemed in good spirits,' said Martha.

'He does like birthdays and I can't believe we've managed to keep his birthday present a secret. I need to pop to the bank this morning and withdraw the cash.'

'Leave Angus with me.'

'Thanks, Gran. I'll drop Finn at school on my way.'

Although Isla had had her doubts when Martha arrived,

she was worth her weight in gold. The children loved her, and Isla was enjoying the company around the place.

Once Finn was safely dropped at school Isla drove over to the bank in Glensheil. As the windscreen wipers frantically swished the rain continued to hammer down. The wind swept through the branches of the trees that adorned the river bank, causing them to sway violently. Luckily for Isla there was a car-park space right outside the bank which she pulled into. Tugging her hood over her head, she ran sprightly towards the revolving glass door. Isla wished she'd withdrawn the money sooner but didn't want to alert Drew, she wanted the alpacas to be a surprise.

'Good morning, Mrs Allaway.'

Isla pushed back her hood and smiled, 'It's brutal out there today.'

Lucy the bank clerk glanced towards the huge glass windows. 'I'm glad I'm safely tucked away in here until five o'clock. What can I do for you today?'

Isla handed over her bank card, 'I'd like to withdraw some cash. It's quite a large amount but I rang through to check that would be okay.'

'Perfect,' said Lucy, tapping away at her keyboard while concentrating on the computer screen.

'Is it for anything special ... a holiday?'

'Would you believe I'm buying my husband a herd of alpacas for his birthday?'

Lucy let out a low whistle, 'Wow! I'd just be happy with a

bunch of flowers!' she said, counting out the cash, placing it in an envelope and sliding it under the counter.

Just as Isla was safely tucking the money away in her bag her phone pinged, a text message from David O'Sullivan. He'd set off early, the alpacas would be with them soon. She smiled to herself, happy with her purchase, and she couldn't wait to see Drew's face.

The second she stepped back inside the farmhouse a jovial Martha beckoned her, 'Come and take a look at the cake.' But hearing the crunch of tyres behind her, Isla spun round to see a truck.

'The alpacas are here!' Isla shouted down the hallway towards Martha. 'Grab a coat and come and take a look.'

Isla sheltered in the doorway as a short bald stocky man jumped down from behind the wheel, thrusting his hand forward for her to shake. 'Nice place you have here,' he said in a gravelly Welsh accent.

'Thanks, we like it. I'm Isla.'

'David,' he said. 'The weather isn't being kind to us today … which field am I letting them loose in?'

Isla pointed and grabbed an umbrella from the hallway before following him to the back of the truck.

'These creatures are responsible for bearing some of the silkiest, most versatile fleece found in nature. Stronger than mohair, finer than cashmere, smoother than silk, softer than cotton, warmer than goose down … you're on to a winner with these beauties. Shorn annually for a good price,' said David.

Isla watched in amazement as he pulled open the door and unleashed numerous docile-looking animals. She couldn't take her eyes away from the magnificent creatures. Isla had never seen an alpaca up close and was mesmerised by their floppy furry tufts, slender necks. They genuinely looked like they were sporting huge grins.

'They are captivating,' said Martha, joining them, not taking her eyes off them. 'How many are there?'

'Twelve,' answered Isla.

Once all of them were unloaded into the field they huddled together, sheltering under the canopy of the trees.

'Thank you so much, we'll look after them, I promise. And I'm sorry to hear about your father.'

'Father?' said David, looking puzzled as he bolted up the back of the truck. 'Oh yes, my father. Thank you. All I need now is the money.' He stood and waited while Isla rummaged around in her handbag and pulled out the envelope of cash.

'Thank you,' he said, not hanging around. He jumped into the trunk, started the engine and was off.

'That was short and sweet ... strange little man. He couldn't get out of here quick enough,' noticed Martha.

'Twelve alpacas, all present and correct. Aren't they wonderful?' Isla squeezed her Gran's arm. 'Let's get out of this rain.'

They'd only been inside a couple of minutes when they noticed Drew's van pull up outside.

'He's here ... quick,' said Isla, unboxing the birthday cake and placing it in pride of place in the middle of the kitchen table. She risked a tentative look in the mirror, ran her fingers through her hair and quickly applied her lip gloss.

As the kitchen door opened, two loud pops erupted. The unmistakable sounds of party poppers.

'Happy birthday, Drew!' Isla moved towards him and planted a kiss on his cheek.

Drew's face didn't crack a smile, he was drenched with rain and Fergus looked even more dishevelled standing next to him with his overalls splattered with mud.

'You poor things, look at the state of you both, all wet through. Let me get you a towel.'

'Never mind a towel,' Drew said, eyeing up the banners pinned to the kitchen wall before locking eyes with Isla. 'For a second I thought I'd come home to the wrong farm.'

'What do you mean?' she asked. 'Aww, because of all this … Finn made the paperchains and of course Flick made the cake.'

'Isla … I could have sworn there are llamas in our field.'

Isla wagged her finger, 'Actually, that's where you are wrong … they are alpacas … Happy birthday, Drew! What do you get a man who has everything? A herd of alpacas!'

Fergus looked suitably impressed, but it was clear by the look on Drew's face that he wasn't quite feeling the same.

'Alpacas? You've bought me alpacas? Where do you think we live, the Peruvian Andes?'

'Beautiful animals,' said Isla, hoping for a better reaction and noting the slight tension that had crept into the room. She couldn't help but feel disappointed, this was not the reaction she was hoping for.

'Where the hell have you got a herd of alpacas from?' asked an annoyed Drew.

'A man called David O'Sullivan came into the teashop and mentioned to Rona that his father had passed away, he didn't know what to do with them and needed to re-home the herd. I thought you'd be happy.'

Drew blew out a breath, he looked relieved as a small smile hitched on his face. 'Why didn't you say ... so he gave them to you? I had visions of you spending a small fortune on them.'

Isla just stared at him. Of course she had spent a small fortune on them and now felt a little guilty because of Drew's reaction. This was not how it was meant to be.

'Isla?'

'Of course he didn't give them to me. They're a prize-winning herd, but what an asset to the farm ... and what a birthday present, too.'

'Isla, I can't believe you can be so stupid,' Drew blurted.

Isla felt infuriated, he was talking to her like she was a child, not his equal.

'And who's this David bloke? You'll have to ring him now and tell him to take them back and get the money back.' Drew was so angry he barely came up for air.

'I can't do that. He'll think I've lost the plot, and anyway, what's the problem? Those fleeces will bring in a small fortune. They'll pay for themselves in the long run.'

'Isla, it matters. How much did you pay for them?' His question was loaded with more than polite enquiry.

For a second, the question hung in the air. 'Isla?'

Martha gave Fergus a nod and they quickly disappeared into the living room, leaving them alone.

Isla narrowed her eyes at him, 'What has got into you? You've just embarrassed me and yourself in front of my gran and Fergus. I've bought you a present, at the very least you could act grateful.'

'An extravagant present, do you think we have money to throw around?' Drew lunged at Isla's phone which was lying on the table. 'David, you say?' he said, scrolling through her last numbers.

'You are acting like a complete idiot. What the hell is going on with you, Drew? It's like I don't even know who you are at the minute.'

'Marvellous ... bloody marvellous,' he said, switching the phone to speaker and throwing his hands up into the air.

'Your call cannot be connected.'

Isla had to admit she felt a tiny pang of worry. Surely it was just because the mobile phone signal was sparse in this region, but before she could voice her opinion Drew jumped in with his.

'My guess is David is a crook, by chance he rocked up here and sold you those animals ...' he pointed towards the window, 'that are probably riddled with disease.'

'Don't be stupid,' Isla was now shouting but had begun to worry. Maybe she had made a mistake. 'His father passed away. They needed re-homing and Rory can give them the once over.'

Drew shook his head, 'Oh brilliant ... more money on our vet's bill. I can't believe you would spend so much on a herd of animals that we know nothing about. Seriously Isla, I just can't understand you sometimes.'

Drew stormed out of the kitchen, slamming the door, leaving Isla to burst into tears. Isla had hoped that this would make Drew happier, be the best birthday present ever, but it seemed it had all gone wrong. She felt like she'd made a terrible mistake. Goodness knows what Martha and Fergus were making of it all in the next room.

'Happy bloody birthday!' she bellowed after him. 'Happy bloody birthday.'

Chapter 9

It was just after six o'clock when Isla heard Drew kick off his boots and throw his overalls into the washing machine. He totally ignored Isla as he entered the living room and instead threw Finn up in the air, who wished him happy birthday.

Out of curiosity Isla had continued to call David's number throughout the afternoon, only to receive the same message as before. Isla had begun to worry that maybe Drew was right and she had been taken for a ride and the alpacas were riddled with disease. But David had seemed so genuine when she'd spoken to him on the phone.

'That's how con-artists operate ... give you a sob story and you fall for it hook, line and sinker. Hand over your cash and they disappear, never to be seen again,' Martha had said, unhelpfully. 'The TV is full of stories like that.'

Isla just wanted the day to end. She'd taken herself off to her bedroom and cradled Angus who was unaware of the sadness that flowed through her veins. As her unhappiness gained momentum, her eyes glazed with glassy tears. She blinked, dripping tears sliding down her face.

'Oh Angus, what are we going to do?' she murmured, kissing him lightly on the top of his head. 'What is going on with that daddy of yours?'

Looking out over the fields, the alpacas appeared to have settled in well, and were happily grazing. She'd texted Rory, who had shown more excitement than Drew about their arrival and promised he'd be over in the next couple of days to give them the full once over.

But now Isla had to get through tonight.

Everyone had been invited to the pub for Drew's birthday. Meredith and Fraser had organised a band and Felicity and Rona had prepared a buffet. Everyone was looking forward to it ... well, everyone except Isla and most probably Drew. He couldn't even look at her.

Maybe her marriage really was in trouble. Thinking about it more and more, it had never mattered how tired either of them had been at night, they'd still curl up together under a fleecy blanket watching late-night films and fall asleep in each other's arms. But lately Drew had started to take himself off to bed early and had been fast asleep by the time Isla had slipped under the duvet.

Finn appeared in the doorway, bubbling with excitement and Isla didn't dare turn round as she blinked more tears away.

With a calming voice she said, 'Finn, go and get changed, put your special shirt on. Daddy will like that.'

He zoomed out of the room with his arms stretched wide while making the noise of an aeroplane. When Finn's footsteps petered out Isla turned to face her husband.

'What's going on with us, Drew?' her voice quivered.

He didn't turn around.

'So, is this going to be our night? Not talking to each other? What's the point of even going out?'

'Because Meredith and Fraser have organised a band, and everyone is expecting us.' And with that he disappeared into the bathroom, shutting the door behind him. Isla felt his words were like a kick in the teeth, she was disheartened. All Drew was bothered about was saving face, not what was going on between them.

An hour later they all headed to the pub. Isla pushed Angus in the pram, thinking about the last twelve hours. All she wanted to do was burst into tears but knew she had to keep that smile on her face. Martha walked quietly at the side of her, obviously sensing the tension. Drew gave Finn a piggyback, his pudgy arms wrapped around his dad's neck, both of them laughing. Isla wished she could feel as happy as they seemed.

The Grouse and Haggis was heaving as they pushed open the door.

'Here he is, the birthday boy!' bellowed Rory above the jangle of voices, and everyone turned and cheered.

Meredith had pulled out all the stops. 'Happy Birthday' banners hung from the wooden beams that crossed the ceiling, and at each end of the bar danced a cluster of colourful balloons.

Isla parked the pram next to the table in the corner by the window and pulled out a stool for Finn, but he'd already spotted Esme and ran off to play with her.

Allie was serving behind the bar and waved across to Isla. Drew joined Rory who was chatting to Fergus.

'Drink?' asked Martha, turning towards Isla. 'I think we need one after today.'

'A very large gin and tonic, please,' answered Isla, sitting down feeling deflated and most definitely not in the party mood.

With huge beams on their faces, Felicity and Polly wandered over to join Isla. 'Loving your new top,' exclaimed Felicity. 'But more importantly, how did the alpacas go down ... did Drew love them?'

Isla looked up, holding on to her tears, 'He hated them.'

Felicity and Polly exchanged worried glances before squeezing into the seats opposite her.

'In fact, he more than hated them,' she blurted. 'He hated them that much, he insisted I rang David to come and collect them, and get my money back.'

'That doesn't sound like Drew,' said Felicity, raising her eyebrows.

Isla shrugged, feeling her stomach churn, 'Well, that's what happened.'

'And has David come back to pick them up?'

Isla shook her head, 'The call couldn't be connected. Drew reckons they are riddled with disease or stolen and is blaming me for wasting his hard-earned cash. If I'm truly honest ...' she took a breath. 'I think my marriage is in trouble.'

The words were out in the open and Isla felt a mixture of relief at being finally able to express her fears and sadness, when she couldn't talk to Drew about how she was feeling.

'Don't be daft, it's just a stupid row. Some people don't like birthdays, it reminds them their youth is slipping further and further away,' reassured Felicity.

'Flick, you aren't listening to me,' Isla kept her voice low. 'My marriage is in trouble, we've been drifting apart for some time. Maybe we were just going through the motions having another baby etc. We aren't even speaking at the moment and somehow I have to get through tonight looking happy and jolly.'

Isla knew she had shocked Felicity, but she was worried. Was this really the end for her and Drew? Flick reached over and squeezed Isla's hand and Isla insisted they change the subject.

Martha returned to the table with Aggie and Rona, and Isla checked on Angus. Despite the noisy chatter in the pub he'd drifted off to sleep.

'Over here ... over here, everyone ... gather round,' Meredith's voice echoed over the microphone in the far corner of the room where a makeshift stage had been erected. Everyone shushed and began to huddle around in front of her.

'Where is the birthday boy?' Meredith looked over towards Isla, who pointed at Drew standing at the bar.

Allie gently shooed him in her mum's direction.

Drew looked suitably embarrassed as he joined Meredith. All eyes were on him, his embarrassed smile glued in place.

Meredith cleared her throat, 'Thank you all for coming. As we all know, today is Drew's birthday and his gorgeous wife

Isla didn't want to let it pass without celebrating with this wonderful husband of hers.'

Isla pinned a forced smile on her face.

Without pausing to draw breath and before Drew could make a quick escape, Meredith exclaimed, 'Bring on the cake!'

Allie dimmed the lights and immediately Rona appeared at the side of them proudly holding a cake with lit candles.

Meredith burst into song and the whole pub followed her lead singing 'Happy Birthday' to Drew, who dutifully took his cue and blew out the candles.

Everyone applauded and Allie shouted for Drew to make a speech.

Isla watched Drew roll his eyes and could tell he was dying on the spot. She wondered whether this would lead to another row between them tonight.

'I'm feeling very humble standing here,' Drew took a breath, looking over the sea of faces. 'Thank you all for coming and thank you, Rona, for this magnificent cake. I'm not sure what all the fuss is about, it's just another year slipping away from my youth.'

Felicity caught Isla's eye. 'Told you,' she mouthed discreetly.

'And I mustn't forget to thank my beautiful wife who organised all of this for me. I love you.'

The crowd looked towards Isla who quickly managed a smile. She was confused, she was not expecting such a loving, loyal declaration. Maybe he was just physically exhausted on the farm and she'd blown everything up out of proportion in her mind ... maybe everything was actually okay and not totally lost.

'And I believe there is a fabulous buffet for you all to devour too,' Drew continued, finishing his sentence with a triumphant uplift as everyone clapped. Isla tried to catch Drew's eye as he stepped down from the stage. He looked relieved stepping away from the limelight, but he didn't look in her direction.

Drew joined his friends at the bar and with his back to Isla, her emotions were all over the place, she didn't know what to think. One minute he was telling her he loved her in public, and the next avoiding her at all costs. It didn't make any sense.

After everyone had suitably piled their plates with the buffet and settled back down, Meredith took to the microphone again. 'Please take to your seats,' she left a little pause until everyone was settled. 'Without further ado please put your hands together to welcome all the way from Glensheil ... Mainly Scottish,' she said gaily.

Everyone began to clap as four men confidently walked on to the stage. Dressed in a Pink Floyd T-shirt and Levi's, the lead singer certainly looked the part, even if he was slightly on the mature side. 'I believe we have a birthday in the house,' he bellowed down the microphone.

Everyone cheered and heads spun towards Drew who was still standing alongside Fergus. He nodded his appreciation and gave a thumbs up.

'We are "Mainly Scottish", and as you have probably guessed, one of us isn't from Scotland!'

The guitarist waved his hand.

'And this one's for you, Drew.'

The drummer banged his sticks together and counted them in and the band began to play.

Isla noticed her gran scrutinising the lead singer. 'Where do I know him from?' she mused aloud.

As he began to sing Martha hurled herself across two seats into the chair next to Rona, leaving Aggie raising her eyebrows at the sudden movement.

'What's up with you?' Rona looked up, alarmed.

'It's him!' Martha said as she nudged Rona with her elbow.

'Who?'

'Please don't pretend you don't know.' Martha's eyes were wide, as though she were willing Rona to remember.

'He's vaguely familiar.' Rona fixed her eyes back on the lead singer.

'What's up with you pair? You are like two naughty school children every time you're in each other's company,' said Isla, chastising her gran.

'It's him ... what was his name?' Martha was now flapping her hand in front of her face, trying to remember. 'Bill! His name is Bill.'

Rona shook her head, still none the wiser.

'Bill from Tinder ... the one you matched with,' Martha shouted and all eyes now turned towards the singer on stage.

'This is meant to be, Mum,' teased Felicity as she looked at her mum who had flushed bright red.

'I'll go and find out,' Martha said, standing up.

'You stay where you are,' ordered Rona, with a look of horror on her face. But it was too late. Martha was in one of her take-no-prisoners kind of moods and ignored Rona as she sprinted to the bar.

Whilst everyone was watching Martha, Isla looked at Drew who was in deep conversation with Fergus and Rory. He looked aghast, raking his hand frantically through his hair, which she knew wasn't a good sign. What were they talking about? And why did Drew look so worried? Isla was about to go and see if he was okay, when Martha returned to the table.

'At least you've been useful getting another round of drinks in while you've been gone,' Rona rolled her eyes as Martha put the tray down on the table.

'I have all the gen from Meredith.'

'I'm not sure I want to hear,' Rona said, as she took a big swig of her drink.

'Well, if you don't want the information ...' Martha replied blithely.

'You pair are acting like a couple of teenagers,' Felicity said, shaking her head in jest.

'Oh, come on then ... put me out of my misery,' urged Rona.

Martha pretended to get comfy on her seat. 'See, I knew you wanted to know ...' she said in a voice holding a note of superiority.

Rona shot her a playful dirty look, to which Martha raised her eyebrow and quirked her lip.

Everyone turned to face Martha and waited patiently.

'He's called Bill Awbery. He's been playing in the band for nearly thirty years and lives over the bridge in Glensheil.'

'So not too far away,' said Felicity, giving her mum a look of encouragement.

'And here is the bit of information you've all been waiting for ... he's single!'

'No shit, Sherlock!' laughed Aggie, joining in the conversation. 'We know he's single, he's on Tinder!'

'That means nothing these days,' confirmed Polly.

They all turned back towards the band except Isla, who was still watching Drew, her uneasy feeling about the conversation he was having growing minute by minute. At any other time, she wouldn't think twice about standing up and joining the boys but after today's row with Drew, she didn't think she would be welcome. She couldn't bear a scene in public, so she stayed rooted to her seat.

Everyone else in the Haggis and Grouse seemed to be enjoying the evening, which only made Isla feel even more miserable. Hamish was tapping his feet, Julia and Jessica were jigging on the spot at the far end of the bar and singing along, and the mood was jovial. Finn and Esme were now jumping up and down in front of the stage, pretending to play air guitar. Bill spotted them and gave them a high five.

'Look at those two,' said Felicity, smiling over at the pair of youngsters.

'Best friends,' observed Aggie. 'At least they'll sleep tonight.'

While the conversation was going on around her Isla had drifted off into her own little world. She slouched back in her chair and her thoughts turned to the alpacas. Obviously, Drew wasn't happy, but the fleeces would bring them vast amounts of money which they could then invest back into the farm. She just didn't understand Drew's problem. Surely, he could see the financial potential of the herd?

Isla jolted out of her thoughts as Angus began to cry. It was always at this time of night he began to get grouchy. She snagged another look over in Drew's direction. He hadn't even spoken to her all night. What was the point of her being here? She may as well take Angus home and get him settled in his cot.

Isla cradled him and whispered to Martha, 'I'm going to make a move.'

'You can't go just yet, the band hasn't even finished playing and it's your husband's birthday.'

'And what's the point of me being here when he's completely ignoring me?'

'Just stay until the interval and then I'll walk back with you,' persuaded Martha, and Isla reluctantly agreed.

After playing for another thirty minutes the band took a break.

'That's your cue to go and talk to him, Mum,' prompted Felicity, giving her mum an encouraging nod. Rona looked suitably horrified.

'Anyway, this is a good time to leave you ladies to get on with your night,' said Isla, once again looking over towards Drew. 'I need to get this one to bed,' she said as she placed Angus back in his pram. He'd become fractious now and was beginning to scream blue murder. His cheeks were turning red and his eyes were watery. Isla tucked the blue woven blanket tightly around him.

'Bottle and bed for this one,' smiled Isla. 'And by that look on his face he's filling his nappy too.'

Martha stood up and grabbed her coat from the back of the chair.

'You stay, Gran ... keep the others company. I'll leave the door off the latch, but don't go waking us up when you stumble in.'

'What it's like to be reprimanded by your granddaughter,' Martha laughed. 'But don't be daft, I'll come back with you.'

'No, I insist. I'll grab Finn and head back. You enjoy the rest of the night.'

Martha kissed Isla on the cheek. 'I'll be as quiet as a mouse.'

Isla rolled her eyes, 'I doubt that.'

Felicity grabbed her attention, 'Come over for breakfast in the morning and we can chat.'

'If I dare,' she whispered discreetly in Felicity's ear as she gave her a hug.

'It's on me and I'm sorry you've not enjoyed your evening.'

'It's not your fault, and I'd better show willing and say bye to my bad-tempered husband, otherwise the village will be talking about us.'

Felicity gave her a sympathetic look; she knew better than most how in such a close-knit community nothing escaped anyone's notice.

'Will you rock Angus while I say my goodbyes and grab Finn?'

'Of course,' said Felicity, taking control of the pram.

As Isla approached the bar Meredith and Fraser were talking in low whispers to Rory and Fergus, with Allie loitering behind them listening. Drew was nowhere to be seen. 'Has Drew gone to the toilet? He's useless after a couple of pints.' Isla was only joking but as they all looked at her nervously, she sensed something wasn't quite right.

'Are you going to tell her?' said Rory, staring straight at Fergus.

The whole group looked towards Isla.

'What am I missing?' asked Isla, uncertain what was going on. 'And where's Drew?'

Silence hung in the air.

'Well, will someone tell me what's going on?' Isla's glare intensified as her heart pounded. She was really starting to worry now.

'Rory,' Meredith looked towards him to do the decent thing.

'Drew's gone.'

'What do you mean, gone?'

'It's probably absolutely nothing to worry about,' said Rory, avoiding her eye.

Isla's heart was racing, and her mouth had gone dry.

'Where has he gone?'

'My guess is home.'

'I don't understand, this is his birthday bash. Why would he have left, and without telling me?'

Rory placed his hand in the small of her back, 'Isla, the police came to the surgery today.'

'And what's that got to do with Drew?' Isla's voice had risen an octave and she noticed Felicity had joined the group, along with Polly and Martha.

91

Feeling uneasy, Isla's tone was firm, 'Rory, just tell me what's going on, please.'

She saw him swallow.

'You know that James Kerr passed away a couple of weeks ago? Even though he was a cantankerous old bugger, my father was still good friends with him and looked after his stock.'

'James Kerr? ... You've lost me.'

'James Kerr ... Clover Farm ... lived in Clover Cottage on the land.'

'The old man whose boys are in jail? What's this got to do with Drew?' Isla felt a combination of confusion and sickness.

'Nothing exactly, but the police came to the practice to warn us that there are rustlers operating in the area and that a herd of alpacas had been stolen from James Kerr's farm.'

Isla gave a nervous laugh and looked straight at Rory, who was shifting uncomfortably from one foot to the other. 'You're joking, right?'

'I'm afraid not, Isla,' Rory replied, his face pale and serious.

'What exactly are you trying to tell me here?'

Rory exhaled, 'I think those alpacas are grazing in your field.'

As Rory's words swam around inside Isla's head, she suddenly felt sick to her stomach. 'You're telling me that I've bought an expensive herd of alpacas from a bloke called David, and they weren't even his to sell? And now I'm more than likely in possession of stolen goods.'

'Unfortunately, that about sums it up,' answered Rory, regretfully.

'I think I need another drink ... make it a large one, please,' she turned to Meredith. 'I feel sick ... do you know how much I paid for those animals?'

Rory nodded, 'Drew just told us. I'm so sorry, Isla,' he said, pulling out a bar stool for her to sit on.

'Do you still have this David's number?' asked Rory.

Isla pulled out her phone from her bag and pressed redial. Once again an automated posh woman's voice sounded out, informing her she was unable to connect the call.

'He's long gone, no doubt counting his thousands.' Isla brought a hand up to her mouth. Drew was right about this being a bad idea, she should have talked it over with him first. 'I could honestly throw up. How could I have been so gullible?'

Everyone fell silent for a minute.

'Okay, so what do I need to do?' Isla felt confused. 'I can't give the herd back to a dead man and I have no clue who the man was I handed over the cash to.'

'Isla has a point. If there's no-one living at the farm, what would have happened to the animals?' asked Felicity.

'Probably shipped off to a sanctuary.'

'And James Kerr's sons are still currently being retained at Her Majesty's pleasure, so they aren't going to be able to re-home them,' chipped in Allie.

'Did you chat it over with Drew before parting with the cash?' asked Meredith tentatively.

Isla shook her head, 'It was meant to be a birthday surprise.'

Martha affectionately rubbed her arm, knowing the arguments that had erupted in the last twenty-four hours.

'But alpacas don't turn up for sale every day of the week,'

said Fraser. 'Surely you'd checked out this David's story before you bought them?'

Meredith was quick to shoot Fraser a stern look and he immediately shut up.

'I never gave it a thought! He seemed so genuine when he said his father had passed away and he was visiting from Wales. And I thought it would be profitable in the long run for the farm.'

'There's no denying James Kerr ran a very profitable business. He was the only alpaca farmer in this region. As much as his boys are crooks and him a drinker, he was still a very astute businessman. He took an idea, ran with it and never looked back. All his profits came from selling their fleeces. It's three times stronger than sheep's wool and there's a niche demand for their fleeces in the fashion industry. Those animals out there have won prizes and earnt him a vast amount of money,' confirmed Fergus. 'Breeding them is profitable too, their young can bring in around four thousand pounds each,' he continued.

'That's all well and good, but technically I'm still in possession of stolen goods,' said Isla, fighting back the tears. 'No wonder Drew is mad with me, I should have talked it over with him first. No doubt whoever that David was, he's currently sipping champagne, counting his cash.'

'What's done is done. We can't change it,' reassured Felicity.

'Let's just sit tight and see what happens,' added Martha. 'Surely, if there are no living relatives other than the sons who are inside, then the herd would need to be re-homed somewhere anyway?'

'But that crook has got away with our money,' Isla wailed, holding her head in her hands. It was all such a mess!

'And we can't change that,' said Martha. 'Obviously, you can report it to the police, give a description, but my guess is that man's name isn't even David. What more can we do?'

'Absolutely nothing at the minute except sit tight and see what happens,' suggested Rory.

'Come on, let's get you and the boys home.' Martha had slipped her coat on and drained the dregs of gin from her glass.

Isla nodded. 'I'm so sorry, Meredith, look at all this trouble you and Rona have gone to, and I've put a dampener on everything.' Isla felt distraught.

'You get yourself home and talk to Drew and don't worry about this lot,' Meredith glanced around the pub at the rest of the villagers who were still busy enjoying themselves.

On the way home Martha clutched Finn's hand while Isla gripped the pram. Martha knew the Kerr family from old and had divulged to Isla that as far back as she could remember James Kerr had always been an alcoholic, often swigging from a bottle before breakfast. His wife Gracie had moved away from Scotland many years ago. The rumours were, she'd been fighting a losing battle trying to keep her boys on the right side of the law and had decided enough was enough – for her own sanity, she'd left.

'Originally Gracie wasn't from around these parts, if my memory serves me right ... Cumbria, I think,' said Martha as they turned off Love Heart Lane towards Foxglove Farm. 'I remember having a drink with her many moons ago and she told me she was from a family of lawyers. She said her parents invested a lot of money in that farm. In the end, I think it was her family who said enough was enough and shipped her out of there to safety. Of course, it might just be village gossip but there's no smoke without fire.'

And whilst Drew had spent every waking moment mirroring his own father working the land, learning to care for the animals and grow produce to make a living, the Kerr brothers had turned their backs on the same farming lifestyle and had instead chosen the life of crime.

Isla felt down in the dumps. Drew was a good farmer, hardworking, and now look what she'd done. She'd brought trouble to their door. 'Gran, I'm dreading facing Drew,' Isla's voice faltered.

'You pair really need to talk. It's no good bottling everything up.'

Isla nodded as she put the key in the door. The farmhouse was in complete darkness, but Drew's shoes were planted in the hallway. He must have taken himself off to bed.

'Come on Finn, I'll tuck you in,' said Martha, taking control. 'You get the wee one to bed, his eyes are closing.'

Isla nodded and planted a kiss on the top of Finn's head 'Thank you.'

She grabbed Angus's PJs that were warming on the Aga and, wearily climbing the stairs with her arms wrapped around the baby, she tiptoed into the bedroom, noticing immediately that Drew wasn't asleep in bed as she had imagined. Feeling deflated, she changed Angus's nappy and tucked him in the cot before stepping quietly along the landing towards the spare room at the far end of the farmhouse. The door was slightly ajar as Isla took a deep breath and peered into the room. She could see Drew nestled under the covers, a bottle of whisky and an empty glass abandoned on the bedside table. Hearing his breathing, she knew he was asleep as she silently crept into the room and set the alarm on the clock for his early wake-up call.

Feeling empty inside, she checked on Finn and kissed him goodnight before getting changed for bed and crawling under the duvet alone.

Even though she was exhausted Isla knew she wasn't going to fall asleep anytime soon. Her head was swirling round and round. The distance between her and Drew seemed to be growing further and further. It felt as though everything was spiralling out of control. Isla thought back to when the bridge had collapsed, cutting the whole village off from civilisation. Everyone had pulled together and despite the disaster, spirits in the village had remained high. Drew and Fergus had been fantastic, distributing eggs, managing food drops to the other farms and houses, and Drew had been a major coordinator, helping the community get back on its feet.

He'd been under pressure then, and money had been tight for them, but they'd got through it. As much as Isla tried to think of a trigger for a change in his behaviour, she couldn't. She just didn't understand it. There'd been a time when they'd talk about everything and anything, but whatever was going on in Drew's head, he was pushing them further apart. But Isla knew she needed to accept some responsibility for this row. Buying the alpacas had been a terrible idea and it was going to cost them. Drew's reaction was understandable, of course he was furious, but this didn't explain why he had stopped talking to her about other stuff.

Sleeping in the spare room had escalating things to another level. How did they come back from this? Was that it now? Every time they had a disagreement, was this going to be the norm? They'd made a pact on their wedding night never to go to bed on an argument, and Isla lay there for a moment toying with the idea of waking Drew up, apologising for being so impulsive and buying the alpacas without consulting him, but what was it going to achieve now ... another row? Everyone was tired and tempers were frayed. She'd wait until the morning when things would hopefully seem better, but the way she was feeling, she couldn't even convince herself that was true. She wept silently so no-one could hear her.

Chapter 10

Isla woke up to the sound of Angus gurgling next to her in the cot. It was 7 a.m. and she could hear the wind rustling through the trees and the rain pelting against the window. The weather was so unpredictable at this time of year and Isla knew milking the cows in this torrential downpour wouldn't help Drew's mood in the slightest. She reached over to the bedside cabinet to grab the mug of tea that Drew always made for her and stopped in her tracks ... there was no drink waiting for her today.

Every morning without fail Drew left her a drink before he headed out to milk the cows. Usually it was barely warm by the time she'd woken, but the thought had been there every morning of their married life ... until now.

Scooping up a wriggling Angus, she changed him before heading downstairs to see Finn bashing the top of his boiled egg with a spoon while Martha was busying herself emptying the dishwasher.

'You look like you haven't slept a wink,' said Martha as she turned to face Isla.

Isla risked a tentative look in the mirror; her eyes were

bloodshot and puffy, her skin looked mottled and she looked downright exhausted.

'Probably because I haven't slept a wink.'

Martha gave Isla a sympathetic look, 'Today is another day.'

'Have you seen Drew this morning?'

Martha nodded, 'He nipped back about ten minutes ago to fill up their flasks and change his overalls. He was already soaked from the rain.'

Isla stood in front of the Belfast sink and looked out of the window. It was bleak outside to say the least and she felt as tired as the dreary-looking landscape.

The wind rattled the windows, the trees bowed and creaked and through the torrential rain, Isla spotted Fergus, his head bent low, hurrying towards the farmhouse.

The door to the boot room swung open and Fergus shouted, 'Isla!'

'Is everything okay?'

Fergus wiped the raindrops from his nose. 'You need to call Rory.'

'Rory? Why, what's the matter?'

'I'm not sure, but one of the alpacas doesn't look well. You need to give him a call to be on the safe side.'

'Has Drew taken a look?'

'Yes, that's why I'm here. He said to ring Rory.'

'Has his mood improved any?' asked Isla, already knowing the answer from the lack of drink on her bedside table.

'He's worried, Isla. He's now paying for vet's visits for stolen alpacas.'

Isla nodded; the extra cost of a vet's visit didn't help the situation in the slightest. 'But we don't actually know if that's the herd that has gone missing from Clover Farm.'

'I think Paddy Power odds would be a dead cert. I best get back to work ... ring Rory,' Fergus insisted before yanking his hood back over his head and disappearing into the pouring rain.

'Weather warnings again,' remarked Martha, switching off the TV. 'A storm is on its way.'

'It's already a stormy start to my day. I need to ring Rory. Apparently one of the alpacas isn't looking too sprightly. Drew said he thought they were going to be riddled with disease.'

'Don't be daft, if they are James Kerr's herd Rory's father looked after them, so they'll be in tip-top condition.'

'But they aren't insured. We all know calling out the vet can be costly. This will be just another thing Drew will hold against me.'

'You and I both know Drew would never leave an animal to suffer.'

'Yes, you're right,' Isla sighed and flicked the kettle on before strapping Angus into his bouncy chair.

'Do you need a bottle for this wee one?' asked Martha, smiling down at Angus who was attempting to chew his fist like it was going out of fashion.

'Perfect, thanks.'

'I take it you didn't sleep well because you had things on your mind?'

'Sums it up. Finn, if you've finished your breakfast go and clean your teeth.

Without question, Finn scraped his chair back and chugged off making noises like a steam train as he hurtled up the stairs.

As soon as he was out of sight Isla turned towards her gran. 'Drew slept in the spare room last night. We haven't spoken about what's going on, because he refuses to even be in the same room as me.'

Martha stopped in her tracks, and her eyes widened.

'And for the first time in all our married life he didn't make me my morning cuppa.' Isla exhaled and slumped on to the chair. 'What am I going to do, Gran?'

'I know this is none of my business but what exactly are you arguing over?'

Isla thought for a second. 'I really have no idea ... Do you think ...' She paused. 'Gran, do you think Drew might be having an affair?'

Martha laughed, 'Don't be ridiculous. He's working all hours at the farm and falls into bed early every night. He only goes to the local pub where everyone knows who he is ... and in this village you would know about it before he'd thought about it.'

'I suppose.'

Last night Isla had barely slept a wink with worrying about the state of her marriage, and when she finally did drift off, it only felt like five minutes later when she woke up. Her eyelids felt heavy, and she felt exhausted, with all sorts of scenarios swirling around in her head as to why Drew's moods had slumped so low, especially towards her. As far as she could see, nothing had really changed for her, she was still managing the house and the children ... she just didn't understand why Drew was so angry and upset with her.

'You pair need to talk, and I mean properly talk. Get it out in the open, whatever it is that's bothering him.'

'I can't make him tell me. Lambing season is nearly here and I know he stresses about that, but never like this ... and now, to make things worse, I've thrown away thousands on a herd that wasn't for sale in the first place.'

'He'll come round. That wasn't your fault.'

Isla sipped her tea. 'Buying the alpacas is my fault. We used to talk about everything and anything, and now it feels like we are ships passing in the night.'

'Couples get stuck in a rut. Children come first, and you and Drew need to remember you are more than just a mum and dad. Set some time aside for just the pair of you. Sometimes you need to be Drew and Isla too.'

Isla knew she and Drew had fallen into a mundane routine, but sometimes life got the better of you and you forgot how to have fun with each other. Sex with Drew used to be wild but now only happened on the rarest occasion, and hardly at all since Angus had been born. Maybe she had neglected Drew and their relationship of late, but didn't that work both ways? She knew he was tired from all the hard, manual labour he put in all day every day, but she was tired too from looking after the kids and the house. When had they stopped looking after each other?

Isla sighed as she dialled Rory's number. She was too tired to think about this now. 'Rory, it's Isla,' she said as he picked up his phone.

Isla explained that one of the alpacas looked under the weather and Rory confirmed he'd be there in the next ten minutes.

'Rory's on his way. I've just caught him before he goes out on his rounds. I'll just nip and change into my overalls ... have you seen my waterproofs?'

Martha nodded, 'Hanging up in the boot room.'

'Are you okay to keep an eye on the boys?'

'Of course I am! That's what great-grannies are for, isn't it?' She gave Isla a loving smile. 'I'll get Finn ready for school. Everything will be okay, you know.'

Isla crossed her fingers above her head as she disappeared upstairs.

When Martha had first arrived in the village Isla had her doubts about her staying with them, but not anymore. In the last few days she knew she would have struggled without her being around. At times, Isla felt isolated and unimportant and the loneliness of being a housewife and a full-time mum took its toll. But now with Martha around Isla had company, adult company. Martha was worth her weight in gold.

Isla saw Rory's car driving towards the farmhouse. The rain was still lashing down as she pulled on her waterproofs and thrust her feet inside her wellington boots and stepped outside. Rory parked the car and hurried towards her clutching his black bag. 'Poorly alpaca, you say?'

'Apparently so, I haven't been out to check yet, but Fergus said she didn't look too sprightly.'

Rory closely followed Isla as she pushed open the wooden

gate and traipsed across the muddy field. 'And here was me thinking spring was on its way,' joked Rory, noticing the chocolate-fleeced alpaca that was shielding itself from the rain under the Shetland ponies' shelter.

'Do you think this is James Kerr's herd, Rory?'

'Unfortunately, yes Isla, I do. I'm sorry.'

Feeling guilt-ridden, Isla exhaled, knowing Drew had every right to be mad at her. 'I should have talked it over with Drew first.'

'What's done is done,' he said, bending down at the side of the alpaca while Isla hovered over him. 'These rustlers are chancers and usually get away with fleecing innocent folk ... no pun intended.'

Rory listened to the alpaca's heart rate through his stethoscope and took her temperature before checking over her mouth and ears.

Isla watched as Rory ran his hand down her spine and across her stomach. He tried to lift the alpaca to her feet but almost immediately her legs bent underneath her, and she was lying down once more.

'I think she's going to have to come in for a scan. She feels a little swollen. But my dad knows this herd inside and out, he'll be the best one to look her over.'

'A scan?' replied Isla, struggling to keep hold of her hood as the wind attempted to knock her off her feet once more.

'Yes, just to be on the safe side. It could be something or nothing, but first we need to get her inside. Have you got an empty stable?'

'Yes, of course.'

'Can you go and lay some fresh hay and maybe rig up a heat lamp, if you can? I'll get Drew and Fergus to help me move her.'

Isla nodded and quickly headed in the direction of the stable.

Ten minutes later, Isla finished setting up the heat lamps and dashed towards the cupboard in the storage area as she heard the tyres of the Land Rover crunch outside and the clanking of the old ramshackle trailer.

'I'm just grabbing some towels to dry off the alpaca's wet fleece. Third stable on the right is set up,' shouted Isla down the galley way.

Fergus and Rory carefully manoeuvred the alpaca into the stable and gently laid her down on the fresh hay. Juggling a pile of towels, Isla stopped dead in her tracks as Drew's voice carried down the block. 'Are you serious?'

She strained to listen. Drew's voice seemed heated.

'I'm afraid so. The Kerr brothers are about to be released from jail,' admitted Rory.

'Oh shit,' Isla muttered under her breath as she plucked up the courage to walk towards them.

'Did you hear that?' Drew's eyes were blazing as Isla locked eyes with him.

'I did,' she answered. 'But what does that actually mean for us?'

'What does this mean? I'll tell you what it means ...'

Rory touched Drew's arm, 'Steady on, mate.'

'Sorry, sorry,' said Drew, realising he'd gone a little too far.

'It depends on what happens to Clover Farm and Clover Cottage. Are the properties left to the brothers in the will? Will they want them? Will they want to live around these parts again? It's anyone's guess,' answered Rory, taking control of the situation.

'And can you really see the Kerr brothers wanting to rear alpacas?' added Fergus.

'I can, actually. Obviously, not to rear them ... they'll probably sell them, as they are actually theirs to sell. Which means we ... in fact you ... may as well have thrown my money down the drain,' Drew replied.

Anger engulfed Isla, and her blood was boiling. How dare he speak to her that way in front of their friends?

She retaliated, 'Actually, last time I checked it was *our* money, and stop talking to me like I'm a five-year-old.' Thankfully her voice was steady even though inside she was shaking with anger. If Drew said one more word she would explode.

Isla turned towards Rory, 'She looks settled. I'll dry her off with these towels and let me know what time the scan is on Monday.'

Rory didn't have time to answer. Drew threw his arms up in the air, 'Oh bloody marvellous, now I'm going to be landed with a vet's bill for an animal we don't even own ... Isn't life just great?'

'I don't think it's much fun for the alpaca either,' Isla answered, throwing Drew a dark look.

'Have you got the money to pay for this?' asked Drew, his lips flatlined as he stared at Isla. 'Did you factor in the extra costs when you bought these animals?'

This was the breaking point of Isla's patience and, before she could stop herself, she hurled the towels she was carrying right at Drew. He stared at her in amazement. In all the years they'd been married she'd never lost her temper like this before, but this time he'd pushed her to her limits.

'You know what ...' she threw her arms up into the air. 'Rory, book the scan, and you ...' she pointed at Drew, 'dry off the animal before she dies of pneumonia, and Fergus ...' she took a breath, 'I'm sorry you have to work with such an unreasonable individual. He's being a total idiot and I wouldn't blame you if you decided to find another boss. God knows, I'd love to do the same!'

Having the last word, Isla tossed back her hair and stormed out of the stable block without as much as a fleeting glance behind her.

Chapter 11

With the anger flowing through her veins, Isla found herself standing outside the pub, dripping wet. She thumped on the door and was taken aback by her own strength. Since she'd flounced away from the farm her phone had been ringing constantly ... seven missed calls from Drew. She switched it off and plunged the phone into the pocket of her overalls. 'Go away,' she muttered under her breath. 'Leave me alone.'

Thud ... thud ... thud ...

Isla banged hell out of the door again.

'Hold your horses, we aren't even open yet,' bellowed a disgruntled Allie from inside the pub. 'Who is it?'

'Allie, it's me.'

Isla waited, shielding herself from the rain under the porch as the bolts clanged and the key jangled in the lock.

As soon as Allie opened the door Isla was overcome with emotion and burst into tears.

'Whatever is the matter? And you're drenched.'

'I hate him ... urghhhhhh.'

Allie was taken back; it took a lot to rattle Isla, who was

usually the level-headed one of the group, hardly ever lost her temper and always saw the good in every situation.

'Hate who?' asked Allie, bewildered.

'Drew ... he makes me so mad.'

'Drew? Don't be daft, you don't hate Drew.'

'I do ... I bloody do and especially at this moment in time.' Isla was that mad, she was tripping over her words. 'And I've left the kids with Gran, but I can't face going back just yet.'

'Isla, breathe,' insisted Allie, pulling out a bar stool. 'What on earth is going on?'

Isla peeled off the top of her wet overalls before tying the arms around her waist, then she plumped herself down on the stool, and with her arms folded on the bar she stared at Allie.

'At the minute it's about alpacas, but that's not how it all started.'

'And how did it all start?'

'You know what, Allie, I've no idea,' said Isla, feeling frustrated. 'I think he's fallen out of love with me.'

Allie narrowed her eyes, and the two women stared at each other for a moment before Allie broke the silence. 'You need a drink.'

'Large G and T, please.'

While Allie was pouring the drink, Isla updated her on the morning's antics. She listened and slid the gin across the bar.

'It's like his body and mind have been taken over by aliens. He looks like Drew, but he doesn't act like the Drew I know.'

'Do you think there's more to this than the alpacas?'

'I do. Allie, my marriage is in trouble and I really don't understand the reason why.' Isla was close to tears again. Every possible scenario had been spinning around inside her head. Was Drew cheating? Did he not find her attractive anymore? Had they grown apart? Was he hiding something from her? Isla was beginning to drive herself insane with worry. To everyone else they seemed the perfect couple. In the past her friends had joked that they wanted to bottle the special kind of love that they shared.

Allie's phone buzzed with a text message. 'It's Rory, he's checking if I've seen you. He says he thinks you might need a friend right now.' Allie turned the phone towards Isla so she could read the message.

'Bless him. I did flounce off after throwing a pile of towels at Drew.'

'You threw some towels at Drew?'

'I'm feeling ashamed about that now,' admitted Isla. 'But he made me so mad! I kind of lost control and I'm not proud of that, but the way he was talking to me ...' Isla's voice trailed off as she wiped away more tears that were rolling down her cheeks.

'Rory mentioned that the Kerr brothers are about to be released from jail, but surely they aren't going to show their faces around these parts again. They wouldn't have the nerve.'

Isla drained the gin from her glass. 'Of course they would. What do they care about anyone or anything? If I had just been released from jail and someone was handing me Clover Cottage, Clover Farm and a prize-winning herd of alpacas for absolutely nothing, I would think I'd won the lottery. I wouldn't give two hoots what anyone thought of me.'

Isla knew she couldn't predict the future and yes, she was feeling stupid and helpless about her decision to hand over such a large amount of money before making more checks on David O'Sullivan. Drew would have insisted he visited the farm to view the alpacas in their environment as well as asking Rory to give the herd a quick once over, but Isla didn't need reminding what a mistake she had made, especially by Drew and in front of their friends.

'We were a team once,' Isla sighed. 'But now I feel like we are worlds apart.'

'What are you going to do?'

'I don't know, I haven't thought that far ahead,' Isla answered, digging deep in her pocket and switching her phone back on. The second it received a signal it pinged in quick succession with text messages.

'Gran's in the teashop looking for me. I feel even more awful now, leaving her with the boys.'

'She'll understand, and whatever is bothering Drew, it will come out in the wash. He can't keep it bottled up forever. Remember, this is good old dependable Drew we are talking about.'

Isla nodded, but wasn't convinced. She hadn't seen good old dependable Drew for some time now.

'Go home and talk to him tonight.'

'I'll try, I know I need to apologise for throwing the towels at him, at least.'

'The way he's behaving, I'm surprised you didn't beat him with a pitchfork.' Allie walked around the bar and hugged her friend. 'Love isn't always easy, it's not always hearts and roses, but I'm always here for you.'

'I know,' said Isla, feeling close to tears again. 'Thank you. I better go and face the music.'

Isla stood in the doorway of the pub and exhaled. Slipping her arms back inside her overalls, she shivered. Her dark mood was a perfect mirror of the black sky grumbling above. As Isla ran from the pub there wasn't a soul in sight and the rain lashed down, soaking her through in seconds as she headed towards the teashop.

The only thing on her mind was Drew. Allie's words playing over in mind, *love isn't always easy.*

In all of their married life Isla had always been willing to compromise and she'd stood by every decision Drew had made – even the terrible ones. There was no need for him to treat her this way, even though she'd made a mistake buying the alpacas. She was a person with feelings too, but somehow in the last few weeks she felt Drew's feelings towards her had changed irrevocably. He'd crossed the line, raising his voice at her the way he had, and she wouldn't stand for it. She thought they were good together, understood each other, but after today, Isla knew this wasn't the way love should feel. She'd lost a little respect for him, and not only that; possibly a small piece of her heart too.

Chapter 12

Isla shivered as she pushed opened the teashop door. The wind and rain had whipped furiously through her hair as she'd pushed it back out of her eyes. Felicity was issuing the bill to a group of ramblers sat on the comfy sofas in the corner of the shop, while Rona battled with the coffee machine. After dropping Finn off at school, Martha was sitting reading a magazine, enjoying a pot of tea while Angus was quite happily chomping on a teething ring. The teashop was busy, the serious hikers all kitted out in the latest walking fashion. Without a doubt the hiking shop over in Glensheil made a small fortune from the walkers that frequented Heartcross Mountain.

'Are we ready?' bellowed a confident elderly gentleman who stood up and banged his walking poles on the floor. 'The storm is coming, so make sure you stick with a partner.' He sounded like a sergeant-major rallying together his troops.

Isla quickly moved out of the way as they trundled out of the shop. Martha looked up and spotted her. 'About time, do you not answer that phone of yours? And look at you, you're drenched.'

'I know. I'm sorry, Gran, for leaving you in the lurch, it's brutal out there,' said Isla, catching her breath as she sat down.

'This weather is sticking around for a couple of days according to the latest weather reports,' added Rona, who appeared at the side of the table. 'Can I get you anything, Isla?'

'Just some tea, thank you.'

Once Rona had left the table, Martha leant towards Isla and discreetly sniffed.

'Gran, what are you doing?' asked an embarrassed Isla, looking suitably offended.

'Have you been drinking?'

'Just the one. I needed it.'

Martha eyed her granddaughter carefully. 'Is this what you and Drew are arguing about? Have you got a drinking problem?'

For a second, Isla was stunned and shook her head in disbelief. Martha was waiting for an answer.

'I'm here to help, you know. You can tell me anything.'

Isla opened her mouth, but no words came out. Feeling humiliated and hurt, finally Isla spoke. 'I can't believe you, Gran. I have not got a drinking problem,' she shouted louder than she'd intended, causing the customers in the teashop to look over in her direction.

'Shush now, keep your voice down, we've had enough scenes caused already today,' Martha soothed, patting Isla's arm gently.

Almost immediately, a worried Felicity appeared at the side of the table. 'Is everything okay?'

'Oh, absolutely hunky-dory. My husband has lost the plot

and I'm the worst wife in the world, and apparently now I have a drink problem.'

Felicity glanced between Isla and Martha, clearly worried about her friend.

'Felicity, can you leave us for a moment, please?' asked Martha with a polite but firm tone.

Felicity looked towards Isla for confirmation, who rolled her eyes while nodding.

'Drew's told me, Isla. He said you were violent towards him today and that sometimes, very early in the evening before he's home, you have a glass of wine and rinse the glass out, hoping he doesn't notice.'

Isla couldn't believe what she was hearing. 'Violent? That's stretching the truth. As God is my witness, my husband spoke down to me in front of my friends, so yes ... I admit I pushed me to my limits, and I flung a pile of towels at him ... That does not make me a violent person or an alcoholic,' fumed Isla.

'And as for having a glass of wine in the evening, why not? I don't smoke, I rarely go out, and after coping on my own with two small children and a boring mundane routine every day, it relaxes me. And why the hell am I feeling the need to explain myself? I'm a grown woman. So, I like a glass of wine while I'm cooking the dinner, nothing more, and nothing less. I'm hiding nothing and don't give me that look like you know best ... because ...' Isla was physically shaking with anger. 'And he's turning you against me now,' she said, feeling frustrated.

'He's doing no such thing,' Martha squeezed Isla's hand.

'And I'm not taking sides, but you have to admit it's out of character for you to throw something. Don't go getting upset.'

'What do you expect me to do, sit here and laugh about it all? Did Finn get to school okay?'

'Yes, but he'll start picking up on the tension in the house, kids aren't daft.'

As Isla picked up the menu which she knew off by heart she pretended to look over it to give her time to gather her thoughts. She couldn't quite believe how her morning was panning out.

Isla wished that, whatever was bothering Drew, he would get it out in the open sooner rather than later, but she knew tonight they were in for a hell of a time. Whether he liked it or not, she was going to have it out with him once and for all.

While Isla was perusing the menu, Felicity visited the table again. 'Is it safe to come over now?' she asked, keeping a careful eye on them both.

Before they could answer a sudden fierce gust of wind funnelled in through the door where a man stood, grinning from underneath his dripping wet hood.

'Now that's a storm and a half brewing out there.'

Isla and Felicity looked over towards him.

He was undeniably good looking, with a mane of blond hair swept back from his tanned face, a chiselled jawline and piercing blue eyes.

'And it doesn't look like it's passing anytime soon. We've not seen you around these parts before,' pointed out Felicity.

The guy gave her a cheeky smile. 'I'm Nate, and my guess

is you are Felicity.' He stretched out his hand while an amazed Felicity shook it.

'Do I know you?' she asked, looking confused.

He towered above her, his bright-blue eyes looking down at her. There was a softness to his gaze and a gentleness to his voice.

'Where have you come from?' she enquired. 'I kind of detect a slight Irish accent.'

'And you'll be right,' he answered, not giving any more away. 'You're the legendary girl who single-handedly raised the money for the temporary bridge. I've seen you on the news quite a lot,' Nate replied and Felicity blushed.

'All I did was post a video ... actually I didn't ... but that's another story,' Felicity paused, thinking of Esme who had accidentally uploaded the video that had started the fundraising. 'Anyone would have done the same.'

'But they didn't, did they?' added Rona, feeling proud of her daughter. She put her hand forward, 'Welcome to Bonnie's Teashop.'

'And you must be Bonnie?' quizzed Nate.

'Rona, I'm Rona ... Bonnie was my mum, she's sadly passed away ... and this is my daughter Felicity, as you already know.'

'Surely not ... you two could be ...'

'Sisters,' chipped in Martha in a sarcastic tone. 'Full of the Irish charm,' she added, laughing.

'Take a seat, Nate, and I'll get you a menu,' Rona said, smiling at Martha comment.

'May I?' he asked, looking directly at Isla and pulling out the empty chair next to her.

'Be my guest.'

He peeled off his sodden coat and stretched his shoulders, his muscles rippling along his damp skin. He placed his phone on the table in front of him, and Rona handed him a menu. 'Can I get you a drink?' she asked.

'Coffee would be great ... thank you. You have a wonderful place here, such a quaint little teashop, and quite famous, I believe,' said Nate before ordering a sandwich.

'What brings you here? Looking to hike the mountain?' asked Felicity, placing his drink in front of him.

'In this weather, not a chance.'

'It takes a few hours to hike to the top ... but it's worth every step.'

They all looked towards the window, and the sky seemed darker and unwelcoming. Through the haze of the rain the mountainous terrain was barely visible.

'It is truly impressive, fancy waking up to this spectacular scenery each day,' said Nate. 'I'm actually here looking for work. Would you pass me the sugar, please?'

Isla nodded, handing him the bowl.

'Work, you say?' asked Martha.

'Due to the coverage on the news I thought there may be an increase in tourism? Maybe some jobs going?'

'Believe me, tourism has increased, Julia at the B&B is turning people away left, right and centre, but as for work, most of the businesses in Heartcross are family run ... just like this place,' said Felicity.

'What about farming?'

'Isla's your girl.' Felicity nodded towards her friend.

120

'Isla, what a lovely name,' Nate looked towards her.

'Sorry, there's no jobs at our place.'

'Just my luck. Can anyone recommend somewhere to stay this evening?'

'If you turn left at the bottom of Love Heart Lane, Julia's B&B is on the right,' said Isla. 'And if Julia is full, I'm afraid you'll have to head over the bridge into Glensheil.'

'Thank you. I'll try Julia's B&B.' said Nate, sipping his coffee.

'Look at that rain,' said Isla, glancing once more towards the window. She knew she had a hundred and one things to do back at the farm but didn't relish the idea of walking back in the torrential rain.

Angus was still happily chewing on his teething ring, his bib soaked with all the dribble. 'Pass him over, Gran, there's a clean bib in his bag.'

'And who is this fellow?' asked Nate, smiling towards the baby.

'This is Angus,' answered Isla, dropping his bib. Nate caught it and handed it back to her.

Nate grinned and tousled the boy's hair.

'We need to make a move soon,' said Martha.

Isla was reluctant to move, she didn't want to bump into Drew just yet but knew she needed to rally some enthusiasm together, otherwise she'd be sat there all day.

'I thought we were done with this bad weather,' chipped in Flick, staring out of the window.

Just at that moment everyone jumped as a flash of lightning struck right across the dense clouds, followed by a boom of thunder.

Angus's lips began to tremble at the sound and he let out a cry. Isla soothed his back and cradled him.

The trees that lined Love Heart Lane began to sway in the strengthening gust. The rain became heavier. Another jagged bolt of white split the sky again, the clap of thunder following immediately.

'Jeez, that sounded close,' exclaimed Martha. 'I'm going nowhere fast.'

Isla gave a sigh. There was no way she was abandoning the warmth of the teashop for another soaking.

'The storm will hopefully pass quickly,' Flick said, disappearing into the kitchen just as another loud clatter of thunder could be heard.

After finishing his sandwich, Nate slid his plate away from him and found himself looking out of the window. 'I best go and see if I can find a bed for the night. I don't fancy being stranded in this weather,' he said, taking a note from his wallet and laying it on the table.

'It was lovely to meet you all.' Nate stood up and slipped his arms back inside his damp coat.

Martha nudged Isla, 'Isn't that your Land Rover?'

A continuous frantic beep of the car horn caught everyone's attention, automatically all heads turned towards Love Heart Lane.

'What's going on?' asked Isla, watching the car speed towards the teashop. She had an uneasy feeling.

The Land Rover screeched to a halt outside the teashop.

'It's Rory,' exclaimed Rona, as they watched him jump from the car and throw open the teashop door.

'Isla ... where's Isla?' Rory looked stricken.

Isla looked across at the sound of her name, but Rory's expression wasn't his usual happy one. Their eyes locked and her heart was speeding fast; she knew something was terribly wrong.

'What is it?' she stammered.

He pulled down his wet hood and wiped the drippy wet fringe from his face.

'The storm ... the lightning ...' Rory was tripping over his words in urgency. 'The lightning's hit the barn.'

'Which barn?' asked Isla, hoping and praying he didn't mean the milking shed. If any of the equipment had been damaged that would immediately put the farm in financial jeopardy. Of course, there would be the insurance, but time was money.

'The old barn, the one where you stack the hay bales ... the one we are moving the pregnant ewes to.'

'Is the barn damaged?' Isla could tell by the sickened look on Rory's face that there was more.

'It's Drew ... The barn's on fire and he's trapped inside.' Rory swallowed down a lump in his throat. He was visibly shaking.

'On fire ...' exclaimed Isla. Then reality struck. 'But the barn is full of hay.' Clutching Angus with all her might, the tears began streaming down her face.

'Oh my God,' whispered Felicity. 'Where's Fergus?'

'He went in after Drew.'

Isla looked at Felicity, all the colour had drained from her cheeks.

Martha took control. 'You both need to go now with Rory,' she said, taking Angus from Isla and kissing her grand-daughter lightly on the cheek. 'Go!'

The tone of her voice jolted Isla, who mechanically nodded her appreciation and shivered. Standing up, her legs felt shaky and panic was mounting inside her.

Rory carried on talking as Felicity grabbed her coat. 'I'd nipped back to check on the alpaca,' Rory was choked up.

Isla's voice wavered, 'We can't lose him, Gran ... we just can't lose him. He might be a pain in the arse, but he's *my* pain in the arse.'

Martha put on her best encouraging smile. 'As soon as you have news, let me know.'

Isla nodded and followed Rory and Felicity towards the door. Felicity was fighting back tears too.

Rona shouted after them, 'Has the fire brigade been called?'

'Yes, they are on their way,' bellowed Rory as they braved the fierce storm outside.

Everyone inside the teashop watched as a distressed Isla and Felicity ran towards the Land Rover and clambered in. The door slammed and everyone stood in silence as they sped off down Love Heart Lane.

Chapter 13

The view through the car windscreen was barely recognisable, frantically the wipers swished back and forth, barely clearing the rain. Everything was blurry as they turned into Foxglove Farm. Then they saw it, the barn aglow with red-hot flames.

Rory slowed the car down and parked in front of the farmhouse.

'Where the hell is the fire brigade?' Isla said, flinging open the car door swiftly, followed by Felicity.

Immediately huge drops of water attacked their bodies, and their clothes were sodden in seconds. Isla's feet pounded heavily across the ground, her legs flailing, the torrential rain turning the grass to mud, making it slippery.

She stopped dead.

A plume of fire exploded in the black sky. Isla was praying with all her might that somehow, just somehow, Drew and Fergus were okay.

Pain and uncertainty gripped her stomach and she retched. Felicity gripped hold of her for dear life. The heat was immense even from five hundred yards away, an inferno fuelled by the hay bales stacked up in the barn. The glowing embers swirled in the air, the sky illuminated, and ash floated to the ground like dirty flakes of snow.

Isla's eyes were glued to her phone, frantically wiping the rain from the screen, willing for a signal.

'There's no service,' she said, inside screaming with frustration. 'Where the hell are they? I'm going in. I can't leave them in there.'

The idea of Isla rushing into the barn was ludicrous and Felicity gripped her tighter. 'Oh no you don't! It's too dangerous ... think of the kids. They need us.'

Isla's face crumpled, all the colour had drained from her skin.

The two women stood helpless, holding on to each other as the wind attempted to lift them off their feet, the rain stinging their cheeks.

'Drew! Fergus!' Isla shouted with all her might, hoping they'd respond. There was nothing except another loud blast, causing them to jump backwards.

They watched in horror as the fire raged on. Not even the torrential rain helped to lessen its heat. Rory paced up and down like a caged animal, raking his hand through his wet hair. They all felt helpless as another enormous explosion punched a fist of orange flames towards the farmhouse. With the force, a window blew out, sending hot shards of glass on to the yard. The eerie gasps and cries of the villagers now gathered at the gates of Foxglove Farm carried towards them in the wind.

The radiant heat was intense, the flames crackled loudly,

the smell of burning was potent. All they could do was stand gripping each other tightly and pray.

Finally, the sirens of the fire engines became noticeable. 'At last!' exclaimed Rory.

It had felt like hours had passed to Isla, but it had only been a matter of minutes. 'Hang on in there, Drew ... Hang on in there, Fergus,' Isla whispered, still clutching Felicity with all her might. She prayed so hard for them both, it physically hurt.

'I'll go and direct the fire engine. Do not move,' ordered Rory, but they didn't answer him. In a trance-like state Isla and Felicity stared into the flames.

Battling hard against the wind and rain, Rory ran the short distance towards the driveway, waving his hands madly in the air to attract the firefighters' attention. The tyres of the fire engine threw up mud as it raced along the rain-drenched drive, followed by two ambulances.

The sirens shut down as the fire engine came to a halt.

'Get those girls moved back,' shouted a firefighter. 'It's not safe.'

But Isla and Felicity were oblivious to the commotion, their eyes still firmly fixed on the burning barn. Soaked to the core, Isla's body was numb from the cold, but the pain in her heart was excruciating. Reality had struck; whatever they were arguing about, it didn't matter. Isla couldn't stand to lose Drew. Despite everything that had happened recently, she still loved him.

Then, without warning, Isla let out an earth-shattering scream, the kind that made your blood run cold. She screamed again and took off towards the barn.

'Isla, stop!' bellowed Rory, sprinting towards her, shielding the heat from his face with his arm. The barn was crackling and spitting flames. As Rory reached her, he was conscious of the heavy boots thumping the ground behind him. Both the firefighter and Rory grabbed Isla's coat and cleanly lifted her off the ground. She kicked her legs like a tantrum toddler. 'Put me down!'

'Get back,' ordered the firefighter, with stern authority. 'It's too dangerous. Take her out of the way.'

'No! Look!' she sobbed, the tears leaving streak-marks down her black sooted face. She pointed. 'Drew!' she screamed. Felicity was by her side, their arms wrapped tightly around each other, shaking with relief as they witnessed Fergus hunched over, dragging Drew with all his might behind him.

The firefighters ran to help him and tears of relief cascaded down Isla and Flick's faces.

'He's unconscious,' spluttered Fergus, barely able to breathe himself.

'Get two stretchers over here NOW,' ordered the chief fire-fighter.

As soon as they emerged, both men were strapped to stretchers and carefully manoeuvred out of the rain into the back of the waiting ambulances.

The paramedics passed blankets to Isla and Felicity. 'You are both shivering, get wrapped up.'

Both did as they were told before disappearing into the back of one of the ambulances to check on Drew.

'Why isn't he awake, why isn't he moving?' Isla was frantic. 'Please help him.'

'Are you a relative?'

'I'm his wife, Isla.'

The paramedic nodded, 'Can you tell me his name, please.'

'Drew ... it's Drew.'

'Okay, Drew, I'm Lenny and I'm here to help you,' he said, hooking Drew up to a monitor.

Drew didn't respond.

'We need you to stand back.'

Isla disobeyed, grabbing Drew's hand. 'Drew ... Drew, can you hear me?'

His eyes were closed, his chest was falling and rising slowly. Wide eyed with horror, Isla caught her breath, her body soaked and shivery, her stomach twisting in knots.

'Drew ... talk to me.'

'We need to get the oxygen mask on him,' said Lenny. 'Please can you stand to the side?'

Isla felt herself crumbling. Rubbing her hands over her face, she did as she was asked and stepped away from her husband. She watched in horror as the barn continued to burn. The front and side of the farmhouse were scorched by the flames and covered in black soot, and the majority of the side windows had blown. Isla put this day down as one of the worst in her life.

Wrapped in a blanket, Rory appeared at the back of the ambulance.

'Fergus is doing okay, just some minor burns and smoke inhalation. How's Drew doing?'

Isla couldn't speak, she attempted to shrug. She just wanted someone, anyone to tell her Drew was going to be okay. Deep breaths, Isla told herself, trying to be braver than she felt.

'He's in the best possible hands,' said Rory, pulling Isla in for a hug. They both watched as the paramedics made Drew as comfortable as possible, before turning towards Isla.

'We need to get him to hospital. He's inhaled large amounts of smoke, there's a large cut to his head and there's a possibility his leg is broken.'

'Can I come with him?'

'Of course.'

'What about Angus and Finn?' she turned towards Rory.

'Martha will look after them. You go, I'll take care of everything ... just go,' reassured Rory.

As Isla sat down she felt emotionally bankrupt. She looked out from the back of the ambulance to see the firefighters trying to bring the blaze under control. She felt devastated, worried that everything she'd ever loved, worked for and struggled for lay in ruins. The desolation she felt was all consuming.

Whatever she and Drew had been arguing about, it didn't matter now. Drew had to be okay, there wasn't another option for their family. Wiping the tears from her eyes, her anxiety levels off the scale, all she could think about was her boys – Drew, Finn and Angus. They were her whole life.

She reached for Drew's hand; he was still unconscious. The ambulance door was slammed shut and they sped off towards the hospital, sirens blaring.

Chapter 14

As soon as the ambulance reached the hospital, Drew was whisked out of sight and Isla was escorted towards the waiting room. The journey had taken approximately ten minutes and Drew's eyes had remained closed throughout, but Isla had never let go of his hand.

Exhausted, cold and still wrapped up in the blanket, Isla slumped on to a chair, the stench of smoke still potent. She shivered, all she could do now was wait.

'Cup of tea?'

Dazed, Isla looked up to see an old man sitting opposite her.

'I've no money,' she answered politely.

The man handed over some coins. 'You look like you need one.'

'Thank you,' she said, gratefully slotting the coins into the drinks machine in the waiting room.

She sat back, cupping her hands around the warm polystyrene cup, her fingers finally coming back to life. 'Isla ... Isla.' The door to the waiting room swung open and Allie and Polly rushed towards her. She fell into their arms, tears falling once more.

'How is he?' asked Allie, sitting down next to Isla and placing her hand on her knee.

'I'm not sure. They've taken him through to another room but he looked lifeless,' Isla swallowed down a lump in her throat. 'I can't believe it ... why us? And do we know how Fergus is?'

'He's suffering with a headache, hoarseness and feels nauseous. He has minor burns to his arms but he's going to be absolutely fine.'

'Thank God. How's Felicity?'

'Relieved, she'll be along in a minute, we've brought her some clean clothes to change into, and here's yours,' Allie held up a carrier bag.

'And the children? Has anyone said anything to Finn?'

Allie shook her head, 'Don't worry, Finn's still at school. Martha's going to take the children to Heartwood Cottage, she'll be with Rona and Aggie. They won't say anything until you tell them to, that's your call.'

'And the fire?' Isla dreaded to think.

'The fire is under control and I know this won't seem like good news, but despite the windows being blown out, there's only smoke damage to the farmhouse, mainly in the living room and kitchen.'

'You can't stay there until the fire brigade give it the all clear. So, you can either say at Heartwood Cottage, Aggie's or the pub,' added Polly.

'Everyone is so kind, I can't even think straight at the minute.' Isla burst into tears, everything was getting on top of her. 'What a mess, barns burnt down, windows blown out and the house must stink of smoke. I'm dreading going home.'

'Don't you worry about anything, Alfie has already got the villagers co-ordinated. He's holding an emergency meeting right at this very moment,' said Polly.

'Hamish and Julia are in charge of the cleaning squad. Hamish is providing all the cleaning materials from the shop free of charge,' chipped in Allie.

Isla felt overwhelmed by the kindness of everyone.

'And Alfie said he'll sort the windows through his contractors at work and you can just pay him back once the insurance money is paid.'

'And this is why I love living in our village. Everyone always pulls together at a time of need. Did we lose any livestock?'

'Not as far as Rory could see, all the pregnant ewes are accounted for, the cows and alpacas are safe.'

At least that was good news, thought Isla. It didn't matter how many years she'd lived on the farm, she never got used to any loss of life.

'But the old fence lifted in the wind. Rory is securing that, along with some guy called Nate? I didn't have time to query who he was but at least the alpacas will be secure.'

'Nate's the Irish guy, turned up at the teashop looking for work and needed a bed for the night. I need to thank everyone when I get home. If nothing else, Drew will have more to worry about now than just the alpacas.' Isla attempted a light-hearted smile, but inside she was far from smiling. The last time she'd seen Drew they'd argued horribly. What if she didn't have the chance to say sorry to him? Or to tell him how much she loved him? She'd never forgive herself.

'Now go and get changed, there's a towel in there too,' said Polly.

Isla nodded her appreciation, 'What if the nurse ...'

'If the nurse comes back we'll come and find you immediately, don't worry,' Allie assured her.

Isla barely had the energy to walk to the ladies toilets as she left the waiting room. She looked solemn and exhausted, her hair bedraggled, wet and limp, the smell of smoke clinging to her body. When she appeared again five minutes later with her wet clothes stuffed in a carrier bag, there was still no news about Drew.

The waiting was killing her. What was taking them so long? Her chest felt tighter by the second and she was struggling to breathe. The image of Drew being pulled from the burning barn played over and over again in her mind.

The three women sat and waited in silence for around fifteen minutes.

'This is awful ... the waiting,' said Polly, finally.

'Why us? Just when you think you are on the up, something happens to put you back to square one.' Isla rubbed a hand over her weary face and tossed her empty cup into the bin. 'Where are they? This is ridiculous now,' she said, the frustration and fear making her worry all the more.

Just then they heard footsteps padding up the corridor and they all sat up straight. The door to the waiting room opened and a doctor and nurse walked in. Isla stood up and looked imploringly towards them for news.

The doctor smiled warmly, 'Isla?'

'At last – yes, that's me.' Her stomach was churning and her hands shaking.

Allie squeezed her hand for moral support.

Isla held her breath as she waited for them to speak.

'Drew's leg is broken, and he's got a couple of broken ribs too. He has a cast on his leg and he'll be on crutches for a while.'

Isla exhaled, 'What about the fire and the smoke?'

'He's suffered burns to his back and fingers, which we've dressed, and he's inhaled a lot of smoke, which will cause him some discomfort. He also has quite a nasty cut to his head, which we've stitched.'

'But he's going to be okay?'

The doctor smiled, 'He's going to be just fine. We'll keep him in for observation, but he will need rest over the next few weeks.'

Relief swept through Isla's body.

'Can I see him?'

'Of course, if you want to follow the nurse.'

'We'll wait here, give him our love,' said Allie.

Isla hugged both her friends before following the nurse up the corridor, her clean white clogs squeaking on the tiled floor as she walked. Feeling apprehensive, Isla followed the nurse into the room. The last time she saw Drew they'd argued and she'd thrown towels at him, and now here he was, lying in a hospital bed after being pulled from a burning barn. She felt guilty for reacting the way she had – what if that had been the last time they ever spoke to each other? Isla couldn't bear to think about it. She'd never ever be able to live with herself.

The tears flowed down her cheeks the second she saw Drew, lying in bed. He was hooked up to a machine that constantly beeped, his head was bandaged, his hair singed, his face charred and his eyes were closed.

'Oh Drew,' said Isla, fraught with emotion. Her big rugged husband suddenly looked fragile and weak. She planted a light kiss on top of his head.

He murmured.

'Are you awake?' She pulled the chair closer to the side of his bed and perched on the edge, leaning towards him. 'How are you feeling?'

'Like I've been hit over the head with a plank of wood.'

'Funny that, apparently you have.'

Drew gulped, and slowly brought his hand up to his throat, his fingers bound in bandages. 'My throat is sore.'

'Don't try and speak. Just rest.'

For a split second he looked like he was about to close his eyes again, then suddenly he seemed startled. 'It's all hazy ... Fergus ... Fergus ...' Drew appeared frantic, fighting for his breath. 'Please tell me ...' His eyes stacked with tears. In all the time they'd been together Isla had never seen him cry.

'He's fine, fine,' she repeated, interrupting him quickly.

Drew's chest heaved, 'Thank God.'

His body relaxed for a moment and he lay back on the pillow looking up at the ceiling. 'That smell is driving me insane.'

'It'll be the smoke.'

'The fire, did it spread to the house?'

'Apparently some of the windows have been blown out. But it's all in hand.'

'Huh?' Drew began to cough. He tried to sit up, but winced in pain.

'Stop trying to talk ... Alfie's been amazing, organised the villagers, cleaning etc ... He's even got his contractors from the council on the job. He said don't worry about any money, he'll sort it out with you once the insurance money is paid. I can't stay at the house tonight but hopefully, if the fire service deem it safe, I can nip back in and grab some things and call the insurance company. Is the policy still in the bottom drawer of your desk in the office?'

Drew looked troubled.

'It's okay, I'll find it. And Rory, he's been working flat out in the rain. The wind lifted the old fence, we've said that needed fixing for a while.' Isla knew she was rambling but she just wanted Drew not to worry about a thing. 'But Rory and Nate have it under control. They've moved all the animals to the far fields, including the alpacas, and Rory is checking them all over.'

'Nate?'

'He turned up in the village looking for work, thought there might have been something going, with the increase of tourism in Heartcross.'

'Stop,' cried out Drew. 'Stop.'

'Are you okay, shall I get the nurse? Are you in pain?'

Isla knew that was a stupid question, his leg was in a cast, his body was full of burns, his head was in a bandage and he could barely talk.

'You need to stop him.'

'Stop who?'

'No windows ...' Drew seemed drowsy. His words were slurred.

'You aren't making any sense, Drew, it'll be the drugs. Just try and rest. Don't you worry about a thing. I'll sort everything at home. You just concentrate on getting better.'

Drew was drifting in and out sleep. Isla bent her elbows and leant on the bed, cupping her hands around his. She exhaled with relief. Drew was her comfort blanket, it had always been Drew and Isla, Isla and Drew. The thought of losing him was a thought she just couldn't comprehend. She never ever wanted to feel the way she felt today. She could never lose him. Whatever they had been quarrelling about was now insignificant. They had each other and were a team. No-one or nothing could ever break that.

'I'm sorry Drew, I love you.'

He didn't move, he'd fallen asleep.

As she stepped out into the corridor, she had to admit she was worried. She didn't know what use she was going to be in the next six weeks, but she made a silent promise, she'd do whatever it took to keep the farm going.

Chapter 15

Knock ... knock ...
Isla rapped on the door softly and waited.

She heard voices and the scrape of a chair before an exhausted Felicity peered around the door of Fergus's hospital room. She immediately fell into Isla's arms and hugged her like her life depended on it.

'Come in,' said Felicity.

Isla stepped into the room to see Fergus sitting up in bed. He looked wide awake compared to Drew, considering the trauma he'd been through.

'Oh Fergus,' Isla walked to the bed with her arms open, the tears again flowing down her cheeks. 'I don't know where all these tears are coming from,' she said, trying to make a light-hearted joke.

'Drew, Drew – how is he?' asked Fergus, hugging Isla. 'Ow, sorry – I'm a little sore,' he said, pulling away his bandaged arms.

'Sorry ... sorry,' she said, drawing away quickly. 'Drew's not on this planet at the minute – drugged, broken leg, ribs, burns, smoke inhalation. He's drugged up on painkillers and not making much sense.'

Fergus blew out a breath, 'But he's going to be okay?'

'He is, thanks to you ... Fergus, I don't know how we are ever going to repay you. If it wasn't for you ...' Isla couldn't control her emotions and her bottom lip began to quiver.

'Don't you start bawling on me, this one hasn't stopped.'

'I can't help it,' Isla attempted a smile. 'I just couldn't imagine, what if ...'

'You can't get rid of us that easily, even though I have to admit, my life flashed before my eyes.' Fergus's voice faltered. 'All I could think about was Esme and you,' he reached out for Felicity's hand, the emotion clearly overwhelming him.

'He told me off for being maudlin, now look at him.'

Isla sat opposite Felicity who poured Fergus a drink of water.

'What happened, Fergus? Can you remember anything?' asked Isla.

Fergus took a sip of his drink then leant back on his pillows. 'It felt so surreal, like I was an actor in a movie, everything felt like it was in slow motion. Lambing had begun and one of the ewes had got into difficulty, and with the weather like it was Drew wanted to move her out of the rain. I'd moved the trailer back to the barn and Drew went to retrieve it while I fetched the Land Rover. The lightning lit up the sky and the boom of thunder made me jump, it was literally seconds away.'

Fergus took a moment to compose himself.

'Then there was another loud bang,' Fergus flinched. 'I glanced up to see orange light dancing through the rain on the windscreen. It took me a couple of seconds to realise the barn had gone up in flames ... just like that. The lightning must have struck something ... I don't know ... all I knew was, Drew was in that barn.'

Isla's pulse was racing, listening to the agony in Fergus's voice.

'I couldn't leave him in there. I didn't think about anything at the time, it was just a gut reaction. I ran to the barn and the heat was already immense, the hay bales fuelling the fire. I could see Drew and shouted towards him. He looked over as there was a loud creak and part of the roof splintered off, collapsing and falling on to him, trapping him. He yelled as the impact of the burning roof hit him, and then there was silence. I shouted and shouted but he didn't answer. The smoke was overwhelming, making me feel dizzy. I kept low and held a rag over my mouth, but the heat from the fire was piercing through my overalls. I reached Drew and pulled him so hard, not even knowing where I got my strength from. I managed to free him, somehow.'

'Thank God you did,' interrupted Isla.

'I knew his leg was broken. Then I heard the sirens in the distance.' Fergus gave a fragile smile.

Isla's tears unleashed once more listening to the horror which both Fergus and Drew had endured. 'The whole thing could have collapsed at any time,' she said, knowing it didn't bear thinking about.

'I know you've not had time to think yet,' said Felicity. 'But what's going to happen to the farm? Fergus and Drew will both need to take some time off.'

'I'm okay, just a sore throat and a few burns,' said Fergus.

Felicity gave him that look which totally dismissed what

he was saying. 'The nurse said no work until you have fully recovered.'

'Absolutely,' agreed Isla. 'I wouldn't expect you back at work, and with Drew the way he is ... I've no idea what the hell we're going to do. It's lambing season, the cows need milking, trips to market, and it's the alpacas' scan on Monday,' Isla's voice was earnest.

She slipped into deep thought. What the hell was the farm going to do? If Gran looked after Angus maybe she'd be able to milk the cows? It would be a struggle, but she'd have to manage.

'I can't thank you enough, Fergus, and you must take all the time you need.' Isla looked over the bed towards Felicity. 'I need to get back to see the boys and take a look at the damage to the house. How are you getting home? Allie and Polly are still in the waiting room, if you want a lift?'

'You go with Isla,' insisted Fergus. 'I'm tired, I'm going to get some sleep.'

'Okay, if you're sure,' replied Felicity, standing up. She pressed a light kiss on Fergus's lips. 'You taste smoking hot,' she grinned.

'Ha, very funny,' Fergus rolled his eyes.

'I'll bring Esme along tomorrow, we'll let you get a good night's rest first.'

Fergus nodded, clearly exhausted, his eyes already closing.

'Oh, Isla?' he said as she was about to walk out the door.

She spun round, 'Yes?'

'When I was dragging Drew out of the fire, he kept saying to tell you he was sorry and that he loved you. He was slipping in and out of consciousness, but he wanted to make sure you knew how sorry he was, maybe about the argument you had this morning?'

'Thanks, Fergus.' This declaration meant so much to Isla. She was sorry too. All this had highlighted how important Drew and her boys were to her. Isla was determined to put their differences to one side. She was going to make sure their marriage got back on track.

All the way home Isla's mind was on Drew and the farm. The alpacas had suddenly paled into insignificance and she had to work out how to keep the farm running.

'You okay in the back?' Allie eyeballed Isla through the mirror, noticing she was extremely quiet.

'My mind is in overdrive. I'm going to have to help on the farm until the boys are back on their feet. Thank God Martha arrived when she did. It'll mean very early starts, but what choice do I have?'

'Hire a temporary farm hand?' suggested Allie.

'Can't afford to. They'll want paying, and we still have to pay Drew and Fergus's wages while they're off sick. The only solution is me,' she exhaled. This is when I step into Drew's shoes and realise how hard it is to run the farm, she thought. She didn't relish the very early morning starts but she could prioritise milking, eggs and the market; all the manual stuff would have to wait.

'With me at the helm,' continued Isla, 'all it'll cost is time.'

'Good job you'll have me to help then, isn't it?' said Polly.

'Huh?'

'Girl power!' Polly high-fived a stunned Isla from the passenger seat. 'I don't need paying, all I'm doing is getting under Felicity's feet at the teashop ... A friend in need ... what else would I do?'

'Are you serious?'

'Absolutely serious, you can pay me in eggs,' laughed Polly. 'Count me in.'

'Done! You are bloody amazing!'

'I know, I know, polishing my halo as I speak,' answered Polly, grinning.

Isla couldn't believe the kindness from people; there was Alfie already sorting out the contractors and windows, Rory fixing the fences and now Polly's offer to help out. She was lucky to have such special people around her. Isla had to admit, she wasn't relishing walking back into Foxglove Farm for the first time. She didn't know what to expect and she wasn't sure she could cope with any more today. All she wanted to do was hug her boys and tell them daddy was safe.

Drew had always been the protector of the family, the one that looked after them, but for the next few weeks it would be Isla's turn. Her first job was to locate the insurance policy and ring them as soon as possible. There was the rebuilding of the barns, new animal feed and hay to be bought. Isla knew they were going to have to tighten their belts until the insurance money came through, and it was going to be difficult for a while.

'Allie,' said Isla. 'Please can we nip to the farm before going back to Heartwood Cottage? Is that okay with everyone? I need to see the damage before I see the boys.'

'Yes, of course,' replied Allie, swinging the car into the drive of Foxglove Farm.

'At least it's stopped raining,' said Felicity, as they all looked towards the farmhouse.

Isla unfastened her seatbelt and shuffled forward to stare between the two front seats out of the windscreen. Everyone was silent.

Isla's eyes started to tear up as she fixed her gaze on the charcoal debris. The barn was completely burnt to the ground. The firefighters had secured the area with red-and-yellow tape and now there wasn't a soul in sight.

'It looks so different,' said Felicity quietly.

'You can see right into the mountains now,' exclaimed Polly.

'We need to be thankful it wasn't worse. At least it didn't spread,' added Felicity.

The wind was still howling as an exhausted and emotional Isla climbed out of the passenger seat and pulled the lapels of her coat up around her neck.

'How are you feeling?' asked Allie. 'If it's too much to go inside, just say ... you don't have to do this now.'

'I honestly feel like I'm watching a movie but like we've said, it could be a lot worse. The barn, the windows and furnishings are all replaceable. Drew isn't.'

With her three friends by her side, Isla pushed open the door to the farmhouse. She didn't know what to expect, but the stench of smoke was still strong in the air. The hallway looked exactly the same, but walking into the living room, it was a different story. Isla was lost for words as she took in the carnage around her. She drew in the fresh air from the open windows and shivered. The smoky curtains were torn and flapping in the wind. There were shards of glass splintered all over the carpet and strewn across the coffee table. The photographs from the dresser were tossed on to the floor and layers of ash covered every surface.

'If I didn't know better, I'd think I'd stepped into a winter wonderland. It looks like it's been snowing inside,' Isla blew out a breath. 'Look at this place.'

All Isla wanted was the cleaning fairies to fly through the open windows and work their magic, but she knew that was wishful thinking.

'It's mainly cosmetic. Once we vacuum up the ash, it'll be looking spick and span in no time at all,' said Felicity, trying to put a positive spin on it all.

Isla walked over towards the sideboard, her boots crunching over the broken glass. She bent down and picked up her wedding photo from the floor. The glass was cracked and she couldn't hold back the tears.

Felicity took the photograph from her and enveloped her in a heart-warming hug. 'It's only a frame. We'll get it fixed.'

Isla nodded, but this was all too much for her. All she could think about was Drew lying all alone in the hospital bed. She'd nearly lost him and their home in a matter of seconds.

'Honestly Isla, let's get settled for the night. A hot bath will do you the world of good. Mum's cooked us all some food and tomorrow all this will look brighter ... it's been a long day,' said Felicity.

Isla nodded, 'I'll just get the insurance policy and we'll

head back to yours. Gran will be out of her mind with worry.'

Isla could hear the girls talking amongst themselves as she wandered through to the kitchen, which was also covered in a grey confetti. Just as she was about to open the door to Drew's study, Isla jumped as a bedraggled Rory appeared in the doorway, followed by Nate.

'You frightened the life out of me then!' exclaimed Isla, holding her hand up to her thumping heart as the girls joined her.

Allie gave Rory a quick peck on the cheek.

'Sorry, we didn't mean to, how's Drew and Fergus?'

Isla explained the trauma they'd both endured and that they would both be off work for the near future.

'What's all this?' asked Isla. 'Why are you still here and why are you dressed in Drew's overalls?' Isla looked Nate up and down.

'We've secured the alpacas' field and I've checked over the ewes and all of them are doing well. And the reason why Nate is dressed in Drew's overalls,' Rory slapped Nate's back, 'is because ... meet your new farm hand, this lad is worth his weight in gold ... where did you find him, again?'

'Huh? What do you mean?' asked Isla, puzzled, knowing full well she couldn't afford to pay another farm hand.

'Nate was here looking for work, he spoke to you in the teashop,' replied Rory cheerily.

'Woah! I'm sorry,' said Isla, holding up her hand. 'As much as we need the extra help at the minute, we can't afford to pay out any more wages. I'm sorry, Nate.' Isla snagged a glance between Rory and Nate, who grinned.

'It's all sorted, so don't worry,' said Rory, 'Martha is taking care of it.'

'Gran?' Isla gave a nervous laugh.

'Martha is going to pay Nate a weekly wage until Drew is back on his feet.'

Isla was dumbfounded, 'Are you serious?'

'Yes!'

'Unless you don't want to be stuck with me?' Nate gave Isla a cheeky lopsided grin.

'Where will you stay? The B&B is going to be expensive for that many weeks.'

'Julia was full, so Nate is staying in my spare room, and if it helps you guys out ...'

'Oh my God, Rory, you are just the best!'

Delighted that the running of the farm wasn't going to be down to just herself and Polly, Isla hugged Rory.

'I'm not sure who smells the worst,' Isla laughed.

She turned towards Nate, 'And thank you. You turned up in Heartcross at just the right time.'

'I did, didn't I?' said Nate with a beam.

Feeling a sense of relief, there seemed to be light at the end of the tunnel. Isla could never imagine living anywhere other than Heartcross. The bridge collapse had shocked the whole community and everyone had looked after each other then, and today was no different. The whole of Heartcross was pulling together once more for her, showing just what an amazing community they had.

'What time do you want me in the morning, boss?' Nate saluted.

'5 a.m. to milk the cows.'

'I'll be here bright and early.'

'I'll be here early but I can't guarantee I'll be bright,' laughed Polly, who hadn't admitted to anyone yet that she was actually scared of cows.

'I can't thank you all enough, now let me grab the insurance policy and we'll head back to Heartwood Cottage.'

Chapter 16

'A nyone home?' Felicity shouted as she opened the door to Heartwood Cottage.

'We're all in here,' shouted Rona.

Martha, Meredith and Alfie were all gathered in the living room.

The second Martha saw Isla, she was on her feet hugging her. 'Were your ears burning?'

'Gran! You can't say that after today.'

'Sorry, sorry, just a figure of speech. We were just saying you should be back anytime soon.'

'Unfortunately, my sense of humour is running low.' Isla looked into the pram. Angus was sleeping peacefully, oblivious to the chaos that had been going on around him. 'Where's Finn?'

'We thought it best if he went over to Aggie's to play with Esme after school. She's giving them their tea to take the pressure off here.'

'I'll pop across in a second to see her,' chipped in Felicity. 'I've spoken to her on the phone, but she'll be so worried about Fergus and Drew. And I need a cuddle from our little girl too.'

151

Isla nodded and watched Felicity accompany Rona to the kitchen. Isla saw them fall into each other's arms, the emotion still very raw for them all.

'I'm filthy,' Isla said as she looked down at her overalls. 'And exhausted.'

'You sit down,' ordered Rona, returning to the room carrying a tray with a pot of tea and a plate of biscuits.

'How are they both?' asked Alfie.

'Bloody lucky,' said Felicity, perching next to her mum on the arm of her chair. Rona clutched her hand.

'If Fergus hadn't managed to free Drew's leg ...' Isla's voice faltered and she squeezed her eyes shut, hoping no more tears would escape.

Martha touched her knee, 'But he did, and they are both okay. Let's focus on the positive.'

'One of my contractors is on his way from Glensheil, we'll get those windows boarded up before dark and make the farmhouse as secure as it can be,' Alfie said, smiling at Isla.

'Thanks Alfie, I'm overcome. Everyone is being so kind.'

Just at that very moment, a van beeped outside and Alfie stood up. 'That'll be for me. You need anything Isla, just ring.'

'I will, thanks again Alfie.'

Once Alfie had stepped outside the cottage, Isla sighed and sank back into the settee. 'Everyone always goes out of their way,' she acknowledged, feeling blessed by all the support. 'And just now we bumped into Rory and Nate up at the farm. Rory told us you are going to pay Nate's wages until Fergus and Drew are back on their feet. Are you sure, Gran?'

'I don't want you to worry about a thing, I'll look after the little one and you can concentrate on Drew and the farm.'

'Thanks Gran, I owe you,' said Isla, entirely grateful.

'You owe me nothing, we look after each other in this family and this village. And Rory told us he couldn't have managed without Nate today. Looks like he turned up at the right time, your knight in shining armour.'

'It's not like this in the city,' surmised Polly. 'I never even knew my neighbours in London. I'm in awe of this place.'

'We are going to stay at Aggie's tonight, if that's okay with you? We'll have to muddle through for the next couple of days until we can get the farmhouse cleaned up,' said Martha.

'Finn will like that,' replied Isla. 'He'll be excited about a sleepover.'

'Now you girls, get a warm cup of tea inside you and there's a pan of chilli bubbling away on the Aga, if you are hungry,' said Rona.

'Yes please!' came the cry of the four girls, suddenly feeling ravenous.

'That's perfect Rona, thank you,' added Isla.

Allie and Polly followed Felicity into the kitchen while Isla hung back.

'Oh, and before I forget, the fire officer gave me this.' Martha handed Isla a piece of paper. 'There will be an investigation, but he doesn't see any problems whatsoever for insurance purposes. He's agreed there's no foul play and, on first inspection, it was due to the lightning hitting the electricity cable … freak of nature. He advised for you to ring the insurance company as soon as possible and he'll get the report to you by early next week.'

'Thank God, that's a weight off my mind. In fact, do you think Rona would mind if I use her land line and ring them now?'

'Of course I don't mind,' said Rona, scurrying into the room. 'The phone is in the hall. Just shut the living-room door if you need some privacy.'

Clasping the policy in her hand, Isla went to the hallway and perched on the bottom stair. She dialled the number and waited.

She felt frustrated by the automated service, which took her through various options before finally connecting her. Isla confirmed all the necessary details and could hear the woman tapping away on a computer as Isla continued to tell the woman all about the storm and what the fire officer had stated.

'Can you just hold the line for a moment please, Mrs Allaway?'

'Yes of course, no problem.'

Isla waited patiently while the annoying pipe music played on.

'Mrs Allaway?'

'Yes, I'm still here.'

'Unfortunately, we can't process the claim for you.'

Isla felt puzzled. 'What do you mean?' she asked, sitting up straight and gripping the receiver like her life depended on it. 'I have the policy documents right in front of me now. We pay this insurance money on a monthly basis.'

'Your policy was cancelled approximately three months ago.'

Isla was perplexed. 'I'm sorry, I think there's been a mistake. Can I speak to your supervisor, please?'

'No mistake. The policy was cancelled by Mr Allaway himself. My supervisor can certainly confirm that detail for you.'

Isla felt baffled, why the hell would Drew cancel the insurance policy? Surely it was a computer error, or a human error ... there was no way Drew would pay all that money into a policy and cancel it out of the blue, without telling her. It didn't make any sense to her at all. What the hell were they going to do now? Once more Isla felt close to tears. Today was taking its toll, she didn't know whether she was coming or going.

Martha appeared in the doorway. 'Everything okay?' she asked.

'Everything is just fine,' Isla replied, telling a white lie, still trying to get her head around the conversation that had taken place with the insurance company. Firstly, Isla needed to discover all the facts.

'Good, good, now get this inside you,' insisted Martha, passing Isla a bowl of chilli. 'You are going to need to keep your strength up.'

Feeling dazed, Isla followed her Gran back into the living room, she couldn't think straight. She tried to cast her mind back to three months ago but couldn't recollect any conversation with Drew about cancelling the policy. Surely, they would have had a conversation about doing something as drastic as that? It had to be a mistake, there was no way on this earth Drew would put his family, home and business in jeopardy.

As Isla sat back down on the chair, she was oblivious to the chatter going on around her. She felt panicked, her safe world was turning upside down. Isla wasn't prepared for this. How could this be happening to her? She felt anxious just thinking about it.

How would they replace the barn, the animal feed and the windows with no insurance money? Everything was crumbling all around her and she tried the best she could to rationalise what was happening. Maybe Drew had changed the policy to a different insurance broker? She exhaled; yes, that would be it. Drew would have found more suitable cover and most probably at a cheaper cost. Now she was mad with herself for doubting him for a moment, but it was strange he hadn't mentioned it to her. Isla decided that as soon as she finished her food and cleaned herself up, she'd nip back up to the farmhouse and take another look at the paperwork in the office.

Chapter 17

After a short soak in the bath and a hot meal inside her, Isla was looking forward to seeing Finn. She and Martha pushed Angus in the pram the short distance over to Aggie's cottage, accompanied by Felicity.

They followed Felicity inside, who announced their arrival while Isla parked the pram in the hallway. Aggie appeared in seconds, drying her hand on a tea towel, her face full of concern.

'Come here,' she said, pulling Felicity in for a hug. 'I know they are both okay, but I've been out of my mind with worry. This weather will be the death of us.'

'It nearly was,' answered Isla, swooping Angus out of the pram and cradling him into her neck.

Esme and Finn came running down the stairs as soon as they heard voices. They both looked like they didn't have a care in the world.

'We've had the best day – baked cakes, watched films and made a rocket out of boxes ... come and look!' said Finn, jerking his head towards the living room and slipping his hand inside Isla's, her heart swelling with love for him. Isla took a glance towards Felicity, noticing her eyes had welled up with tears. They gave each other a look that meant, *This could have played out so differently.*

'How's Daddy? Did he get stuck in the storm?'

'Daddy is absolutely fine, but he's broken his leg and it's in a cast. He will be resting in hospital for a few days.'

Finn's eyes widened, 'Does that mean we get to draw all over it?'

'I'm sure Daddy will let you,' smiled Isla, thinking being a child was simple and carefree.

Esme and Finn squealed with delight before racing towards the dresser in the corner of the room.

'Where are you going now?' asked Isla, watching Finn fling open the door to the dresser. Finn was happy, unaware that today he could have lost his father. Isla tried to push that fact to the back of her mind. They were lucky, Drew was lucky. This could have turned out so differently. Isla was thankful that she wasn't standing here, coping with a very different outcome.

'To sort out the pens to draw on Daddy's leg!'

'Of course you are!' Isla laughed.

'I've made up the spare room for you both,' said Aggie, touching Isla on her elbow. 'There's fresh towels on the bed, just help yourself to whatever you need. Finn can go in with Esme if that's okay by you?'

'He'll love that. Thank you.'

'And Meredith is opening up the pub an hour early tomorrow so Hamish and Julia can organise their troops.'

'Troops?'

'The cleaning squad.'

'We are your fairy godmothers, except there is no way you're getting this body squeezing into any sort of tutu at my time of life.'

'Or mine, for that matter,' laughed Isla.

'What's the state of the farmhouse?' asked Aggie.

'The windows are non-existent, broken glass and ash everywhere, but it could be a lot worse.'

'I'll take the curtains down in the morning and run them over to the dry cleaners in Glensheil on my way to visit Fergus. Oh, and Rory said there was spare feed and bales of hay over at Clover Farm. He's going to get it transported across on Monday. There's no harm in taking it, it'll only go to waste,' said Aggie.

'I can't go pinching feed from James Kerr's farm, I'm already in possession of his stolen alpacas.'

'Well look at this way, you're taking the food to feed his alpacas. Who is going to argue with that?'

Aggie had a point. At the moment, the alpacas were the least of Isla's worries. She'd telephoned the hospital just before she left Rona's and had been told Drew was comfortable. She planned to go across to the hospital first thing in the morning to visit him.

'I know I've only just got here, but do you mind if I nip back home? I'd like to grab Drew some clean clothes, ready for tomorrow.'

'I'll go if you want to rest?' offered Martha, knowing that Isla hadn't stopped all day.

'Thanks, but I want to check on the ewes and the alpacas too.'

'You're turning into a proper farmer already,' teased Martha. But Isla wasn't listening, rumbles of doubt were still in her mind over the insurance policy. She needed to search through all the documents and find the correct one as soon as possible.

Isla's phoned pinged, 'It's Alfie, all the windows are boarded up,' she said, reading the message out loud. 'At least the place is secure. That man needs to be bottled ... I'm going to go now and then I can settle the boys down and hopefully bed down for a good night's sleep.'

As Isla shut the cottage door behind her, deep inside she didn't have a good feeling at all about the insurance policy. Her gut feeling was telling her there was more to this situation, but she didn't know what. Isla felt nervous that she was going to uncover ... actually she didn't know what she was going to uncover, and that was what she was afraid of. She looked behind her towards the cottage window and saw Martha was watching her. Plastering a fake smile on her face, she waved back.

She'd put her heart and soul into her family and life. She just hoped Drew hadn't let her down ... somehow.

Chapter 18

As the wind pushed Isla along the drive of Foxglove Farm the smell of burning still lingered. The farmhouse looked deserted, the boards on the windows made it look run-down and in desperate need of some tender loving care, but Isla was thankful that Alfie had sorted that so quickly, she wouldn't have known where to start.

Wandering over to the stable block to check on the alpaca, Isla was amazed to see Rory and Nate still milling around the place.

'Have you pair not got a home to go to?'

'Well actually ...' grinned Nate.

Isla rolled her eyes, 'You know what I mean.'

'Lambing has started,' said Rory. 'And so far, so good. But I just wanted to check on the alpaca before I head home.'

All three of them leant on the wall looking into the stable. The alpaca was settled on the hay.

'The scan ... on Monday, I've organised for our own van to come and pick her up, that's one less worry for you, except ...'

'Except?' interrupted Isla.

'You'll need someone to travel with the alpaca.'

Isla looked towards Rory, 'What time are we talking? There's milking first and we've got Polly pitching in too.'

'Just before 9 a.m.'

'I can do that,' offered Nate. 'You'll be better staying at the farm keeping an eye on the lambs. We will have finished the milking by then?'

'Yes, milking will be finished by then. Are you sure, Nate?'

'Yes, if that's okay with you?' Nate looked towards Rory.

'Fine by me. I'll see you at 9 a.m. sharp.'

Isla nodded her appreciation towards Nate. He seemed to have slotted in straight away, in a matter of hours. It was like he was one of the gang.

'Okay, this one seems to be settled for the night,' said Rory, glancing at his watch. 'And I don't know about you, but after today I'm in need of a pint.'

'Tell Allie the drinks are on me, I'll settle up with her tomorrow.'

'I'll hear of no such thing, the good thing about my girlfriend owning a pub is my drinks are always on a tab, which never seems to be settled.' Rory patted Nate on the back.

'You've landed on your feet, I've often dreamt of my girlfriend owning a pub ... hypothetically of course,' joked Nate.

Isla noticed the pair of them seemed in good spirits despite all of their hard work today. 'Thanks for everything you've done today and thanks for stepping in,' she turned towards Nate.

'Honestly, it's not a problem, I could do with the extra cash and it's no hardship working in a place like this with spectacular scenery,' he said, taking his phone out of his pocket as it beeped. He took a quick glance at the screen then quickly tucked it away in his pocket.

'Everything okay?' asked Isla.

'Yes,' he said. 'But I'm ready for that pint.'

'Are you coming?' Rory asked Isla.

'No, I'm just collecting a few things for Drew, then I'll head back to Aggie's to put the boys to bed.'

Rory nodded, and he and Nate headed along the driveway.

Isla let herself into the house. Everywhere seemed dark and dingy and for the first time it didn't feel like home. She felt like she was trespassing as she switched on the table lamp in Drew's study before pulling open the drawer in his desk. She took out the folders that were all neatly labelled – water, gas, electricity, bank statements – and stacked them up in front of her.

Firstly, she flipped open the blue wallet and thumbed through the insurance paperwork. The home insurance policies went back ten years, all with the same insurance company. Isla couldn't find any new policy. She poured herself a strong coffee before opening the next file.

Everything seemed in order – all the cars, the farm vehicles and animals were insured, and nothing seemed untoward. So why would Drew cancel the policy? Maybe it was a genuine mistake by the insurance company, a computer error. All she could was talk to Drew when she visited him tomorrow.

Isla opened the drawer on the other side of the desk and was taken aback; there she found unopened envelopes stuffed on top of each other and an old accounts book with numerous sheets of paper slipped inside. She cleared a large space on the desk and stared in horror at the paperwork in front of her.

Isla had always left the farm business to Drew, who'd always seemed capable of taking care of the farm, in fact he'd always insisted on it. But Isla felt suddenly dazed, an entire stock of emotions running through her body. What the hell was going on here? How had Drew let things slide so badly? This wasn't like him at all. There was no denying these accounts were in a terrible state. They looked like they hadn't been kept updated in a long time. She began to rifle through the loose bits of paper, receipts and invoices, trying to sort them out into date order. She'd no clue if any of the invoices had been paid, there seemed to be no logical system at all. 'Oh Drew,' she mumbled under her breath, then let out a long shuddering sigh.

Slurping her coffee, she would have preferred a very large gin and tonic as she powered up her laptop. There was only one thing for it, she'd have to start right at the very beginning and go back to basics. Month by month Isla deciphered the figures and began to enter the data on to the screen. In the middle of the table she made a pile of invoices that she wasn't entirely sure about; she would need to ask Drew whether they had been paid or not.

Two hours later Isla's mood plummeted to an all-time low as she discovered a number of unopened red-letter bills stuffed in the back of the book. Why hadn't Drew opened any of these? Some even had 'Final Demand' stamped all over them. The more envelopes Isla opened, the more she began to worry. She felt sick to her stomach. They owed money everywhere.

The only thing that seemed to be paid on time was Fergus's wages.

Isla collapsed in the chair as a feeling of dread engulfed her. Things started to make sense, was this why Drew's moods were erratic? Was this why he was adamant she needed to get a job, because their finances were all over the place? Isla contemplated how they were going to get out of this mess, they were about to lose the farm and in order to make ends meet, they needed a miracle to happen. And as a lottery win wasn't looking likely, Isla had no choice, she would have to go back to work.

Isla exhaled and took another look. She was getting angrier and angrier by the second as she found more and more invoices that hadn't been paid. No wonder Drew had been getting tetchier as time went on. How on earth had he been able to sleep at night? And how was he planning to put all this right ... by robbing a bank?

Isla noticed, from what she could decipher from the mess of the paperwork, that the farm had begun to lose revenue when the bridge had collapsed, which made sense. The tankers hadn't been able to get into Heartcross to transport the milk, and thousands and thousands of gallons had been lost. But what Isla didn't understand was why Drew was keeping all this to himself. When was he going to tell her, the day the bailiffs knocked on the door? How dare he do this to her and her boys?

Isla needed to take control and face up to things, and fast. First, she needed to work out which bills were of most importance and which ones they could pay. The only obvious way out of this mess was to try and bring in some more income, but with Drew out of action that seemed impossible. She glanced at her phone and noticed two missed calls from Martha, who must be wondering where she was.

'Sorry Gran, phone was on silent. I'm still at the farm. Will be back soon,' she texted, not wanting to talk to anyone at this moment in time. She felt so livid with Drew and tears of frustration blinded her. Isla knew she couldn't cope with much more. She wondered again, why had Drew hidden this from her, and if he could hide this from her, what else hadn't he told her? She began to question whether she knew her husband at all.

Shutting down her laptop and taking her empty coffee cup back to the kitchen, she blew the ash off the local paper that was lying on the kitchen table. Isla perused the job section. Granted it was full of jobs, but ones with unsociable hours or not enough hours and none that filled her with any excitement. Taking a broken crayon from Finn's pencil case, she circled the shop-assistant post in the chip shop over in Glensheil, followed by a cleaner in a care home. She took one last look at the paper before letting out a breath.

Isla suspected she couldn't be fussy and would need to secure any type of employment to try and make ends meet. But she'd also have to wait until Drew was back on his feet and could take over the running of the farm again. And if Martha upped and left anytime soon, these jobs wouldn't even cover childcare costs. They would barely have two pennies to rub together.

Isla knew she needed to come up with a plan B, but she

just didn't know what that was yet, and she was so tired she couldn't even think straight. How dare Drew do this to them. She didn't even want to see him tomorrow, she didn't even know what she was going to say to him, he'd left her completely speechless.

As Isla locked the door behind her, emotion poured through her body and tears brimmed her eyes. Foxglove Farm was her life ... was her family's life. She stood on the doormat and looked up at the picturesque farmhouse that had been in Drew's family for generations and took a breath. The thought of losing it filled her with fear. If those accounts were anything to go by, it was certainly a realistic possibility. This was their home and their livelihood, and Drew had let it spiral out of control without even confiding in her. She'd gone looking for an insurance policy that didn't exist and had uncovered a nightmare.

Isla sullenly ambled up the long path and stared out over the fields. She could see the alpacas grazing, mingling with the sheep. No wonder Drew had gone ballistic when she'd bought them. But what she didn't understand was why Drew had stopped paying the bills when there was still money in their bank account. None of this made sense. Isla gazed up at the majestic scenery beyond the lush farmland. The landscape was beautiful – rolling hills, thick woodlands, towering mountains and glittering lochs. She spotted far-off goats rambling up the hillside and stood and watched for a second.

The depressing truth was, she was about to lose everything she had ever loved and believed in, and the way she was feeling right now, that included Drew too.

Chapter 19

Isla ended the call to the hospital, who confirmed that Drew had had a comfortable night. This morning they were redressing the burns and it was possible that the doctor would discharge him in the next couple of days. Isla knew he was already fed up to the back teeth lying in the hospital bed because he hadn't stopped texting since the minute she'd turned on her phone, but as yet Isla hadn't replied to him because she wanted to reduce the temptation of saying something she shouldn't.

Everyone was sitting around the kitchen table when Isla ventured downstairs carrying Angus who was ready for his feed. Finn and Esme had drawn faces on their boiled eggs and were currently giggling as they bashed the tops of their eggs with a spoon.

'Good morning!' chirped Aggie, pouring Isla a tea from the pot. 'Did you sleep well?'

'I did, thank you.'

'Would you like a boiled egg? I believe they come from the best farm in Heartcross.' Aggie gave Isla a wink.

'That would be perfect,' said Isla, giving a small chuckle and noticing Rory pass the cottage window.

'Good morning!' Rory said cheerfully, opening the front door of the cottage. 'Is Isla around?'

'In here,' Aggie shouted from the kitchen.

'Is everything okay?' asked Isla, meeting his gaze. 'Was the milking okay?'

Rory and his dad Stuart had kindly offered to milk the cows until Isla had settled into a routine.

'It all went very smoothly, I'm just driving over to Clover Farm to pick up the animal feed and hay bales that's left over in James Kerr's barn to get you restocked, but we need somewhere to store it. What's in that old dilapidated barn at the end of the farm? It's locked up with a rusty old padlock.'

'As far as I can remember, that barn is full of those old campervans and caravans. Remember Drew and Fergus's brainwave? They bought them at auction with the intent to restore them to sell them on ... except they didn't. They have no engines, and flat tyres and are no doubt full of spiders and goodness knows what. I'm not sure there's even room in there. But once I've been to the hospital I'll nip to the farm and find the key for you.'

'Perfect,' Rory said, waving his hand over his head and leaving the cottage.

Aggie placed a boiled egg down in front of Isla, 'You get that down you, while I'll go and get these children washed and dressed.' Aggie ushered Esme and Finn out of the kitchen, leaving Martha quietly staring at Isla.

'Why are you looking at me like that?' asked Isla, feeling under scrutiny.

'Where were you last night? You were gone for hours.'

'I just had stuff to do up at the farm,' answered Isla vaguely, not wanting to elaborate on her findings until she'd spoken to Drew.

'I'm worried about you Isla, there's something going on.' Martha's voice was soft.

Her Gran's caring nature nearly reduced Isla to tears. 'There's nothing going on. It's just been a hell of a couple of days.' Isla felt her voice wobble, she was worried sick about visiting Drew and confronting him.

Standing up, Isla couldn't make eye contact with her gran. She bit down on her lip, hoping that her gran wouldn't notice the tears in her eyes. 'I'm going to go to the hospital now. Drew must be bored out of his mind.'

'What about your boiled egg?'

'I'm not hungry,' Isla replied, kissing Angus on top of his head before slipping her feet into her pumps and picking up her keys. She closed the front door to Fox Hollow Cottage behind her.

As Isla put the key in the ignition, she was feeling anxious. Lying on the passenger seat next to her was a bag stuffed with the unpaid bills and invoices which she was going to use to confront Drew. She had no idea how he was going to react or what he was going to say, but she wasn't going to leave until she got answers.

Starting the engine, Isla noticed that Love Heart Lane

seemed brighter and prettier this morning, despite the storm. Thankfully, the rain had stopped, and the sun was shining. Julia was hanging a colourful basket of blooms outside the B&B and Isla gave her a quick beep of the horn as she drove past. On the edge of the village a few children were up and out early, splashing in the puddles from the heavy downpour last night, and as she switched up the car radio and approached the bridge out of Heartcross her mind was fixed on the conversation she was about to have with Drew.

In the distance she could see Clover Farm standing on the hill. Curiosity got the better of Isla, and taking a detour, she indicated left and followed the long winding country lane for about half a mile. Then she saw it, the old wooden sign hammered into the ground outside the farmhouse gates, which were in need of some tender loving care. 'Clover Farm', she read, pulling over in the layby. Climbing out of her car, she rested her hand on the gate and peered up the driveway.

Standing in the grounds was the ramshackle white-walled ivy-covered cottage where James Kerr had lived for as long as anyone could remember. It was an average-sized cottage which looked dreary and winter-beaten. The windows had never been modernised and the frames were tired and flaky. Many years ago this cottage had been built to impress, picturesque and sitting proudly on the crown of the hill. But looking at it now, it was clear that James Kerr had let it go to rack and ruin, which surprised Isla, considering the substantial revenue he must have made each year from the alpacas.

'You're not considering buying it, are you? It's most likely a death trap inside. It'll suck all your money out of you.'

The voice behind Isla made her jump and she spun round.

Isla was faced with a slim woman in her late sixties. Her brunette hair fell below her shoulders, her chiselled cheekbones were streaked with blusher and she wore a pencil skirt with a cashmere jumper, not the usual clientele they were used to in these parts.

'No, I was just passing.'

'Just being nosey, hey?'

'Yes, I suppose I was. Are you from the estate agents?' asked Isla.

The woman laughed, 'No,' then she narrowed her eyes at Isla, giving her a quizzical look. 'You have a look of Martha Gray about you.'

Isla was completely taken aback by the mention of her gran's name.

'She's my grandmother. Do you know her?'

'You were a small bairn last time I clapped eyes on you ... you must be ... Isla?'

'I am ... but who are ...' Isla didn't finish her sentence.

'I'm Gracie Maxwell,' she said, thrusting her bony hand forward.

Looking puzzled, Isla was still none the wiser but shook the woman's offered hand.

'I was once Gracie Kerr before I remarried. James was my ex-husband. I lived there once, in Clover Cottage.' She nodded towards the property sitting on the hill.

Isla had to do everything in her power to stop her jaw from falling somewhere below her knees.

'I don't suppose you would remember,' said Gracie. 'I've not been around these parts for many years.'

For a moment they both stood in silence and stared towards the farmhouse.

'Clover Cottage was once a happy home, believe it or not.' Gracie's eyes swept towards Isla. 'Then it all went wrong. Have you seen much of James in recent years?'

Isla shook her head. 'To be honest, I can't remember the last time anyone saw him.'

'I honestly thought he'd turned his life around. I saw him in a farmer's magazine a few years back, there was an interview about him and his prize alpacas. Goodness knows what's happened to them. No doubt he sold them for booze.' Her tone was curious rather than accusatory, she clearly had no idea the expensive stock was currently grazing in the fields at Foxglove Farm.

Isla could feel nervous butterflies swirling around the pit of her stomach. She knew the right thing would be to admit there and then where the alpacas were. Maybe she could pass it off that they were just looking after them temporarily, but she felt nervous and couldn't bring herself to tell her.

'So, you married again?' Isla said instead, steering the conversation away from the animals.

'I did, it was the best thing I ever did, leaving this place, but I did marry another farmer, would you believe it? ... Glutton for punishment,' she rolled her eyes and chuckled.

'And recently we've bought a little property in the South of France to retire to.'

'That sounds like a fantastic way to retire.' To say Isla was a nervous wreck asking the next question was an understatement: 'And your boys? Do you still see them?' she asked, fearful of the answer.

'So, you know about my boys. Always one for gossip, this village.'

'I'm sorry, I didn't mean to offend.'

'You haven't,' she said, patting Isla's arm. 'They've been released from prison, I'm sure you've heard the story,' the words tripped off her tongue. 'That's why I'm here.'

Her words spun in Isla's mind ... already released from prison. Isla could feel her heart beating faster and she prayed her voice sounded normal as she spoke: 'Are they coming back here to Clover Farm ... Clover Cottage?'

Gracie shrugged, 'I would imagine so. Who else would James leave this lot to? That's why I'm here. They've been inside for so long, this farm is all they have ever known, the only home they've ever had, the only area they've ever lived in. I thought they actually might be here ... silly, I know.' Gracie sounded wretched. 'All I know is, they were released a week ago and I've no idea where they are. I thought they might be here, but I'm clutching at straws ...'

Isla blinked slowly, not knowing what to say. Avoiding the conversation was her preferred approach. While she hesitated, Gracie stepped in: 'How is Martha?'

'She's great, thank you, staying with me at the farm at the minute.'

'Farm?'

Isla kicked herself for even mentioning the word 'farm'.

Gracie tilted her head to the side, waiting for Isla to elaborate.

'I married Drew Allaway, he took over his dad's farm.'

'Allaway ...' she screwed up her eyes whilst thinking. 'That would be Foxglove Farm?'

'Yes, that's the one. Anyway, I best be going, it was nice to meet you,' said Isla, beginning to perspire at the very thought of the conversation continuing.

'How is the farm?' asked Gracie, holding Isla's gaze and, unfortunately for Isla, not letting the conversation drop.

'All is good,' answered Isla, sounding more convincing than she felt.

'Still rearing beef ... providing Glensheil dairies?'

Isla nodded.

'Have you ever thought of owning alpacas? Apparently, it's becoming more fashionable by the minute.'

'Al ... pac ... as,' Isla strung the word out. Isla knew again this would be the time to come clean about the alpacas but again, with a feeling of dread in the pit of her stomach, she knew there was a possibility they would be whipped from underneath them sooner rather than later. Cringing inside at her own dishonesty, the only words that escaped from her mouth were, 'Never really thought about it.'

Standing side by side, Gracie exhaled and took a swift glance back towards the decrepit farmhouse. 'All those years ago I had such happy hopes of this place, but sometimes things are just not meant to be. I hope you're taking better care of Foxglove Farm.'

Painting a smile on her face, Isla lied, 'We are.'

'Why did you say you were here again?' Gracie looked Isla straight in the eye and was totally oblivious to Isla's discomfort.

Feeling panicky, Isla was saved by the ringing of her mobile phone in her pocket. She quickly pulled out the phone and saw Drew's name flashing on the screen. She should have been at the hospital by now. He'd be impatient, wondering what was keeping her.

'Sorry Gracie, I need to run, but lovely to bump into you. Take care of yourself and enjoy the South of France,' she said, feeling shifty.

'You too. From what I remember, the Allaways were good honest people – you did well there.'

Gracie's kind words caused Isla to feel a twinge of guilt. Isla didn't feel like a good honest person; after all, she'd had the opportunity to come clean about the alpacas and hadn't taken it. Isla's legs trembled as she walked towards the car. She looked back over her shoulder and smiled bravely at Gracie who was standing watching her. What were the chances of bumping into her after all this time?

With the car engine running, she rested her hand on the gearstick, her heart pounding as she pushed down on the accelerator. She wanted to get out of there fast.

Chapter 20

Tucking her hands inside the pockets of her coat, Isla stood and stared up at the hospital building. She wasn't looking forward to this conversation and wasn't even sure how she was feeling about Drew at this moment in time.

Nervous butterflies began to flutter around her stomach as she walked through the entrance of the hospital and through the gleaming-white corridors towards Drew's room.

The conversation she was about to have with her husband played over and over in her mind like a broken record, and Isla took a second to compose herself as she hovered outside his room. Taking a deep breath, she felt herself beginning to tremble – nervous didn't come close to how she was currently feeling. Drew must be aware this argument was coming. He couldn't have hidden the fact that there was no insurance forever.

Isla slowly pushed open the door and stepped inside the room. The sun shone through the cracks in the blinds, catching Isla's attention before she turned her gaze towards Drew, who was fast asleep under a white cotton sheet with his plastered leg sticking out to the side. For a second Isla watched him,

Drew looked so tired and fragile. Quietly she slid on to the blue plastic chair and placed the bag of unpaid bills and invoices by her side. Isla felt angry at the predicament Drew had put them in, she was hurt to discover there was no insurance from a stranger on the phone. She debated whether to wake him or not, but in the warmth of the hospital room she suddenly began to feel tired herself.

The next thing Isla knew, her knee was being touched and, opening her eyes wide, she saw Drew staring at her. Almost immediately Isla felt a weird tension in the air.

'Good morning,' she said politely, like she was passing a neighbour in the street and not like she was greeting her husband after he'd been fighting for his life in a fire. 'How you feeling?'

Drew shifted self-consciously in his bed and slipped his hands underneath his bum before pushing himself up. 'Sore, tired, drained. I just want my own bed with my own things around me,' he offered Isla a smile. 'You took your time getting here, everything okay?' Did Drew sense that Isla already knew about the insurance?

'There was the milking, collection of eggs, and don't forget I'm staying at Aggie's. But luckily Nate has it all in hand.'

'And who is this Nate guy and how come he's suddenly appeared on the scene out of nowhere. Isla, we really can't afford to pay him.'

Isla knew full well they couldn't afford to pay him.

'Martha is covering his wages until you are back up on your feet.'

'Who is he? Has he a background in farming?'

180

Isla shrugged, 'I really don't know, Drew.'

'Well, you're letting him work on the farm. Have you asked him?'

'I am, it was the simplest decision and funnily enough, I've not had time to carry out a full-blown interview and check references. I've been a bit busy in the last twenty-four hours, but Nate worked extremely hard yesterday to help us. He turned up at the right time. We only need him until you are back on your feet. Honestly Drew, everyone is pulling together. We have more important things to worry about.' Isla held Drew's gaze, encouraging him to be honest with her, but he shiftily looked away and reached for the glass of water on his bedside cabinet.

Isla carried on, 'Alfie boarded the windows and has organised for the glass to be replaced first thing Monday,' she said. 'He's been amazing, got everything under control. He even said he'd wait for the insurance money to come through so we didn't need to worry about paying him straight away,' she said, watching Drew bristle as she gave him another opportunity to come clean.

'Drew, are you okay? You've kind of gone a funny colour. Shall I get a nurse? Are you in pain?'

She stared at him in quiet contemplation.

But before Drew could answer a nurse breezed into the room.

'Good morning, I've come to do your observations,' she said, perusing the chart hanging from the bottom of his bed.

Drew remained subdued and let the nurse carry out her observations.

When she was finished, she logged the results and handed Drew an appointment card. 'This is your first physiotherapy appointment.'

'Thank you,' he said, taking it from her.

'I can't stress how important these appointments are. They'll help to maintain and regain muscle strength, movement and flexibility. There will be specific exercises to do before and after the cast is removed.'

'How often do I need to come in?'

'Every week.'

'Every week?' Drew blew out a breath.

'Yes, every week,' reaffirmed the nurse.

The nurse looked towards Isla, 'Drew's recovery can't be rushed. The broken bone may not be fully healed even when the pain has subsided. And no driving.'

Drew looked deflated.

'And about the other matter, the doctor has your prescription. He'll see you on his rounds for a chat.'

'Thank you,' said Drew, looking uncomfortable with the conversation.

As soon as the nurse left the room, Isla asked, 'And what is the prescription she was talking about?'

'Just sorting out my painkillers,' said Drew, not making eye contact.

Isla couldn't stand beating around the bush any longer, 'The fire ...' she took a breath, 'brought it home to me how lucky we are as a family. You're safe, we're safe and thankfully it was only the old barn that burnt to the ground and only a few windows were blasted out in the farmhouse. And we have insurance to cover that, don't we?' said Isla, goading Drew into telling the truth while carefully watching his reaction.

Drew was silently staring down at his hands that were clasped in front of him.

'And you know what, we can build a better barn when the insurance money comes through. At least a new one will be watertight. You always said it needed pulling down and we can get a brand-new steel barn. I've already emailed out for quotes.' Isla was scrutinising his reaction. But still Drew said nothing, which was now causing Isla to get increasingly annoyed. 'But the funny thing is, Drew ...'

He looked up for a second but couldn't hold Isla's gaze.

'The funny thing is,' she repeated, 'when I telephoned the insurance company, they said that we didn't have a policy with them. I knew that would be a mistake on their part. However ...' Isla took a breath. 'Last night I searched the house looking for an up-to-date policy, because I know that you ...' Isla looked straight at him now, her tone firm. 'I know that you would never have cancelled the policy because A, why would you ever put your family in a position where they could potentially lose their home? and B, you would have discussed it with me first, because we're a team, a partnership, and that's what married couples do. Isn't it?'

Isla could hear her voice getting higher and higher, her heart was beating faster. If Drew wanted to speak there was no way Isla was going to let him get a word in edgeways. Drew remained silent and rested back on the pillow, he'd paled and closed his eyes. He slowly exhaled. It was obvious to see he was finding this conversation unsettling.

'But then I opened the next drawer and guess what I found, Drew?' Isla picked up the bag at the side of her chair and, for dramatic effect, emptied the contents all over Drew's lap. 'The accounts abandoned, unpaid invoices, red-letter bills that haven't even been opened.'

Isla was furious now, the anger bubbling inside.

Visibly shaking, she waited for an answer.

'I'm sorry Isla,' Drew said finally. 'I'm really sorry.'

'Last night I spent over two hours sitting in a house with no windows, ash all over the place, trying to decipher what was going on. There were numerous thoughts racing through my mind, one being, are you having an affair or even, do you have another family that you're supporting? You hear of people living double lives.'

'No, that's not the case,' he interjected.

'So what is the case? We've even discussed whether you have a gambling addiction.'

'We? Oh, great, so now you are discussing our business with everyone.'

'Says you! Going behind my back, asking Jessica for a job for me, without discussing it with me first? Now I know why, looking at those accounts. The farm is in serious trouble, isn't it? Have I at least got that bit right? If you couldn't keep up to date with the accounts, why didn't you just ask me for help?'

Isla shook her head and gestured her arms towards him, 'What's happened to you, Drew? I don't even know you at the minute.'

'I'm sorry.' Drew looked broken. 'Things spiralled out of control.'

'Tell me how, Drew. Why have you cancelled the policy? We've got Alfie sorting out the windows, how are we going to pay him back?'

Isla fixed her eyes firmly on Drew. 'I suppose it's not all bad – at least we've still got a roof over our heads.'

'For the time being,' Drew said, his eyes cast down.

'What did you just say?'

Drew looked up sheepishly, 'I said for the time being, anyway.'

'And what is that supposed to mean?' asked Isla, her heart thumping fast. 'What have you done?'

Drew looked guilty, hardly daring to look Isla in her eyes. 'You remember when we re-mortgaged the farmhouse to build the milking sheds and purchase all the new machinery and tractors?'

Isla nodded, her eyes wide, with a feeling of sickness overwhelming her.

Drew gestured towards his wallet, which Isla passed to him. He pulled out a folded bit of paper and shamefacedly handed it to Isla.

'What's this?' she said, sitting back down on the chair and smoothing it out.

Isla bit down on her lip, her eyes locked on the letter in front of her. Through blurred eyes she looked up at him, the knots in her stomach taking her breath away.

'What have you done?' Isla replied to herself before Drew could draw breath. 'You've defaulted on the mortgage payments. How could you do this to us?' Isla's voice was shaky. 'How has it come to this?'

Drew hung his head, 'I'm so sorry ... Isla, look at me.'

Isla shook her head, barely bringing her eyes to meet his.

'We are threatened with the bailiffs.' She flapped the crumpled letter in front of him. 'But this can't be right, can it, Drew? Because we are a partnership and you would have spoken to me about this sooner.'

'I tried, but ...'

'Drew, this is serious.'

'I know ... I'm so sorry ... and I know I keep saying that,' Drew broke down. Isla witnessed him physically shaking. He couldn't look at her. Drew knew he'd let his family down, but the financial situation wasn't meant to spiral this much out of control. 'I thought I could put it right.'

'And when you couldn't put it right you still didn't tell me,' said Isla, hurting. Her eyes burnt angrily as she re-read the letter which stated that the mortgage was in arrears of three months and needed to be immediately brought up to date, otherwise further action would be taken. Isla felt like her heart had been ripped out. 'When were you going to tell me about this? When the bailiffs knocked on the door?'

'It won't come to that,' said Drew, trying to offer a little reassurance.

'Really? That's not what this letter says,' she placed the letter down on the bed in front of him.

'Well, it wouldn't have done until you bought those stupid alpacas.'

'So all this is my fault, is it?'

Drew shook his head, 'Not really, but you should have talked to me about it.'

'They were a birthday present,' she said, feeling the need to defend herself.

'I'd nearly sorted everything, until you spent the money on those stolen animals. Someone will come knocking for those sooner rather than later.'

'I know Drew, and I'm sorry. They were an impulse buy but I just thought you'd love them and they would be a good investment for the farm ... There is something I need to tell you.' Now it was Isla's turn to look sheepish.

'Please don't tell me someone has already been to collect them?'

'Not exactly ... but the reason I was running a little late this morning was because I bumped into Gracie Maxwell.'

'Huh? Who's Gracie Maxwell?'

'Gracie Maxwell was Gracie Kerr.'

Drew's eyes flickered as the penny dropped. Running his hand through his hair, he exhaled and stared into space before turning back towards Isla.

'Did she come to the farm?'

Isla could feel her chest rising and falling as her heart pounded fast. 'No, I saw her up at Clover Farm.'

There was silence.

'What were you doing there?'

'Just curious.'

Drew quirked an eyebrow, 'Curious about what?' The tension between them increased for a second.

'Does it matter?' She cut him off crossly. 'Gracie just turned up and she confirmed that the Kerr brothers have been released from jail. She recognised me ... well, recognised that I looked like Gran, and we got chatting.'

'Chatting? Did you mention Foxglove Farm?'

'Yes.'

'Why would you do that?'

'It was just polite conversation. I said I'd married you and we took over the farm.'

'And did you mention you were harbouring the stolen animals?'

'I didn't, no. I lied through my teeth, which I don't feel good about, and Gracie assumed that John probably sold the alpacas to fund his drinking habit.'

Drew was quiet.

'Why did you cancel the insurance?' asked Isla, suddenly realising she hadn't got to the bottom of that one yet.

Drew held his throat and his eyes drooped with shame. 'I'm sorry,' were the only words he could muster up.

Isla was close to tears, too; suddenly all the arguing felt so pointless and unnecessary.

'I was hunting around for a cheaper option to try and save money but never got round to putting any in place. Isla, I was just trying to save some money, honest. I didn't know we were going to be struck by lightning.'

'That's the whole point of insurance.'

Drew's face looked pained, he knew he'd made a huge mistake. 'I just thought a few months without paying the cost would give us some breathing space ... then I forgot all about it.'

'But if we can't even pay the mortgage and we have all these unpaid bills, how come there was money in the account, Drew?' asked Isla, puzzled.

'Because I'd taken out a loan to pay the mortgage arrears and as soon as the money hit the account you spent it on the alpacas. Your timing was impeccable.'

'You're kidding me?'

'Honestly, I couldn't believe it ... the money landed and by the time I'd logged on to transfer the money, it had disappeared ... puff ... like magic.'

Isla rolled her eyes. 'Timing, eh?'

Drew nodded his head shamefully, 'I know I've made a mistake.' He reached out to take Isla's hand. 'But I'll put this right. I promise.'

'How, Drew? How are we going to get out of this mess?'

'I'm not sure yet, but we'll think of something.'

Feeling mentally exhausted, Isla stood up.

'Where are you going?' Drew asked.

'Home, to see the boys, figure a way out of this mess,' she said, gathering up all the paperwork.

'You will be coming back for me, won't you?' asked Drew, sounding like a little lost boy.

She nodded before letting the door swing shut behind her. Isla loved Drew with all her heart and, fighting back the tears, she knew she needed to be strong. She didn't know what the future held, or whether they were going to lose their beautiful home. All Isla knew was, everything was worth fighting for – her marriage, her boys – and she was going to do everything in her power to get them out of this mess.

Chapter 21

Isla pulled her coat around her and huddled on the bench outside the hospital. Despite the sunshine there was still a cool breeze in the air. She was hoping if she sat for a short while she would be able to calm her thumping heart and think straight before she headed back to Foxglove Farm, but with her thoughts in a whirl she couldn't see a way out of this mess.

She sighed, her life felt as dull as the bin lorry that was parked on the other side of the road. Isla fully understood that the bridge collapsing would affect business, but not once had Drew suggested that the farm was in a financial mess. Of course, she wouldn't have bought the herd of alpacas if she'd known about the situation, but to take out a loan to pay the mortgage was ludicrous. How did Drew ever envisage getting on top of it all, especially now with a broken leg?

There was nothing else for it, they needed to tighten their belts, and as soon as Drew was back working the farm she would have to find a job. Angus was tiny and she didn't want to miss him growing up, his first words, his first steps, but she would do absolutely anything to ensure her family kept Foxglove Farm. That her boys would have a home.

Isla's thoughts were interrupted by a text message from Martha. Everyone was up at the farm, apparently the cleaning squad were out in full force and already five lambs had been born this morning.

Isla closed her eyes for a second and sighed before walking back towards the car. Within fifteen minutes she was back at Foxglove Farm. The alpacas were grazing happily, and Isla noticed that the poorly one had joined them. Rory must have released her into the field.

Noticing the hive of activity inside the farm, she stopped and stared for a moment. She could see Hamish and Julia laughing, Polly and Allie were hoovering, and Jessica was dusting.

'Damn,' said Isla, powering her legs to the house. She could see inside the house, the boards over the windows all gone. Isla thought the windows were being put in on Monday, and Alfie needed to stop right this second. They couldn't afford to pay him.

Isla opened the farmhouse door and raced up the hallway towards the living room.

Martha grinned at her, 'Here she is now. I told you she'd be amazed at how much we've achieved already. Finn is upstairs playing with Esme and Angus is in his cot, but gurgling contentedly,' Martha nodded towards the baby monitor.

The whole place had been hoovered and dusted, the curtains were gone, and the cushions stripped, but the only thing on Isla's mind was finding Alfie.

'And look,' said Martha, sweeping her arm towards the window. 'Alfie has pulled out all the stops.'

Isla didn't mean to appear rude, but overcome with worry, she closed her eyes fleetingly.

'Gran, he needs to stop now.'

Martha looked perplexed, with her hands cupped around the handle of the broom.

'Don't be daft, he's finished the job, worked his magic, he has – got the guys here on a Sunday. He left a couple of minutes ago.'

Isla closed her eyes and exhaled.

'And why would Alfie need to stop? You can't move back into a farmhouse with no windows.'

Isla was oblivious to the fact that everyone in the room had stopped cleaning and was staring at her.

Martha looked over towards Allie, who simply shrugged.

Ushering Isla out of the room, Martha asked, 'What's going on, Isla? Take a deep breath and tell me.'

Isla sat on the bottom stair and looked up at her gran, and everything came spilling out. The lies, the lack of insurance, the fact that they could lose the farm. Isla spilled it all.

'Oh my,' said Martha, looking flustered. 'Are you sure? That doesn't sound like something Drew would do at all.'

'Absolutely sure. Gran, he's taken out a loan to pay the arrears of the mortgage, there are unpaid bills, final demands and I've bought the herd of alpacas with the money from the loan.'

'What a mess. What if the house had caught fire or, even worse, something had happened to Drew?' Martha queried.

'Then me and the boys would have been left with nothing.' Deep down Isla was disappointed in Drew and hurt that he hadn't confided in her.

'Gran, I'm going to have to find a job,' the tears welled up in Isla's eyes at the thought of leaving Angus with a stranger. 'We could lose everything and I just don't know what to do!' Isla broke down as the situation finally overwhelmed her.

Martha looked horrified.

'That is not going to happen, let's get our thinking caps on. Come here,' Martha held out her arms and smiled.

Isla stood up and forced a smile back. She was understandably subdued and pushed her hair back out of her eyes. 'It's all a mess.'

'And one we will sort together,' said Martha, hugging her granddaughter.

Martha's kind words could easily make Isla cry again, but she had to hold it together. There was a roomful of people helping to put her life back together on the other side of the door.

'What are people going to think of us if we lose the farm? It's been in Drew's family for generations.'

'People can mind their own business, otherwise they will have me to deal with,' said Martha with authority. 'And don't worry about the cost of the windows, I've some money put by for a rainy day.'

'But that's your money.'

'And I'm your grandmother. If I can't dig you out of a hole, who can?'

Isla felt embarrassed that they needed to be dug out of any kind of hole, but at this moment in time she wasn't going to turn her gran's kind offer down. 'We will pay you back.'

Martha was just about to return to the troops in the living

room when she remembered, 'Rory's with Nate at the moment, they need the key to that other old barn, apparently there's a padlock on it, you were going to find the key.'

'Yes, that's right, the key is in the boot room,' Isla said, trying to summon the energy to get behind the daily grind of running the farm.

'And I'll walk over with you,' said Allie, suddenly appearing from the living room and hovering in the doorway. 'I need some fresh air – I think I've swallowed my body weight in ash.'

Isla nodded, even though she knew it was more than likely Allie wanted to quiz her about what was going on. 'Sorry Allie, I didn't mean to be ungrateful, I can't believe the amount of work everyone has done for us,' said Isla, sincerely.

As soon as Isla and Allie stepped outside, Allie asked, 'How's Drew? Did he have a comfortable night? Felicity's texted, Fergus is allowed home today.'

'That's good for Fergus, I'm pleased. But he still needs to rest.'

'Any news when Drew will be allowed home?'

'I'm not sure Drew will have a home to come home to,' said Isla, the words out of her mouth before she could stop them.

'What's that meant to mean?'

For a moment, Isla didn't say anything, she folded her arms on top of the wooden gate and tilted her face towards the sky, breathing deeply.

Cautiously Allie spoke, 'Come on, I'm listening. I know you and Drew are having a few problems at the minute but ...'

'A few? You don't know half of it,' interrupted Isla, staring up at the spectacular view in front of her. 'Can you imagine not waking up to that each day?' Isla nodded towards the mountain. 'Because that's what could potentially happen to my life, thanks to my husband.'

Isla fixed her gaze on Heartcross Mountain. At this moment in time she couldn't make her mind up about her feelings towards Drew. She was angry he'd chosen to put them in this position, but also sad that he felt he couldn't talk to her about it – yet she still loved him. Of course, Isla knew love didn't always have to run smoothly but it had to be real, a partnership, no keeping secrets. Isla felt the over-whelming and undesirable feeling of lack of trust running through her veins, and once the trust had gone, was there any point? For the first time in her relationship with Drew, she doubted their future. In all the years she and Drew had been together, they'd never been through a rocky patch as bad as this.

'We are in trouble Allie, financial trouble, and I mean this when I say I don't want you discussing it with Felicity.' Isla knew this was a big ask, as the three of them were the best of friends, but Isla didn't want Felicity worrying about Fergus's job until Isla knew for sure what was going to happen.

'Whoa! Now you do have me worried. When have we ever kept secrets from each other?'

'Let's walk and talk. I need to give the key to the boys.'

Within the next couple of minutes, Isla had brought Allie up to speed about the whole sorry situation.

'Bloody hell Isla, I wasn't expecting that,' said Allie, aston-ished. 'Drew has always been the sensible one.'

'Not any more. I've got to find a job and fast. The loan needs repaying, the mortgage arrears and all the unpaid bills. I thought the alpacas would be profitable, but I'm waiting for the knock on the door when the Kerrs come to reclaim them. Nothing seems to be going right at the minute. There's an evening shift going in the chip shop over in Glensheil, it was in the paper this week.'

'You are not working in a chip shop,' exclaimed Allie in horror.

'Beggars can't be choosers,' said Isla, feeling saddened. The look on Isla's face and the tone of her voice said it all.

Allie gave her an affectionate nudge of the shoulder, 'We'll think of a plan, us Heartcrossers ...' she made a heart shape with her hands before swiping her finger down her chest and back up the other way in the shape of a cross, '... stick together.'

Allie's actions brought a smile to Isla's face. As teenagers that sign had been their pact between them all, it meant they would always look after each other.

Isla smiled and held on tight to Allie as they made their way over to the ramshackle barn at the far end of the farm.

'I remember playing in here when we were at school,' Allie said.

'Me too, it feels like a lifetime ago.'

'What's this place use for?' asked Allie, standing behind Isla as she prised open the rickety old door.

'To house a million and one spiders, by the looks of things. Rory and Nate will have their work cut out moving this lot to make some room for the hay bales.'

'And what are those doing hiding away in here?' Allie raised a shoulder half-heartedly. 'If things get that bad, you could live in one of those,' she joked, pointing towards three old VW campervans and a handful of vintage caravans. 'They haven't even got wheels!'

Isla smiled, 'These vans are here due to another one of Drew's hare-brained schemes that never took off. He and Fergus decided that they were going to recondition them and sell them on for a profit, but as you can see, they never got round to it … and they've been here for a few years now.'

'They look as though they should be condemned,' laughed Allie.

'They are condemned,' confirmed Isla, walking towards them. 'But those VW campervans look pretty cool, don't they?' She flicked her eye over the vans.

'They are pretty cool, I'd love to take off for a week, rambling around in one of those, parking up in a field … living the dream,' chipped in Allie.

The cogs in Isla's mind were turning fast. 'Oh my God Allie, I've got it.'

'Got what?' asked Allie, narrowing her eyes at Isla.

She slapped Allie in her stomach and took off at the speed of light. 'Come on,' Isla gestured, waving her on.

Allie tried to keep up with her, 'Slow down, where are we going?'

Then Isla stopped dead in her tracks.

'What's got into you?' asked Allie, after she caught her up.

Isla was grinning and flung her arms open wide, 'Look! This is my favourite part of the farm, the orchard, the stream, the bridge and a view that stretches for miles. Even in winter when the trees are bare there's a magical feel about this place. I can imagine fairy lights draped over the branches ... chimineas burning wood ...'

'I don't understand,' said Allie, confused.

'Come on, all will be explained.'

With a spring in her step Isla led the way back to the ramshackle barn.

'What are we doing back here?'

'Those,' said Isla, pointing at the VW campervans, 'are the future. Drew always said these vans were our future ... maybe he was right. Julia is turning away bookings at the B&B, she can't keep up with the demand since our little village became famous. And that's exactly why Bonnie set up the teashop all those years ago ... passing ramblers knocking on the door, as it was the last cottage on Love Heart Lane before heading up over the mountains,' said Isla enthusiastically. 'How amazing would all these caravans be with a bit of a facelift? Can you imagine waking up to that spectacular scenery every morning?' She spun round and pointed to the mountain. 'And with the sound of the stream trickling, the sun streaming through the windows and the Shetland ponies and alpacas grazing nearby? Okay, granted we'll have to wait and see how the alpaca situation pans out, but the rest is all a hundred percent ours.'

A glimmer of a smile played on Allie's lips, 'You are certainly a tonic, Isla.'

Isla's face lit up. 'I'll clean these caravans up and persuade

Rory and Nate to somehow move them over to the field. There's already the outside toilet block that the boys use in the day – it would need a fresh lick of paint, mind.'

'I think it's a genius idea,' grinned Allie, grabbing her arm.

'Me too!' Isla squealed. 'Foxglove Camping – Camping With a Difference.'

'And it's much better than tents! With vintage campervans you won't even be treading on Julia's toes, it's unique! Your very own little business.'

'I can direct them to the teashop for breakfast if they don't feel like cooking,' enthused Isla. 'And I won't have to leave the farm. Win/win. What do you think?'

'I think you are on to a winner. I'd run it past Julia first, but if she's turning people away from the B&B she could send them in your direction. I'm sure she won't mind in the slightest – it's extra tourism to Heartcross, isn't it?'

Isla clapped her hands in delight. Okay, there wasn't going to be an influx of money straight away, but if she put her business idea to the bank, surely something could be worked out about the mortgage and loan repayments? Feeling hopeful that things were possibly going to be okay, Isla's thoughts were running away with her. She wanted this new idea up and running right this very second. It would be the perfect solution, she wouldn't have to work in a dead-end job and would still be around for her boys. And maybe, just maybe, they would get to save their home.

Chapter 22

'No ... no,' murmured Isla, this was madness. She recognised the excitement, the goose bumps, the tremble of anticipation, she felt like a teenager again.

He didn't listen and she didn't fight him off. She knew it was wrong but the thrill and excitement of it all spurred her on. She wanted more. He tugged at her dress, inciting desire and panic. Tumbling on to the bed, his naked body covering her, her breath caught and she was dizzy with desire. He was a stranger, but she wanted him, she needed to feel wanted. He leant in, his lips briefly brushing against hers, not giving the consequences a second thought.

BEEP! BEEP! BEEP!

Isla bolted upright in bed and stretched out her arm and banged off the alarm with her hand. She quickly looked at the space next to her in the bed and felt relieved to see it empty. Thankfully, it was only a dream. Lying back down, Isla stared at the ceiling, what the hell had prompted that dream? But Isla knew the answer to that question. She felt lonely, the distance between her and Drew was immense.

She wanted to feel loved, she wanted a pair of strapping strong arms to envelop her in a tight hug and for someone to tell her this whole mess was going to be okay. There was no face to the stranger but feeling a twinge of guilt, feeling unfaithful, she pushed the dream to the back of her mind and thought of Drew. She wondered how he was feeling, had he slept? She checked her phone but there was no message from him.

Isla wished she hadn't drunk that bottle of wine last night, but once she'd poured one glass she couldn't stop.

Drew's state of mind, his dishonesty, had been playing on her mind.

Pulling on her overalls and pushing her feet into her boots, Isla grabbed her coat. This morning she was milking the cows with Polly. At 5 a.m. the cockerels were crowing and the hens were scratting about the gravel as she headed towards the cow field.

Isla couldn't believe her eyes, Polly was already ahead of her, standing by the milking shed.

'Reporting for duty, boss,' she saluted.

Isla looked Polly up and down and sniggered.

'What are you laughing at?' asked Polly, a little bewildered.

Polly was dressed in a pale-blue cashmere sweater, a skater skirt, opaque tights and ballet-type shoes.

'What are you wearing?' Isla answered, trying to keep a straight face at Polly's inappropriate dress sense. 'You can't milk cows dressed like that, whatever are you thinking?'

'You didn't say I had to touch the cows. I'm assuming I don't have to sit on a stool and pull and squeeze.'

'I think times have moved on since then Pol,' laughed Isla, thinking that would take forever. 'It's simple, the cows line up and enter the milking parlour.'

'Do we have to take a register?' joked Polly, thinking that every cow looked exactly the same.

Isla rolled her eyes. 'I inspect every cow, we clean all four teats, enter them in the stalls and attach them to the milking-machine cluster. The milk is piped directly to the bulk tank where it's chilled. It takes less than five minutes per cow. They know the routine off by heart. Oh, and once they've finished milking, they exit the parlour that way,' said Isla, nodding towards the exit. Isla watched in amusement as the cows began to filter in and Polly looked horrified.

'My, they are so big,' said Polly, her voice wobbled a little.

'Honestly, they are harmless ... look ... watch.' Isla bent down to clean the teats. At that very moment a strange gurgling sound was released from the cow's mouth, followed by a swish of its tail, leading Polly to step back in alarm – into something squelchy.

'Oh shit!' she announced, pursing her lips together.

'Yep, it's definitely shit,' laughed Isla. 'Do you think Drew and Fergus have this much fun milking the cows?' Isla teased.

'Call this fun?'

Hearing laughter behind them, they swiftly turned to see Nate peering around the door as if he was acting like an international spy.

'You can come out now and what are you doing here?' asked Isla, tilting her head to one side, waiting for an answer.

'Rory mentioned you may need some extra help this

morning, but I can see you have got it all under control,' replied Nate, stifling a laugh while cocking a cheeky eyebrow towards Polly's shoes.

'Polly came dressed for the occasion!' teased Isla, thankful Nate had arrived.

'I've stood in dung ... YUK ... and look, it's seeped over the edge of my shoes,' said Polly, screwing up her face and trying not to retch. 'It stinks.'

'And I'm trying to milk the cows with a bunch of amateurs present.'

'Who are you calling an amateur?' objected Nate, raising an eyebrow but smiling.

Isla looked down at Polly's shoes. 'I think you might need to go and change those shoes, there's a pair of overalls and wellies in the shed.'

Polly stepped back hesitantly, avoiding another swish of the cow's tail.

'In fact, go and make us a cuppa,' suggested Isla as Polly sprinted out of the milking shed.

'Tea, one sugar, for me,' Nate shouted, grinning. 'Was she really milking cows dressed like that? She looked more like she was going for a job interview,' Nate shook his head in jest, and rolled his eyes.

'Talking of interviews, apparently my husband thinks I should have interviewed you to work here. He won't have just anyone working on the farm, you know.'

'And what's your take on that, boss?'

'If Rory is singing your praises ... then that's good enough for me.'

Isla stepped back and stumbled over the edge of the galley, falling on her backside.

Startled, Nate yanked her to her feet as quickly as she fell.

Isla looked straight into the eyes of Nate, who had a massive smile etched on his face.

'Now who's working with amateurs?'

Feeling like a fool, she brushed herself down, 'Are you laughing at me?'

'Why would I be laughing at you?' His smile was slow and crooked. 'Maybe a little, are you okay?'

'I'm fine, it's just been a while since I've been in here. Now, I take it you know how to milk a cow?'

'Of course,' Nate said, giving her a lopsided grin.

Just as they were about to start milking the cows they heard a muffled scream coming from outside.

They swivelled their heads towards the entrance of the milking shed. 'What was that?' asked Isla.

Nate shrugged and took off after Isla, who was now running down the gangway.

'Polly,' shouted Isla. 'Is that you? Where are you?'

'I'm in here. HELP!'

Isla and Nate locked eyes. 'She's in the shed,' said Isla, swinging open the door to find Polly balancing on top of a quad bike, staring down at Robbie, the buff Orpington rooster who was following her every move with his watchful eyes.

Isla burst out laughing. 'What are you doing up there?' she asked, amused.

'Trying to change into those overalls but ... that thing, with its spiky beak and that red flappy body part dangling under its chin, looks like it's going to kill me!'

'I get the impression you don't like him much,' teased Nate, enjoying the entertainment. 'He's a fine specimen.'

The almighty creature hopped on to the handle bars of the bike, leading to Polly squealing again.

'Shall I help you down?' Nate's smirk didn't go unnoticed. 'Please!'

Nate held out his hand which Polly gratefully took.

'You are definitely not cut out for this farm life,' joked Isla.

'City girl through and through,' laughed Nate.

'Now, can we get on and milk those cows?' asked Isla, in a playful tone. 'And did you make us a cup of tea?'

'No, I couldn't find any milk!'

Everyone burst out laughing.

'You just can't get the staff, if I knew being a farmer was as much fun as this, maybe I'll pack Drew off to a dead-end job and I'll take over the farm.'

Walking back towards the milking shed, Polly kept one eye over her shoulder, making sure the rooster wasn't following her.

'We'll make a farmer out of you yet,' winked Isla.

Polly didn't look convinced.

'We'll break you in gently, I don't want you upsetting my cows. Milk means money and believe me, I need every penny right now.'

Isla walked back up the gangway. Nate had already wiped down the first five cows and attached them to the milking cluster. For a second Isla watched him, he knew how to milk a cow. He looked up and caught her looking at him, and arched an eyebrow.

'You are a remarkable woman, aren't you?'

'What makes you say that? Even though I'll take the compliment.'

'Look at you, up at the crack of dawn, stepping into the role of farmer. Your husband is a very lucky man,' said Nate, the intensity of his eyes making her stomach flutter.

'It's a shame my husband doesn't know how lucky he is.' The words were out of Isla's mouth before she could stop them.

Nate narrowed his eyes at her before taking the milking cluster from one cow and attaching it to the next after it wandered into the stall.

'Problems?'

'Just the usual mundane married stuff,' she answered, suddenly feeling disloyal towards Drew. They milked in silence for the next five minutes until Isla shouted over to Polly, who was sitting on a high stool swinging her legs, playing on her phone: 'Are you okay up there?'

'This farming malarkey is so easy!' Polly shouted back.

'That's the spirit, don't work too hard,' teased Nate.

'She better not let Drew hear her say that! ... Urghh, I can't get this cluster to stay on,' said Isla, who was all thumbs and fingers.

'Here ... let me try,' immediately Nate placed his hand over hers. 'There, you just need to be firm.'

'Thank you.'

'When's Drew home?' asked Nate, moving the next cow on.

'Hopefully today,' Isla answered as Nate's phoned beeped. 'That's an early morning text,' she said, looking over at Nate, who seemed distracted by a message on his phone.

'Everything okay?' asked Isla.

'Yes, sorry,' he said, slipping his phone back into his overall pocket.

'Rory mentioned last night you'd come up with a new business idea,' said Nate, making conversation. 'Something about refurbishing the campervans? I think that's a brilliant idea. Mind you though, you do need a licence.'

'A licence?' Isla wasn't aware she needed one.

'Yes, I'm sure you do, but the guy who put your windows in will know.'

'Alfie ... yes, I'll check with him. I've not even spoken to Drew about it yet but it may take time to get it all up and running.'

'You'll get those vans clean and refreshed in no time at all.'

'Have you seen the state of those vans?' exclaimed Isla.

'I have actually, but I can take a closer look after we've finished milking. There's plenty of time before Rory picks me up for the alpaca's scan.'

'Thanks, Nate.'

This was the encouragement Isla needed.

'I think it's a no-brainer, the old vans are sat there, there's no initial outlay ... you can still work at the farm, which is handy for the children. I think you have it all worked out.'

Isla liked Nate, he was good company, easy to be around. It certainly would make her working day pleasant.

'Call it instinct, but I think you have the making of a good business-woman. From what I've seen, you're one determined lady.'

Isla mulled over what Nate was saying. His encouraging words carried reassurance. Those vans wouldn't take long to clean out, she'd check with Alfie about the licence, and the thought of owning her own little business filled Isla with excitement.

As Nate attached the last cow to the milking cluster, she watched him. His bright eyes, his rugged cheekbones and those lashes ... Any girl would die for those lashes. He looked up and cocked an eyebrow, 'Have you seen?'

'Seen what?'

Nate nodded towards Polly, who'd fallen asleep on the stool. Her head was bent low, her arms folded.

'I don't think she's up to the farmer's life,' chuckled Isla, following the last cow down the gangway towards the exit.

'Now go and wake up your friend, and let's take a look at those vans.'

'Thanks, Nate. And thank you for helping us out at the farm and turning up in Heartcross when you did.'

'You don't need to thank me, I'm only doing it for the money,' he said, grinning.

Isla swiped his arm playfully. Nate was going to be good to have around.

Chapter 23

'So what do you think, Gran?'

'I think it's a genius idea!' exclaimed Martha.

'Foxglove Camping ...' said Isla out loud. 'It's got a ring to it ... I'm really going to do this!'

The adrenaline was pumping through Isla's body, as she shared her new business idea with Martha over early morning coffee. Isla would be working the farm for the next six weeks, which would give her plenty of time to spruce up the vans and apply for a licence. Her gran agreed it was a perfect plan, and with Julia turning away custom left, right and centre, Isla was in no doubt the vans would bring in a steady income.

'Nate thought it wouldn't be a huge task to move the vans, the tractor would have no problem pulling them over to the orchard.'

'You seem to have it worked out ... good for you,' said Martha.

'I've got a good feeling about it ... Nate said I need a licence, but I'll have a chat to Alfie about that. Nate said he was sure it's not going to be a problem.'

'Nate's doing a lot of saying,' said Martha, narrowing her eyes at her granddaughter.

'What's that meant to mean?' asked Isla, feeling slight irritation.

'Nothing, I'm just saying.'

'Now it's you who's doing a lot of saying,' replied Isla, arching an eyebrow. She stopped what she was doing, 'Honestly, Gran, that man is an absolute godsend. The gods were shining down on us when they sent him to Heartcross,' she said, meaning every word. 'He's going to help me clean up the vans and we're going to make a start as soon as he gets back from the alpaca's scan. You know Gran, it's been a good morning. Even though all the financial crap is hanging over my head, it's good to keep busy, and that's exactly what I'm going to do. I can't wait to get stuck into cleaning those vans up.'

Isla stood up and, with a spring in her step, she went to wake Finn up for school and check on Angus who was still sleeping, leaving Martha cracking eggs ready to make Finn's favourite, scrambled egg and bacon on bagels.

Finn looked like he had been wrestling with his duvet when Isla gently shook him. 'Time to wake up, breakfast then school.'

Finn opened his eyes and instantly smiled, 'Will Daddy be home when I get home from school?'

'I hope so,' answered Isla. 'I've got to ring the hospital in a minute and check. Come on, Great-gran's making you breakfast.'

'Scrambled eggs and bagels?'

'Exactly that!'

Finn jumped out of bed, 'I like Great-gran staying with us, she's a better cook than you too!'

'Oi cheeky,' laughed Isla, playfully chasing Finn down the stairs.

Martha was dishing up Finn's breakfast and immediately he tucked in the second she placed the plate in front of him.

'How was Polly at milking?' asked Martha, sitting down next to Finn.

Isla told the story of Polly stepping in dung in her inappropriate footwear, which made Finn laugh so much he spluttered his juice everywhere.

'She would never make a farmer's wife,' chuckled Martha.

'It's only me,' shouted Rory, opening the back door. Finn jumped out of his seat and ran towards the door, 'Rory!'

'Good morning champ,' said Rory cheerfully, stepping into the kitchen and ruffling Finn's hair.

Finn flung his arms in the air, 'Spin me round ... spin me round.'

Without hesitation, Rory lifted a squealing Finn high off the floor and spun him round.

'You've started something now,' said Isla, laughing.

'Are you here to make the alpaca better?' asked Finn, looking up at Rory as he placed him safely back on his two feet.

'I am, we are going to load her up now. Is Nate out on the farm?' asked Rory, turning back towards Isla.

She nodded towards the kitchen window. 'He's heading this way right now.'

Nate sauntered across the courtyard, his mobile phone held to his ear. Isla watched him for a second; whoever he was talking to, by his facial expression he looked serious. Just before he reached the farmhouse, he seemed to plunge the phone quickly back into his overall pocket.

'Nate is here now,' Isla stepped outside with Rory.

'Are we ready to load up this alpaca?' asked Nate cheerily, which Isla immediately thought was strange as she'd just witnessed Nate looking irate.

'Yes, two minutes,' answered Rory. 'Before I forget ... the alpacas ... their fleeces need to be sheared.'

'But you know the situation with the alpacas, Rory,' said Isla, giving him a look that meant she didn't want to talk about this in front of Nate. Rory knew these alpacas weren't technically hers.

Rory turned towards Nate, 'Are you okay to fetch the alpaca?' he asked, handing the head collar to him.

As soon as Nate was out of earshot, Isla said, 'Rory, I can't go shearing those alpacas!'

'All I'm saying is, I'm looking after the welfare of those animals, and with the summer months on the way, those fleeces need to come off as soon as possible. Those alpacas are in your possession, so sell those fleeces. Pete, the guy who shears the sheep, is over in Glensheil in a couple of weeks' time, so get him booked in.'

'How much would we get for each fleece?' she asked curiously.

'About a grand per fleece.'

Instantly, Isla felt like she'd won the lottery, this would solve all their financial problems. It would certainly take the pressure off them and pay off the majority of the debts.

'I think you should go ahead, technically you've bought them, they are grazing in your field and, for the welfare of the animal, the fleece needs to come off.' Rory delved into his pocket and brought out a piece of paper. 'Here, take this. Dad knew James Kerr very well. They were friends, despite his reputation, and Dad quite liked the old bugger. This is the name of the buyer that James dealt with. Give them a ring, we can get the fleeces shipped over to them on the same day.'

'Thanks Rory, you know what, as soon as I get back from picking Drew up, I'll give them a call.'

Rory turned and looked down the yard. Nate was walking towards them leading the alpaca behind him.

'Look at her, she looks a little overweight but she's up on those feet fine now,' remarked Rory, taking the alpaca's lead from Nate. 'Come on, let's load her up.'

Isla leant against the wall in deep thought. What would the consequences be of getting the alpacas sheared? Would the Kerr brothers really demand the money back? Or was Rory right and they were doing what was best for the welfare of the animals? The money would certainly get them out of a predicament and Isla made up her mind, those alpacas were going to be sheared.

Chapter 24

As Isla drove towards the hospital she was deep in thought. The radio was on but she was oblivious to the songs being played. The only thing on her mind was the alpacas, getting them sheared as quickly as possible and using the money to pay off the debts. It would certainly make for an easy life, but what were the chances of it coming back to bite her on her bum?

As she drove, Isla concentrated on the road ahead, the pretty cottages and farm houses whizzing past with their colourful blooms hanging from baskets. She tried to dismiss all her negative thoughts and keep in a positive frame of mind. Drew had gotten them into this mess, but maybe the alpacas were the way out of it.

It didn't take long to reach the hospital but, judging by the third missed call from Drew, he was at his wits' end waiting for her to arrive.

The hospital car park was almost full, and Isla manoeuvred into a space at the far end before anyone else spotted it. Stepping out of the car, she was feeling apprehensive; she and Drew still had a lot to sort out between them.

Inside the entrance Isla grabbed a coffee from the small café situated on the ground floor before following the corridor towards Drew's room. As she pushed open the door to his room, Drew was sitting up in the raspberry-coloured wingback chair next to the bed. His coat was already fastened and his leg was stretched out in front of him, his crutches resting next to the bedside table.

'Morning,' she chirped, hoping her voice sounded happier than she felt. She was still worried about the state of their relationship and the financial mess that they were in. She automatically popped a polite kiss on his cheek.

'I didn't know whether you would actually pick me up,' Drew said.

'That was actually a possibility,' she replied, giving him a half-hearted smile. He was still very much in her bad books but what was done was done. She couldn't change any of it. Isla just had to make sure they were never in this situation ever again. 'But I'm not sure the boys would forgive me. We do have a lot of sorting out to do, Drew.'

Looking exhausted, he nodded his understanding then pushed himself up on his crutches. Inside Isla still had mixed feelings. Of course she was thankful to have her husband home after such an ordeal, but deep down Isla knew they needed to learn how to communicate again and build up the trust that had been lost, especially by her. The next six weeks were going to be difficult. She knew Drew would find it hard recuperating in such close proximity to the farm without being able to work, and Isla knew she wasn't used to having him under her feet inside the farmhouse twenty-four/seven.

'I just want to get home,' said Drew. 'Sleep in my own bed.'
Isla picked up his bag while Drew battled with his crutches.
'These things aren't as easy as they look.'

'I can imagine,' answered Isla, holding the door open for
him.

At first, the journey back to Foxglove Farm was very subdued.
Isla could feel slight tension bubbling under the surface. Both
of them knew they needed to talk properly to get everything
out in the open. Isla didn't fully understand why Drew had
kept everything hidden from her. Drew sat slumped in the
passenger seat with his cast stretched in front of him. The
radio played in the background, but neither of them was
listening to the music.

Isla bit the bullet: 'You do know we do have to talk, don't
you?' she said, staring at the road ahead and not giving Drew
a sideward glance.

Drew sighed, 'Not now Isla, I'm exhausted. All I want to
do is see my boys and give them a hug. I don't want to argue.'

Isla nodded, of course she knew the trauma that Drew had
been through, it had been harrowing for them all. But they
still needed to talk and Isla couldn't help but feel Drew was
trying everything to swerve away from the conversation.

They drove on for another five minutes before Isla took the
plunge once more. She was nervous about sharing her
camping idea with Drew, in case he wasn't keen.

'I've come up with an idea to help us get back on our feet.'

Drew carried on staring out of the window. 'What's that?'
he asked.

'Those old campervans and caravans, the ones you and Fergus bought at auction ... I'm going to spruce them up, drag them to the orchard and open up my very own business.'

Drew swung a glance her way, 'What sort of business?'

'Camping with a difference. Julia is turning away customers left, right and centre ... so why not take advantage of that ... put those vans to good use ... all they are doing is sitting there.'

Drew was quiet for a minute, then his eyes skimmed towards Isla. Her stomach was performing double somersaults waiting for him to speak.

Thankfully Isla was relieved to see the corners of his mouth begin to lift. 'You know what Isla, you may have something there, but don't you need a licence?'

'Yes, I need to have a chat with Alfie about that, but on the whole you think it's a good idea?'

'Actually, you know what, I think it's a very good idea,' he said encouragingly, which lifted Isla's mood.

'And I'll still be around for the children,' she added excitedly. 'I can get it up and running in the next six weeks whilst working the farm, and fingers crossed, we'll soon have another income ... Nate said he'll help me spruce up the vans.'

'And this Nate, he seems alright, does he?'

'Yes, he's a hard worker, I think you'll like him when you get to know him.'

Drew didn't answer but stared out of the window again.

Isla took a deep breath, 'You aren't feeling threatened by Nate, are you? Because there's no need, he's a really nice, down-to-earth bloke.'

'Are you kidding me? Why would I feel threatened by him? It's my farm.'

'*Our* farm,' Isla corrected, noticing that Drew had suddenly become agitated. 'What's happening to us, Drew? It feels like sometimes you don't even like me anymore. You've barely shown any interest in me of late, we don't even talk anymore. One minute you're fine and the next you are snapping at me. And look at the financial mess. I don't even understand why you would have kept any of that from me. The bridge collapsing wasn't our fault, lots of businesses were affected and lost money.'

'Isla, please. I said not now. I just want to get home.'

Feeling frustrated with Drew, she wasn't going to let this lie. She indicated left at the roundabout and they drove the rest of the way home in silence.

Drew had been up and down, huffing and puffing, that many times in the last half hour that Isla had lost count. Since he'd been home her irritation towards him was growing, he just couldn't sit still.

'Why are you even at the window?' she asked, not hiding the frustration in her voice.

'Where are they? There's jobs to be done on the farm. We aren't paying him to skive.'

'You aren't even paying him,' Isla reminded him. 'Martha is. And Nate isn't skiving, he's accompanied Rory to the alpaca's scan. Drew, just sit down and relax. There's no need to be stressing yourself out like this.'

This was only day one and Drew was already climbing the

walls. Isla knew that Drew would be itching to get back to work but he needed to take his recovery seriously.

'They should be back by now,' stated Drew, still glued to the window.

'Drew, they will be back soon and please be civil to Nate when they do arrive back, the last thing we need is him walking out on us,' said Isla, scooping up Angus from the midst of all the soft baby blocks on the floor and lying him under his activity centre.

A few minutes later Isla noticed the Land Rover driving through the farm gates. Drew was still at the window, balancing on his crutches. He watched as Rory and Nate jumped out of the van.

'Are they my overalls he's wearing?' Drew dramatically spun round towards Isla.

'Yes,' she said firmly. 'What do you expect him to be working in, his hiking gear?'

'Did you check out this guy's references?'

'References? Drew, what's gotten into you? You break your leg and at very short notice some kind soul has stepped in to help out with lambing, and you are asking for references?'

'It just seems strange to me that some bloke turns up out of the blue looking for work in a village that's in the middle of nowhere. It's not sitting right with me.'

Isla was exasperated. 'You haven't even spoken to the man, give him a chance. You might even find you like him.'

Hearing footsteps behind them, Isla was embarrassed to see Nate now standing in the doorway. She wanted the ground to swallow her up, surely he would have heard every word of their argument.

'Hi, you must be Drew,' Nate walked towards him with his hand stretched out. 'It was the broken leg that gave it away,' he said with a beatific smile.

Drew looked uncomfortable as he shook his hand.

'Nate ... Drew ... Drew ... Nate,' said Isla, introducing them.

'How you doing, mate?' asked Nate.

'Glad to be home,' Drew said.

'It's good to have him home,' added Isla, trying not to roll her eyes.

'I bet you're proud of your wife, what a fantastic business idea ... Foxglove Camping – Camping With a Difference. I hope you don't mind,' Nate turned towards Isla. 'But we saw Alfie on the way to the scan and he's going to come over this afternoon and talk you through the process of applying for a licence.'

Isla's mood lifted, 'Thanks Nate! That's brilliant.' The quicker Isla could get the ball rolling, the quicker income would start flooding in.

'And we can work on the vans this afternoon, if you like? Unless you would like me to do something else?' Nate directed his question at Drew.

'That'll be perfect,' said Isla with a smile, before Drew could answer. 'It's going to take a while to clean all those vans and get the toilet block up and running.'

'Nah, not too long,' chipped in Nate. 'I can help in the evening, all I'm doing is sitting around at Rory's. We'll have you up and running in no time.'

'I can't ask you to do that, you'll be shattered after working on the farm all day. Drew is always fit for nothing in the evenings.'

'That's not so,' answered Drew, feeling like he had to defend himself. 'I always pull my weight.'

Isla shot him a warning glance, 'You know that's not what I'm saying.'

Drew looked forlorn.

'And anyway, where's Rory? What's the news on the alpaca?' asked Isla.

Nate's face lit up and he grinned, 'I'll leave Rory to tell you all. He's here now. I'm just going to grab some lunch, then I'll be back to help with the vans.'

'Thanks Nate,' said Isla, holding the door open for Rory, who walked in with a huge beam on his face.

'Drew, you're back. You had us all worried there for a while,' said Rory, patting him on his back. 'How are you?'

'I just want to get back to work.'

'He's already driving me insane and I've another six weeks of this,' said Isla, blowing out a breath.

'Well, I've got some news that will cheer you up!'

'What's going on?' Isla's expression changed with a jolt, but the way they were grinning, it had to be good news.

'The alpaca isn't sick, she's pregnant!' exclaimed Rory.

'Pregnant?' repeated a surprised Isla.

'And there's more. She's expecting twins!'

Isla gasped, 'Are you serious?'

'That's what the ultrasound showed. The gestation period is eleven and a half months and Gemma ...'

'Gemma?' interrupted Drew.

'Yes, Gemma the alpaca, because she's a gem, an absolute diamond ... I came up with name,' said Rory, looking pleased with himself.

'Well, we'll go with it for now,' chuckled Isla. 'Go on Rory, what were you saying?'

'It's very rare for alpacas to give birth to twins or for even one of them to survive.'

Isla's face dropped, something uneasy descended over her, 'So what are you saying?'

'I'm saying we need to make her as comfortable as possible and hope for the best. Fingers crossed for all of them.'

Isla felt mixed emotions, she didn't know whether to feel happy with the news or sad that the alpaca might lose one of her babies.

'Crias – that's what they call baby alpacas – bring in good money,' said Rory, raising his eyebrows at Drew.

'But you're forgetting we may have to give them back,' sighed Drew.

'Isla and I have spoken about this. Those animals need shearing and as far as you're concerned, you bought them in good faith. Pete is coming to shear them. Have you spoken to the fashion house ... the number I gave you?' Rory looked towards Isla, who shook her head.

'I'll do that now.'

'Fleeces bring in approximately a grand each. Those fleeces have to come off.'

Drew caught Isla's eye. She was clearly thinking the same as him.

'And alpacas instinctively give birth during the morning to early afternoon which enables the young to suckle before the temperature drops at night. So, we need to keep a twenty-four-hour watch on Gemma,' added Rory. 'Anyway, I best get back to the surgery.'

As soon as Rory left the room, Isla said, 'Shearing those alpacas will clear the loan and the mortgage repayments.' She stared at Drew. 'What do you think, Drew?'

'I think those alpacas may just save this farm,' he said, smiling at Isla. This was the first time she'd seen him soften in a long while.

'Can I leave it to you to ring the bank and set up a meeting to talk to them about the mortgage ... and ring Pete too?' said Isla. 'The sooner we get those alpacas sheared the better.'

'I'll do it now,' he said with a sudden spring in his step. Thankfully, Drew seemed happier than he did five minutes ago.

'And keep your eye on Angus, Alfie's just arrived.'

'I will,' said Drew, manoeuvring himself to the chair and staring at Angus with warmth.

'Do you need anything before I go?'

'No, I'm all good.'

'Everything is going to be okay, isn't it Drew?' asked Isla, looking for reassurance and still trying desperately to make sense of it all.

She perched on the edge of the sofa, waiting in anticipation. She wanted to push for the conversation Drew was avoiding at all costs, but she knew this wasn't the right time.

They stared at each for a moment.

He nodded.

Isla saw his smile but his eyes still looked sad.

His mood swings couldn't be any more extreme. One minute he was irritable, next he was melting her heart with the way he was with Angus. Isla used to think she always had the measure of Drew, but it was safe to say at this moment that she really didn't know what was going on inside his head.

'Let's talk later,' she said, standing up, knowing Alfie was waiting outside.

Feeling relieved, Isla felt the conversation had gone well. Had they turned a corner, were all his mood swings to do with all the financial worry? Isla hoped so. Maybe, just maybe they were back on track, which she felt good about.

Chapter 25

Alfie was hovering with his clipboard at the side of the burnt-out barn as Isla walked towards him.

'You look like you're taking it all in your stride, considering all that you've been through,' said Alfie, peering up from his clipboard.

'I'm excited, Alfie, about this whole project and Drew's arrived home, which makes things a little easier,' said Isla, feeling like a huge weight had lifted off her shoulders after the conversation they'd just had. 'And thanks for coming over so quickly.'

'I think it's a brilliant idea, Foxglove Camping, waking up to that scenery each morning will take their breath away. Let's have a look at this shower block.'

'Do I need a licence before I can set up?' asked Isla, leading the way.

'Yes, you do, and it really needs to be in place before you go into business, but as you soon as you get your vans spruced up you could be good to go. You don't need a licence straight away if the site is more than five acres and there are only three or less caravans on the field for twenty-eight days or less a year.'

'I'm not going to make much money only renting out three vans,' said Isla, feeling defeated.

'No, you don't understand ... at first you can rent out just three vans while we apply for the licence.'

Her excitement rose again, 'Which means I can still get up and running.' Isla was eager to get started.

'Yes, exactly that, and also that will ease you in gently.'

'Brilliant, thanks Alfie. That's great news!'

Alfie unclipped a piece of paper from his board and handed it to Isla, 'There's still a lot of things to do, health and safety and all that. Washing facilities need to be in place, working toilets and showers. Once you submit your application a councillor will visit and advise how the site should be laid out, and they'll look over the vans and inform you of what work needs to be done.'

'But it's all doable, isn't it?' asked Isla.

'It's all doable,' smiled Alfie.

'Thanks Alfie. And whilst you are here, I need to talk to you about the windows,' Isla swallowed. 'There was no insurance.'

Alfie's eyes widened, 'No insurance? Is everything okay, Isla?'

'It will be Alfie,' she said, suddenly feeling a little down-hearted again, 'but please don't worry, Martha is going to pay you back for the windows. I'll make sure I sort it as soon as possible. Can you let me know the cost and thanks so much for helping with this, I can't tell you how grateful I am.'

Alfie left, and spotting Nate sprinkling corn for the chickens over by the stables, Isla ran towards him waving the piece of paper in the air with a huge beam etched on her face.

He looked up and grinned, 'You look like the cat that's got the cream.'

'It's actually happening. I'm going into business.' Isla couldn't quite believe it, the idea had been hatched on a whim, but now it was becoming very much a reality.

'We best fill those buckets and get scrubbing those vans, then.'

'I best feed my husband first and my child, then I will be right back out here.'

'I'll be waiting.'

Suddenly the idea of opening up her very own business gave her a spring in her step, she couldn't wait to get all the vans up and running. The new project gave her a glimmer of hope, something to look forward to. All she had to do now was to check with Drew that a meeting had been arranged with the bank, and hopefully their home would not be in jeopardy any longer. Everything was coming together.

Chapter 26

'Anyone home?' came Fergus's familiar voice filtering through the back door.

Isla rushed into the kitchen and flung her arms wide open as she stepped towards Fergus, this was the first time she'd seen him since he came out of hospital. 'You are not coming back to work just yet,' exclaimed Isla. 'Tell him he's not coming back to work just yet.' Isla looked towards Nate who was standing behind Fergus.

'Well, what a welcome that was!'

'You know I'm always glad to see you,' she said, giving Fergus a swift kiss on the cheek. 'But you are still not coming back to work.'

'There's sandwiches on the table and fresh tea in the pot,' piped up Martha, who appeared from the utility room. 'If anyone wants anything.'

'You, Martha, are an absolute gem,' said Fergus.

'I know, I know,' she said, blushing at the compliment.

'And where is he?' asked Fergus, kicking off his shoes and looking towards the living room.

'Drew? ... Using the bathroom ... And how are you doing?' asked Isla.

'Bored is what I am,' said Fergus, pulling out a chair and sitting down at the kitchen table.

'You sound like Drew now. Some people would be glad of time off work.'

'Everyone keeps telling me to rest ...'

'And they'll be right,' interrupted Isla. 'You've been through the mill.'

Fergus rolled his eyes and tucked into a sandwich. Nate sat down next to Isla.

'And that rain is coming in again,' Fergus nodded towards the window. 'The last time I saw a black cloud like that, all hell broke loose.'

'This weather can't make its mind up,' said Isla, pulling the platter of sandwiches towards her. 'One minute you think spring is on the way and the next, we are being blown across the fields ... The joys of living in the Scottish Highlands,' she added, bouncing Angus up and down on her knee.

Nate gazed at Angus and then began to play peek-a-boo. Angus chuckled.

'He is a fine chap,' he said, stretching out his hands to take him from Isla, then quickly retracting them. 'You don't want this little one stinking of dung, I didn't think,' he grinned.

'Believe me, he'll be falling into all sorts when he starts toddling, best get him used to the smell now.' She grinned, remembering the time Finn had started walking around the farm. She handed him over.

Nate wasn't awkward at all with Angus in his arms. He handled him well, even Fergus looked impressed.

'You look a natural with kids, mate. Have you any children?' asked Fergus.

'Me ... no ... but one day.'

'There's still time, mate,' encouraged Fergus. Stuffing another sandwich into his mouth, he pointed at Martha. 'You are the best sandwich maker,' he announced.

'Don't let your mother-in-law-to-be hear you say that,' said Martha chuckling.

'Or Felicity,' chipped in Isla, laughing.

'Good point.'

Finally, Isla heard the clonk of Drew's crutches on the wooden floor, 'Here he is.' Isla glanced up to see Drew in the doorway.

Immediately, Fergus scraped his chair back and stood up. Without warning he locked Drew in a tight bear hug.

'You had me worried there for a moment,' said Fergus, his voice trembling.

Drew exhaled, his eyes misted with tears. 'Mate, I can't thank you enough ... if it wasn't for you ...' Drew squeezed his eyes shut, overcome with emotion. 'I thought I was a gonner.'

'As if I was going to leave you.' Fergus patted Drew on the back.

Isla watched the tearful reunion, she too felt all emotional and brushed away a tear that was rolling down her cheek. The boys had known each other for a lifetime, their friendship held the strongest unbreakable bond. It could have all panned out so differently.

She could be here, grieving with her boys, their life in ruins, losing the man she loved and the father of her boys, but Fergus saved them, he saved them all. As far as Isla was concerned Fergus was a hero, she'd be forever grateful. She stood up and enveloped him in the tightest hug. 'If it wasn't for your bravery ...' Isla pressed a kiss to his cheek.

'Drew would have done the same for me,' said Fergus, looking towards Drew.

Drew hesitated then grinned, 'Of course I would, who else would put up with me as a boss?'

Isla watched as Drew took a moment, then extended his hand towards Nate. 'Thank you mate. I don't know who you are or where you've come from, but we appreciate you helping us out.'

Nate gave him a nod and shook his hand. Isla swallowed down a lump in her throat, she felt proud of Drew and remembered all the reasons why she had married him. He'd got himself in a mess trying to protect her, but surely now he realised like she did, that they worked better as a team.

'But as I'm the boss at the minute,' joked Isla, 'sit down and let's eat.'

Everyone laughed, Martha poured the tea and the mood was jovial.

Fergus took a bite of his sandwich, 'Rory said Pete's coming to shear alpacas?'

'Should have been in a couple of weeks, but he's coming at the weekend, the fleeces are being transported early next week.'

Nate spluttered on his drink and Fergus's immediate reaction was to thump him on his back, 'You okay, mate?'

'Sorry, sorry, it went down the wrong hole,' Nate said, still coughing into his hand.

'Here, have this,' said Isla, pouring him a glass of water and handing it to him.

Nate took a swig then looked over towards Drew, 'I thought Rory said it would be in a couple of weeks' time?'

'He's had a cancellation and the sooner we get them sheared, the better,' said Drew. Isla couldn't agree more, knowing the arrears of the mortgage and the loan would be paid off quicker, which meant she could sleep better at night without worrying.

'Now come on and eat up, otherwise these sandwiches will be curling at the edges,' Isla pushed the plate to each of them in turn. 'And Fergus, don't think you're sneaking on to the farm, I'll be watching you. Get yourself home and rest.'

'I kind of get the feeling you are going to be a harder boss to work for when I do come back, compared to this one.'

'You better believe it,' she joked. 'I run a very tight ship.'

Once they'd all finished eating, Isla and Martha began to clear away the plates.

'Shall I go and check on the lambs and then we can make a start on those vans?' asked Nate, standing up as the rain began pelting against the window. 'Here we go again, it's coming down hard, this weather.'

'It was only earlier today I was thinking how colourful everywhere was looking, with the hanging baskets and the daffodils dancing, and now they'll all be drooping under the weight of this rain,' said Isla. 'Clearing out the vans is a good idea in this weather, at least we'll be under cover. Is that okay with you, Gran?'

'Of course, you go and do what you need to do,' Martha replied as she took Angus in her arms. His eyes were drooping and he was ready for his afternoon nap.

Isla was still looking out the window when Nate left through the back door and hurried towards the jutted-out corrugated-plastic roof at the side of the pigsty to shelter from the downpour. Isla noticed his brow was furrowed and he was looking intently at his mobile before putting it to his ear. She could see his mouth moving fast and his hand thrown up in the air. Isla thought this was strange, as only two minutes ago Nate was all calm and smiles, sitting around the kitchen table. His whole demeanour seemed to have changed in a split second.

Nate moved his weight from one foot to another and looked somewhat shiftily towards the kitchen window. For a split second he caught Isla's eye and she could have sworn she saw a look of panic cross his face, but as the rain was lashing against the window and blurring her vision, she couldn't be certain.

Chapter 27

As Isla pulled back the barn door, she was fizzing with excitement. This was her first-ever business venture and she was brimming with ideas and plans.

Nate was back to smiles until Isla handed him a pair of yellow marigolds. 'You'll need them,' she grinned.

'I'm not wearing those,' he said, looking perturbed.

'You are definitely not in touch with your feminine side, are you?' she teased, handing him a bucket of water and a sponge before opening the door to the first van.

'Blimey!' Nate cocked an eyebrow. 'Is it just my imagination or have these vans never seen the light of day?' he said, peering inside the first one.

Isla had to admit, close up they did rather look dilapidated. 'I'm thinking deluxe prices for the VW campervans ... they ooze vintage charm.'

'Deluxe? Vintage charm?' grinned Nate. 'I'm not sure those are words I'd use to describe these things.'

Isla playfully swiped him with a cloth, 'I'm thinking the smaller vans for ramblers, and the two larger ones for families or larger groups.'

'And when are you hoping to have your first guests in your deluxe vans?' Nate raised an eyebrow at the hundreds of cobwebs and dead flies hanging in the corners of the vans.

'As soon as possible. I spoke to Julia earlier, she's turning away guests all the time, so she's agreed that if she's full, she will recommend me.'

'There's no flies on you ... unlike this van,' said Nate, laughing. 'Come on, we best get cracking.'

Isla watched in amusement as he pulled on the yellow marigolds.

'And you can take that smirk off your face, I'm not having anyone telling me I'm not in touch with my feminine side.'

'Let's start with this one,' said Isla, bumping her shoulder enthusiastically against Nate's as the water slopped over the side of the bucket. 'You go first,' she gestured, then stood behind him.

'Why am I going in first?' he asked, as Isla peered over his shoulder.

'If I'm truly honest, I'm not that keen on any sort of creepy-crawlies,' she replied.

'Now she tells me,' Nate laughed.

As they stepped inside, the musty smell was intense. Isla placed the bucket on the table and looked around in dismay. She didn't know where to start.

'Maybe I've bitten off more than I can chew,' she said, feeling a little disheartened.

'We aren't giving up that easily, I'm not wearing these for the fun of it,' Nate waggled his hands in the air, causing Isla to laugh.

'But no wonder Drew and Fergus didn't do anything with them, they need fumigating,' she added, wrinkling up her nose in disgust.

'But how romantic is this?' swooned Nate, bringing his hand up to his heart and ignoring Isla's concerns.

'Very romantic, if you want to share your van with a thousand spiders, cobwebs and dead flies,' shuddered Isla.

'Which we are about to dispose of ... Look beyond all that and think of the potential. We'll soon have this van cleaned up. Think vintage, think bunting ... gorgeous soft furnishings, rose-coloured quilted duvets and beautiful fragranced hand soap,' said Nate.

'Bloody hell, you are in touch with your feminine side – I take it all back,' Isla laughed.

'You better believe it!'

As Isla took another look around her thoughts turned towards Drew. She knew she'd hit a blip in her marriage, something she'd never had to deal with before. Having fun and banter alongside Nate whilst cleaning the vans only highlighted the fact that she missed her relationship with Drew. At one time fumigating the vans would have been a fun task she'd undertake with Drew, but over time he seemed to have become more and more focused on the farm, and she on the children.

It was only now she realised how much she missed the old days, how sacred her marriage vows were, for better or worse. How much she loved Drew. Unfairly to Drew, Isla had always put him up there on a pedestal, but now she understood he was only human, had feelings, his own struggles. They may be going through a difficult period, but he was her life. She'd nearly lost him and never ever wanted to feel that suffocating, devastating feeling ever again.

Battling with the windows, finally Isla opened them and the air began to circulate.

'It's actually like a proper miniature house inside,' said Isla, standing back in amazement, before soaking her sponge in the water. 'How about we get rid of all these old furnishings, then we can start scrubbing inside and out.'

They set to work, Isla pulling down the curtains as an explosion of dust mushroomed into the air.

'Oh my God,' she spluttered then burst out laughing. 'Look at the state of us already.' They were both covered head to toe in dust and cobwebs. 'And what's that?' said Isla, her eyes fixating on something long and thin sticking out from under the bed. She screamed and jumped off the floor straight into Nate's arms.

'What are you doing, you loon?' he said, smiling.

'There ... there,' she pointed, 'it's a mouse's tail. Don't put me down,' she insisted, her heart beating fourteen to the dozen. Breathless, she clung to him, his long arms roped with muscle hanging on to her.

Nate stepped back for a better viewpoint and howled with laughter. 'It's a twig, you eejit!' he said, gently lowering her to the floor and picking it up.

She held her hand to her chest, 'Are you sure?'

He waved it in front of her eyes, 'I'm sure.'

Isla relaxed enough to smile at him then jumped out of her skin as a big spider ran across the floor.

'Steady,' he said, holding her arm, and Isla told herself firmly to pull herself together.

For the next hour, they stripped out all the furnishings, washed down all the walls and cupboards, then stood back and admired their work.

'Tea for the workers,' shouted Martha, as she appeared at the doorway of the van, bearing a tray covered in a gingham cloth.

Isla threw her sponge down into the bucket. 'Great timing, Gran.'

'Well, well, well. Look at this ... you have been working hard.'

'Thanks Gran. Where's Angus?' she asked, peeling off her rubber gloves and taking a biscuit from the tray.

'Sat with Drew,' answered Martha, handing out mugs of tea before having a proper look around the van. 'It's actually quite roomy in here,' she said in amazement.

'And before I forget, Julia has just rung the farmhouse ... you aren't going to believe this,' Martha raised her eyebrows with a glint in her eye.

'Go on?' urged Isla, waiting.

'She's full the week after next and has passed on your number.'

'Are you kidding me?' exclaimed Isla, beginning to panic. 'Look at this place, it's not in any fit state for anyone to stay in!' She was filled with trepidation and excitement at the very thought.

'Not yet, but in a couple of weeks it could be. You can do this, Isla,' said Nate.

Isla looked towards Nate, did he really think she could pull this off? He gave her a nod of reassurance, 'If anyone can do this ... you can.'

Isla and Martha exchanged a glance and Isla took a breath. 'The vans will need to be moved, the toilet block needs to be painted. And we'd need bedding, curtains and cushions ... the list is endless.' Isla's mood drooped a little. 'Could I really do this?'

'Yes!' replied Martha and Nate in unison.

'Now get to it, I'm so proud of you,' said Martha, gathering up the empty mugs and placing them back on the tray.

'She may not have always been a textbook granny,' said Isla with a smile, 'but she's definitely come back into our lives at the right time. Now get those rubber gloves back on, Nate, and get to work!'

Nate saluted, 'Yes boss!'

For the next hour they scrubbed, rubbed and cleaned everywhere in sight. They lost count of the number of buckets of dirty water they disposed of and the amount of cloths they used, but the pair of them chatted away without a care in the world until Isla let out her second earth-shattering scream of the day. She jumped up, banging her head on the cupboard door.

'What now, not another twig?' Nate spun round then burst into laughter.

Poking his head into the van was Charlie the Shetland pony, chewing on the torn material from Isla's overalls that he'd taken a bite from.

'I think he thinks you are tasty,' said Nate. 'A pony of good taste.'

Isla collapsed into a fit of giggles. 'Ow ... that hurt,' she exclaimed, rubbing her backside and noticing there was a tear in her overalls.

Charlie went in for a second bite but Isla moved quickly, pushing Nate, who toppled over and landed on the bed, doubled over in laughter.

'What the hell is going on here?' Drew was standing in the doorway, looking far from amused.

'Have you seen my bum?' said Isla seriously, bending over.

Nate stifled a smirk.

But Drew gave her a hurtful look before turning and hobbling away on his crutches.

'Drew ... wait ... it's not what you think ... it's just Charlie ...' Isla shouted after him, suddenly feeling guilty, realising how it must have looked to Drew.

Such bad timing.

Isla pushed Charlie out of the way and ran towards the courtyard. 'Drew!' she shouted, but he was nowhere to be seen.

Low spirited, she walked back towards the barn. She knew she could have checked whether Drew was in the house but Isla didn't want the situation escalating. She'd let him calm down first and hopefully he'd realise he'd overreacted. Isla knew she was struggling with her own emotions that were yo-yoing up and down. One second she was on a high, thinking she was back on track with Drew, and the next her mood had slumped past her knees. She felt disappointed in Drew. Why would he even think that way of her? In all the time they'd been together, her head had never been turned by any other man. Drew was her life.

'Did you find him?' asked Nate tentatively as Isla stepped back into the van.

Isla shook her head, 'I'll talk to him later when we've finished this,' she said, picking up her sponge and carrying on with the cleaning. With Drew's arrival the banter had evaporated; for Isla, the fun had been squeezed out of the task.

Happily Nate hummed along but the only thing on Isla's mind was Drew as they continued to spruce up the vans. An hour later Isla was exhausted, but feeling proud, she stood back to admire the now pristine white caravans and the sparkling VW campervans. Once they were towed to the field, she knew they would look perfect in the green grassland, with the stream trickling by, bordered by the old drystone walls. There was something enchanting about it all. The vans gleamed inside and out. And Isla wished Drew was here to share this moment with her.

'I can't thank you enough for today,' said Isla, turning towards Nate.

'In a strange kind of way, I've enjoyed every second,' Nate said. 'But no rest for the wicked,' he added, looking at this watch. 'It's time to milk those cows again.'

'It just doesn't stop,' said Isla, swilling out the last bucket of dirty water on the path outside the barn.

After pushing the ramshackle barn door shut, Isla sauntered towards the cowshed with Nate ambling by her side. She took a swift glance back towards the farmhouse. If the truth be told, in a weird way Isla felt relieved by Drew's jealous reaction, in fact she felt comforted by it. To her this meant that Drew did still love her, and after the cows were milked she'd go and talk to him.

Chapter 28

Feeling shattered, Isla stripped off her overalls and boots at the back door, and even though she felt apprehensive about seeing Drew, she smiled to herself as she heard Finn's laughter filtering up the hallway.

As she walked into the room Finn was kneeling up on a chair and rummaging through what looked like an assortment of material on the kitchen table. Angus was strapped into his pushchair, kicking his legs.

'That's a dress?' exclaimed Finn, not noticing Isla standing in the doorway. 'It looks like something they'd wear in the dinosaur days,' he said, in all seriousness holding up the dress.

'You are a cheeky moo,' Martha laughed, ruffling his hair.

'What's going on here? It looks like a jumble sale,' questioned Isla, popping a kiss on the top of Finn's head.

'It is a jumble sale,' laughed Martha, immediately handing Isla a glass of wine. 'I thought you might need one of these.'

'Cheers! This is very much needed. Every muscle in my body is aching,' said Isla, gratefully clinking her glass against Martha's. 'I need a long soak in the bath.'

'Eat your tea first, then I'll run you a bath.'

Isla looked through the doorway to the living room, 'Where's Drew?'

'He's having a lie down ... his leg is feeling uncomfortable, he's taken some painkillers. He seems down in the dumps ... poor thing, that leg must be driving him insane.'

Isla didn't elaborate on what had happened earlier and felt sorry she hadn't gone to talk to him sooner, but she would as soon as he woke up. Now she pulled a chair out from underneath the table and sat next to Finn.

'So, what is going on here?

'These are Great-granny's old clothes.'

'I wish you wouldn't call me that, it makes me feel old.'

'Not quite as old as the dinosaurs,' Finn said and gave a cheeky smile.

'Mmm, I think there's a compliment in there somewhere and that deserves a kiss,' said Martha, impulsively taking his cheeks in both hands and kissing him noisily.

'Eww, get off,' giggled Finn, frantically wiping his cheeks.

'And why are your clothes strewn all over the table?' asked Isla, picking up one of the dresses. 'This is actually very pretty and good quality.'

'Which is why it's here ... Laura Ashley, that is.'

'Very posh,' exclaimed Isla, taking a sip of her wine.

'And it would make perfect cushions for your vans.' Martha gave Isla a knowing look. 'What do you think?'

'Gran, you can't go cutting up your clothes to make soft furnishings!'

'I can ... they don't fit me anymore and I was actually sorting them out for the charity bag when I thought it would help save some money. I've noticed you've still got the sewing machine in the back bedroom ...'

Isla's eyes widened. She knew her gran was a whizz on the sewing machine because when she was a little girl she'd often made her clothes to wear. She remembered a pair of red crushed-velvet pantaloons that tied at the knee. She'd been ten and everyone at the local disco had thought they were amazing and wanted a pair.

'Are you saying what I think you're saying?'

'There's no point buying material when we have all this. I can soon whip up some curtains for the vans ... cushion covers ... you name it, we can kit it out for next to nothing.'

Isla gasped in delight, 'You, Granny, are just wonderful! You have got all this under control, haven't you?' Isla was amazed. 'You need to be bottled.'

'Why would we put Great-gran in a bottle?' asked Finn, alarmed.

'It's just a figure of speech,' said Martha chuckling away.

Isla had to admit that this time yesterday she'd had a queasy feeling swirling around in the pit of her stomach as she'd worried about the farm. But within twenty-four hours, how things had changed. Life twisted and turned in mysterious ways and here she was, about to set up her own business, and hopefully the fleeces from the alpacas would fund the outstanding debts payments.

Sitting sipping her wine while waiting for Drew to wake, Isla watched Angus happily dribbling on to his bib while chewing a teething ring. Finn had taken himself off to the living room while Martha was clucking around the kitchen like a mother hen. Isla suddenly felt overwhelmed. There was no way she ever wanted to lose her home or Drew.

'You take your wine up and go and have a bath, get cleaned up, food will be waiting, and then we can take a look at this material properly and decide what you want.'

'Thanks Gran, you are a marvel.'

With the bubbles swirling around in the hot water, Isla slipped into her bathrobe and pulled the belt tightly around her waist. She padded across the landing and peered through the crack of the door. Drew was sound asleep and she watched for a moment. He looked peaceful lying there. Isla would never tire of that handsome face.

With a roll of her aching shoulders and a heavy sigh, she walked back to the bathroom and stared at her own reflection in the mirror.

Isla knew she and Drew had a lot to work through but knew her marriage was worth fighting for, she just hoped he felt the same.

If anyone had said a year ago to Isla that her marriage would go through such a rocky patch, she'd have thought they were deluded.

Bending down, she picked up Drew's wash bag that was slung on the bathroom floor. He hadn't even bothered to empty it. Unzipping the bag, she reached inside and placed his toothbrush back in the holder. She took out his aftershave, the one he'd worn every day since the age of seventeen. Then Isla noticed a small black purse at the bottom of the bag. Pulling it out, she looked at it but didn't recognise it. She couldn't help but open the purse, her stomach churning as she pulled out a packet of white pills and numerous empty packets. What the hell were these? Isla's heart thumped against her chest as she thumbed the packets. She was confused. Was Drew a drug addict?

'Don't be so stupid Isla,' she said out loud, hoping to reassure herself, but maybe that would explain his mood swings and erratic behaviour. Maybe the financial trouble they were in was down to this. Isla questioned again whether she knew her husband at all. What else had he been keeping from her?

Chapter 29

Eyeballing the door to make sure no-one was coming, Isla quickly typed the password into the laptop and waited patiently for the Google webpage to load.

'What the hell are they?' said Isla, knowing the tablets she'd found weren't just your bog-standard type of painkillers.

Isla typed in the name on one of the packets – citalopram – and her eyes quickly scanned the screen as she read the loaded results. She could see instantly that the tablets were antidepressants.

She slumped back in the chair and flipped over the six empty packets at the side of her, which meant this was not a new diagnosis for Drew.

Drew was taking antidepressants? Why? Isla felt a roller-coaster of emotions – confused, worried and sad for Drew. How come she didn't know anything about this? Why had he never told her?

As Isla slipped into the bath, she cast her mind back as she tried to think of a catalyst for Drew's depression, but she couldn't think of anything. The thought of him visiting Dr Taylor without even telling her made her feel even more miserable. Why all the secrets? Why couldn't he just be honest with her?

Isla didn't stay immersed in the water for long, she couldn't relax. There were too many questions flying around her head and only one person could give her the answers – that's even if he wanted to. She had no clue where they went from here, but she knew she needed to talk this over with Drew ... tonight.

'Are you out of that bath yet? Finn and I are starving,' Martha shouted up the stairs. 'Tea is on the table in two minutes.'

'Coming,' shouted Isla, drying herself and slipping into a pair of comfy joggers and a sweatshirt. As she walked downstairs she noticed the door to the spare bedroom was wide open, which meant Drew must be awake and up.

The table was set, with three plates of delicious-looking chilli accompanied with garlic bread. 'That smells divine Gran,' she said, taking Angus in her arms and snuggling him into her neck. 'But why only three places? Who's not eating?'

'Drew.'

'Drew?'

'I think he and Fergus are getting cabin fever, you know what they're like, moan they work too hard but then get bored doing nothing. Rory's picked him up and they've gone to some evening auction or something. He said he'll grab food when he's out.'

Isla felt peeved. 'Nice of him to tell me,' she said, feeling a wild combination of hurt as she tucked into her food.

'Are you okay, you look a little peaky,' asked Martha, noticing Isla was very quiet.

'Maybe that's what hard work does for you.'

Martha narrowed her eyes, 'Are you sure that's all it is?'

Isla nodded, she couldn't talk to her gran about her findings just yet, that would be unfair to Drew.

After tea, Isla sat down in the living room with Finn and Angus. She could barely keep her eyes open, and now she understood why Drew was fit for nothing after a day on the farm. The work was tiring with its early-morning starts and late evenings, and not to mention physical. Isla came to realise how hard Drew worked for her and the boys. She was finding it tough after only a couple of days.

After they'd eaten, Isla and Martha colour-coordinated all of Martha's garments and chose which ones would work for the different vans. Isla had discovered numerous old duvet covers in the airing cupboard and Martha had already transformed them into glorious cushion covers that looked like they were straight out of a soft-furnishing shop.

'See, if we sew these two covers together it'll give us a reversible set. One quite feminine and one masculine ... according to who books the van,' said Isla, feeling pleased with herself. Her enthusiasm about the vans hadn't wavered even though her eyelids were beginning to droop, but she'd spent most of the evening wondering when Drew was going to walk back through the door.

'Do you need to go and check on the pregnant alpaca?' asked Martha, switching the material around and pushing it under the foot of the sewing machine.

'No, Nate's doing that,' Isla answered, tapping Finn on his shoulder. 'Time for bed, young man.'

'Aww, I don't get it, how come Angus is younger than me and goes to bed later, it's not fair.' Finn looked at Isla with his big wide eyes.

'Because he's a baby and the longer I can keep him up, the more sleep I'll get, hopefully. Now go and get those PJs on and brush those teeth.'

'You've not been your usual self tonight,' said Martha, not looking up from the sewing machine.

'I'm just shattered and I've another early start in the morning.' Isla yawned.

'You get yourself to bed, snuggle Angus down,' said Martha, smiling up from the sewing machine. 'There's no point watching me sew, I'll finish up here after this one and I'll take the measurements for the curtains tomorrow.'

Isla was grateful for the offer, but she wanted to wait up for Drew, they couldn't keep avoiding each other.

'I bet you didn't imagine this much work when you turned up in your jam-packed Mini.'

'That's what I'm here for, to help in any way I can.'

'Will you be okay to look after Angus again tomorrow?'

'Of course, it will be my pleasure.'

'Thanks Gran, you know what, I'll go and read Finn a story and settle this one down,' she said, scooping up a gurgling Angus then kissing Martha on her cheek. But she knew she would have one ear listening out for Drew to come home.

Chapter 30

It was gone eleven o'clock before Isla heard the crunch of car tyres on the gravel outside. She heard voices then the sound of a car door slamming, before the car drove away. Hearing the key turn in the lock, Isla sat up in bed. Now was probably not the time to confront Drew, but when would be the right time?

Pulling her dressing gown around her and pushing her feet inside her slippers, she could hear him huffing and puffing about in the kitchen. It must be frustrating trying to manoeuvre crutches whilst trying to pour a glass of water.

She settled a hip on the arm of the chair and waited for him to appear. Drew looked startled when he hobbled into the living room. 'What are you doing up?' he asked, bypassing her and heading towards the hallway. 'Late nights and milking cows is a killer, you know.'

'I can believe that ... I kind of get the feeling you're avoiding me.'

He stopped and looked towards her, 'It's late Isla, I'm too tired for this.'

'Too tired for what?' she pushed.

He didn't answer.

'What's going on with you? Us?' asked Isla, holding his gaze. 'We are never like this. Drew, this isn't us.' Isla floundered, swallowing down a lump. 'We always talk, discuss things, decide what's best for us and our family. But that's changed Drew, and I don't know why.'

'I don't want a fight,' he answered. 'I just want to sleep.'

'What are these?' Isla held up the black purse she had discovered inside his washbag.

Drew's eyes grew wide, 'What are doing going through my stuff?' Immediately he was agitated. 'You have no right to go through my stuff.'

'When have I ever gone through your stuff? I emptied your washbag, put your toothbrush back where it belonged, then found this.' Isla kept her voice calm, she needed Drew to talk, not argue with her.

'I'll sit here till the cows come home,' she said, trying to lighten the mood. 'Drew, talk to me? Why won't you talk to me?'

'How can I? You obviously know what they are.' Drew crumbled, his eyes welled up with tears.

Isla was devastated, her heart breaking seeing Drew broken. 'Of course you can talk to me! I'm your wife, your best friend. We've always been able to talk, about everything and anything. Then I discover you're on antidepressants. I knew nothing about it, and not only that, but it's been going on for at least six months.'

'How do you know that? Dr Taylor shouldn't be discussing my personal stuff with you.' Drew sounded alarmed.

'Dr Taylor hasn't been discussing anything with me.' Isla laid the six empty packets on the coffee table. 'These were inside the black purse, so I kind of assumed it wasn't a new diagnosis. Why, Drew?'

Momentarily, his gaze flickered towards their wedding photo on the dresser. Then his wounded eyes locked with hers.

'What's the point, you wouldn't understand.'

'Try me Drew, I want to understand.' Her voice was soft, urging Drew to talk.

'Some days I don't even want to be here.' Drew was staring at the floor. He couldn't look at Isla and she got an uneasy feeling in the pit of her stomach.

'Here in general ... at the farm?'

Drew was physically shaking and took a breath. 'No, in life ... altogether.' There was no denying, by the tone of his voice and the look on his face, that he meant it.

The words hit Isla like a knife being twisted through her heart. She was shocked, lost for words. Every inch of her body wept in pain for Drew, for her family. 'What are you telling me Drew? I don't understand.'

'That's the point, Isla. No-one understands unless they've been there, in a place where's there no way out.' This was the first time Drew had looked at her properly and she felt distressed. How did she not know Drew was feeling this way? Discovering the truth threw Isla into turmoil. His glazed eyes looked sad, empty of feeling. Isla could understand a little; after Finn had been born she'd felt sad, hopeless and had lost interest in things she enjoyed, but it was never on this scale. A pang of guilt hit her, how had she not realised? It felt like her whole world was crashing down all around her. She stared at him, listening. 'Go on.'

'Some days Isla, I feel like there's no way out, like I'm clawing my way to the top of a deep black hole, everything is being poured on me ... I can't stop it ... and when I reach the top someone stamps on my hand and I fall right to the bottom and the journey begins again.'

His eyes teemed with tears.

Fighting a mixture of compelling emotions, Isla's thoughts had catapulted into disarray, her heart sank to a new depth. She moved next to him on the sofa and reached out for his hand, he didn't pull away. Her eyes met his, he looked lost and frightened. 'Drew, what about me ... what about the boys? We love you.'

The tears were now rolling down his cheeks. 'It's not about you or the boys. God, I love you all too, so much. But I've no control over how I feel, sometimes I just think you'd all be better off without me. You deserve better Isla, you deserve the best.'

'You are my best,' she said, her thoughts falling all over the place to make sense of it. 'So, what are you saying? Are you saying you want to end us, our marriage ... split up our family? Because I won't let you.' Uncertainty about Drew's feelings rushed to the fore.

Drew was shaking, the tears freely flowing as he wiped them away. Isla watched as he tried to compose himself but he couldn't.

'I'm so sorry Isla, it's not because I don't love you or the boys.'

'Why then?' asked Isla, trying to understand.

'I just don't know.'

Isla was devastated, lost for words, all she could do was reach out to him, cradle him like a baby in her arms as he cried.

'Have you shared with your friends how you're feeling ... Fergus ... Rory?'

Drew looked up and shook his head, 'How can I?'

'I talk to my friends.'

'It's different for women.'

'Why is it different for women?'

'Can you imagine, if I shared any of this with my mates? They'd just tell me to man up, and have another beer.'

'Men have feelings too, Drew. You never know, they may feel exactly the same sometimes,' said Isla, but she knew it was difficult for men to come forward, open up and talk about their mental health. 'You did well to go and talk to Dr Taylor, did that help?'

Drew shrugged, 'He suggested therapy, gave me a leaflet, it's hidden in the back of the sock drawer.'

'Well it's no good in there, is it?' smiled Isla warmly, trying to lighten the mood a little. 'It's nothing to be ashamed of, you know.'

'Why does it feel like I am, then?'

'Do you know what triggered all this? What changed, Drew?'

'I don't know; the bridge, the loss of income, you giving birth to Angus at home and me feeling utterly helpless. If anything had happened to either of you ...' His eyes filled with tears again and he blinked them away. 'Everything was out of my control and I felt like I was sinking fast.'

'But why didn't you speak to me about it? We are a team, we could have sorted it out together. We could have lost you, Drew, and not just in the barn fire.'

He nodded, 'If I hadn't survived you would have discovered what a lousy husband I was. I can't even provide for my own family.'

'Hey, we are a family and we all provide for each other – love, support and money.'

Drew exhaled and raked his hand through his hair. 'I couldn't tell you about the financial mess I'd gotten into because ... I couldn't bear for you to think of me as a failure. There, I've said it now.'

'The bridge collapsing was beyond your control and so was the storm. Whatever would make you feel like a failure?'

Drew clasped his hands across his chair and stared at the floor, before taking a deep breath, 'You.'

That one word hung in the air. A word Isla was not expecting to hear.

'I don't understand,' she stuttered, her heart pounding, tears brimming in her eyes.

'Look at you, Isla. Everything you touch turns to gold. You run this farmhouse, cook all the meals, make having a baby look like it's the easiest thing in the world. And every night I come home and there's my tea waiting on the table.'

'You're making that sound like it's a problem. Some men could only dream of that.'

'And after all that you play with the kids, read with Finn and build the best Lego towns anyone has ever seen ...'

'Well that's not in dispute,' said Isla with a slight smile, but she was struggling to see where this conversation was going.

'I'm up before you wake, when I get home I'm physically knackered and falling into bed, sometimes even before the kids.'

'You are up at 4.30 a.m. to milk the cows; of course you will be going to bed early, even at the weekends you don't get a lie-in.'

'I just feel like I'm useless to you.'

'Drew, that's crazy!'

'I knew you wouldn't understand.'

'I'm trying,' she said, amazed that Drew felt this way.

Isla had always respected that he was the backbone of the family and admired his hard-work ethic. Rain, hail, snow or shine, he would be up to milk the cows, followed by a day of hard manual labour, or herding the stock or taking produce to market. Drew had never had a day off sick in his life, until now.

'I love you ... the boys love you ... and we need you. All of us, even Martha,' she added, hoping that was a bonus.

'But we never get time to do anything as a family, just me, you and the boys. I don't want to be a dad in name only.'

Isla swallowed down a lump, she dabbed her eyes, she too was emotional. Sometimes she felt the same – that she never really spent quality time with the boys, but just looked after them. 'You could never be that. You are an incredible dad and all Finn wants to do is be just like you. Sometimes work gets in the way, that's just the way things are, but we need to make sure we set time aside for each other, make sure each other is okay.'

Drew took a breath, 'I can't even get the financial stuff right. I've got into a mess ... I know I have,' he admitted. 'And then as soon as you discover the accounts, there you are taking control, up and running your own business before I'm even out of hospital.'

'We can sort the accounts together ... and look at the mistakes I make, Drew ... buying a herd of stolen alpacas,' added Isla, hoping that would make Drew feel a little better. 'You were right, I should have checked David out and been more careful with our money.'

'At least their fleeces will hopefully clear the debts, as long as no-one claims them back before the weekend,' Drew said, a small smile touching his lips.

'Drew, maybe we should just talk to each other, like we used to. When we don't talk, look at the mess we get ourselves into. And the bank will be okay, I'm sure of it. We've been customers for a long time and never defaulted on payments before.'

'And how are we going to build a new barn? I'm out of action for six weeks,' Drew said in a solemn tone. 'And ...' Drew took a moment, he looked pained. Isla waited for him to speak. 'Sometimes, I think I'm not good enough for you, Isla.' His voice cracked.

A terrible sadness bled through the room. Isla felt deeply shocked by Drew's honesty. He had bared all.

Feeling like her heart was being ripped out, Isla took his

hand, she was distressed seeing Drew this way. 'No!' she gasped, trembling. Her throat was tight, 'Don't ever say that ... Look at me, Drew Allaway. You are all I've ever wanted ... the boys are all I want ... we are a family ... we have each other,' the tears were now freefalling down Isla's cheeks.

Drew nodded, 'I'm sorry.'

'I'm sorry too, but please, no more secrets. It's okay not to be okay, but we don't need to hide it from each other. Promise?'

Drew nodded, 'I promise.'

'Come here,' Isla held out her arms and hugged him tightly, like their lives depended on it. 'I do love you.'

'I love you too,' he said, pulling away slowly.

'We are going to get you well again, we are a team ... we are going to be alright.'

Drew nodded, tilting Isla's face towards his. He held her head gently in his hands and slowly pulled her lips towards his. He kissed her softly and slowly, his thumb caressing her cheek.

Every inch of her body tingled with his touch. Isla felt safe with his strong arms wrapped around her, this was what she missed. All their troubles instantly falling away. This was where they belonged, together. From now on they needed to look after each other.

'Can I come back to my own bed?' asked Drew, pulling away slowly with a glint in his eye.

'Let me think about that for a second,' murmured Isla, kissing him again. 'But you just remember, I'm up early, milking those cows.'

'Well, that means one thing ... it'll be my turn to wake up to a cup of tea in bed.'

Isla smiled, she felt emotionally drained and it was safe to say she had no idea how the evening was going to pan out. Drew's honesty had taken her by surprise, but at least she had some answers and now she felt they were back on track.

Chapter 31

What seemed only moments later Isla was woken by banging on the front door of the farmhouse. The sun was shining through the opening of the curtains and she tried to create a gap between her upper and lower eyelids in a vain attempt to read the display on the clock radio. The space next to her lay empty, Drew must be already up. Finally, the red digits came into focus. She couldn't believe her eyes, 10 a.m. Next to the clock stood a mug of cold tea.

Isla bolted upright in bed; she'd slept right through the alarm! The cows, the cows, she hadn't milked the cows. Feeling flustered, she threw back the duvet and swung her legs to the floor.

There it was again – the banging on the door. Isla cursed under her breath before staring into the cot. Angus wasn't there, where was everyone? Why hadn't anyone woken her?

Pulling herself together, she jumped out of bed and grabbed her dressing gown before literally flying down the stairs. She flung the door open to find a smiley red-cheeked delivery man holding out a parcel. 'A delivery for Mrs Isla Allaway.'

Isla peered over his shoulder, 'You haven't seen anyone on the farm?'

The delivery driver looked baffled, 'No ma'am, I'm just delivering a parcel ... can you sign here please?'

Isla took the black contraption from his hand and attempted to scribble her name before scooping up the parcel from the mat. 'Priority Delivery' was stamped across the brown parcel in bold red ink. Isla couldn't think of anything she'd ordered as she carried it into the kitchen and placed it on the table. She saw Finn's favourite cereal bowl on the draining board, which meant Martha had taken him to school, but the house was deadly silent and she knew she was on her own.

Suddenly hearing the click of the front door, she rushed into the hallway to find Martha trundling through the front door with a smiley Angus gurgling away in his pram.

'Morning, sleepy head,' Martha smiled, unbuttoning her coat.

'Why didn't you wake me?' said Isla, all flustered, pulling off Angus's hat, the static leaving his hair standing on end.

'Because it would have been a shame to wake you ... and everything is under control.'

'I haven't milked the cows.'

'Fergus is back – he insisted, before you ask – and he milked the cows this morning.'

'And where's Drew? Please tell me he's not back on the farm?' asked Isla, feeling a tiny bit redundant that the morning routine had run like clockwork without her and she'd slept through all the early morning chaos.

Unstrapping Angus from his pram, Isla planted a kiss on his head.

'Sorry, I should have left you a note, it's a lovely morning out there.' Martha flicked on the kettle and draped her coat over the back of the kitchen chair. 'Finn is safely dropped at school and Drew ...'

'What about Drew?'

'He's been rather busy this morning, but I'm saying no more until you've eaten breakfast.'

Isla narrowed her eyes at her gran, 'What are you hiding?'

'Nothing! But he told me all about last night. Come here,' she said, holding her arms out wide. 'You pair have been through the mill, hopefully you're back on track now?'

Isla hugged her gran tight, 'I had no clue how he felt, Gran.'

'But we do now, so we support him the best we can.'

Isla nodded, feeling relieved she had the support of her gran.

'Now what's in this parcel?' asked Martha, intrigued, looking at the bright-red lettering.

'There's only one way to find out,' said Isla, settling at the table with the parcel in front of her. 'I'm not expecting anything.' She began to open the old-fashioned brown paper, the postmark was smudged which didn't give anything away.

Isla trembled with excitement when she unfolded the tissue paper and gasped.

There in front of her was a beautiful cream-coloured wooden sign with Foxgloves painted in striking colours in the background. 'Foxglove Camping,' she said out loud as she read the lettering, not able to take her eyes off the sign.

'Well, just look at that!' exclaimed Martha, peering over her shoulder. 'What's the card say?'

Isla peeled back the envelope:

Good luck with your new venture,
You'll smash it!

All my love,
Drew x

Isla was overwhelmed and happy tears brimmed her eyes, a huge smile plastered her face. How thoughtful of Drew. Even though he had the weight of the world on his shoulders trying to keep the farm afloat, he always thought of her.

In her mind, Isla had already hung the sign on the post at the entrance to the farm. She pictured the sun beating down in the height of summer with a steady stream of ramblers frequenting the campervans.

'There's something else,' Martha pointed to the parcel.

'So there is ...' Isla delved back into the parcel and let out a tiny gasp. 'A diary ... for my bookings.'

'It's all coming together,' Martha squeezed her granddaughter's hand. 'I'm so proud of you.'

Isla's heart was beating like a drum with excitement, her eyes twinkled, and her smile was wide.

'Now that smile suits you. This little business is going to be the making of you ... I can feel it in my old bones,' said Martha, giving her a wink. 'Now go and get a shower, because we are off to the charity shops today to source out bargains for those vans.'

After taking a long hot shower Isla was beginning to feel human again. She tugged a brush through her tangled locks and sat down at her dressing table. For the first time in a long time she brushed blusher across her cheekbones and applied some lip gloss. How things had changed in just twenty-four hours.

'Are you nearly ready?' Martha shouted up the stairs.

'Coming,' shouted Isla, wandering into the kitchen to find her gran bouncing Angus up and down on her knee.

'You look refreshed,' admired Martha, noticing the sparkle back in her granddaughter's eye.

'It's amazing what a good night's sleep does for you,' said Isla, tapping Angus playfully on the nose before turning towards Martha.

'Ready when you are.'

The day flew by so quickly. They'd grabbed lunch in the new bistro and enjoyed a cheeky glass of wine. Isla was on a massive high when she ambled back up Love Heart Lane towards Foxglove Farm with her gran by her side.

Stored in the bottom of the pram were carrier bags full of bargains they'd rooted out from the charity shops: vintage crockery, cutlery and other paraphernalia to spruce up the vans. Isla couldn't wait to get it all cleaned up and show Drew what she'd bought.

As she pushed a sleepy Angus through the gates of the farm something caught her eye. She held her breath and stared. There, swinging in the light breeze, was her new sign. Another lovely surprise from Drew.

'Foxglove Camping,' she whispered under her breath. Isla felt like she was flying high, just like the sign, and it was a far cry from how she had been feeling at the beginning of the week. Her heart gave a flip and Isla knew she would give her all to her new business venture.

Opening the farmhouse door, Isla shouted Drew's name. 'Come and look at the bargains we bought!' But there was no answer, only the sound of silence.

Martha pointed to the envelope propped up against a jam-jar of flowers. Her name was written boldly on the front. Tearing it open, she read these words:

Isla,
  When you get back meet me in the orchard.
                                         Love Drew x

That was it, there was no further clue to what was going on and Isla felt a tingle of excitement.

'What's all this about?' asked Isla, giving her gran an inquisitive stare.

'I'm saying nothing!' Martha's cheeks stretched into a gigantic smile.

'You know something, tell me!' Isla tilted her head to one side, waiting for her to answer. 'Were you under strict instructions to keep me away from the farm today?'

'I'm saying nothing! Go on ... go and find out!' Martha placed her hand around Isla's shoulder and gently shooed her out of the front door. 'Don't keep him waiting!'

Isla had no idea what was going on, but she hurried down

the path and stood at the foot of the wooden bridge. As she cast her eyes across the orchard she caught her breath. Dotted around the lush green meadow stood two campervans and the caravan. Isla had no idea how Drew had managed to transport them from the barn with his broken leg, but he had done it and she couldn't thank him enough.

The sun shone down on the vans and they gleamed. Everywhere looked so peaceful and pretty, and lanterns draped through the trees of the orchard. Someone had been busy. Isla had always thought this was the most romantic place on the farm: delicate pansies, cheery daffodils and poppies freckled the scenic meadow, and there was something timeless about the whole place. Isla couldn't tear herself away, it all looked so perfect. Goosebumps prickled her skin and her face was alight with excitement, her cheeks aglow.

As she walked full circle around the vans, she couldn't help feeling thrilled, and she flashed the biggest smile ever. This was her new business ... all hers.

She opened the first campervan door and gasped. Her eyes filled with happy tears. Polka-dot bunting crisscrossed the walls. The small pine table was adorned with a jam-jar of fresh flowers picked from the meadow. The musty smell had been replaced by fresh, clean aromas and the whole van had been given an instant facelift. Vintage-style cushions were scattered on the front seat of the van, which had been upgraded (presumably by Drew) to create a small sofa, and on the hob was a duck-egg-blue kettle which would match perfectly the crockery she'd picked up from the charity shop.

Isla pulled the door shut and walked over to the next

campervan. The vintage violet van had the original awning attached to the side which provided extra space. Isla again stepped inside and was amazed at how hard Martha and Drew must have worked to make this happen. Everywhere was spick and span and even the jam-jar of purple crocuses was colour co-ordinated.

Last but not least she made her way to the caravan. Until she secured the licence she could only rent out three vans at a time, but hopefully, once the toilet block was refurnished, it wouldn't take too long for the council to grant permission for further vans.

She tugged on the door and jumped out of her skin.

'You took your time.'

Startled by his voice, she met the smile of Drew, her heart beating wildly. Bringing her hand up to her thumping chest, she tried to catch her breath.

'You frightened the life out of me.'

Drew was sitting on the settee sporting a huge grin. Isla was amazed to see the table was set and a small candle flickered away. She threw him a smile. 'What's all this?'

'Would you like a glass of wine?' he asked, leaning over and taking the chilled bottle from the fridge.

For a second Isla was speechless. 'You've done all this for me?'

Drew took Isla's hand, 'I know it's been a challenging few months, having a new baby in the house, me not being honest with you, but I never want to lose you, Isla. I'll do anything I can to get us back on track and I want you to know you're doing a fantastic job.'

Isla felt choked.

'And I want you to know how much I appreciate what you do for me and our boys,' he added.

Feeling emotional, Isla flapped a hand in front of her face, 'Stop ... you're making me cry.'

He looked ridiculously good-looking sitting there with his grey tight T-shirt clinging to his muscular toned torso. Her body tingled in his presence.

'I know you will make this business venture work and I'm behind you one hundred percent.'

'Oh Drew, thank you.'

Drew slipped one arm around her waist, bent his head and kissed her neck. Her mouth hitched into a huge smile. 'You smell better than you normally do,' she teased, inhaling his elegant and stylish aroma.

'Are you hungry?'

Isla was ravenous.

Drew nodded towards the free-standing cooker in the caravan.

'No way, you've cooked? You are a keeper, aren't you?'

'Well, maybe I had a little help from your gran, but I thought we'd best try out the oven before your first guests arrive.'

'I knew she knew something about this.'

Drew handed Isla a glass of wine and they stood in the doorway looking out across the orchard.

'I have to say, this is my favourite spot on the whole farm ... peaceful ... tranquil.' Isla chinked her glass against his.

'Here's to you, and Foxglove Camping,' he said, holding her

gaze. 'I think I have a genius of a wife who took an idea, an opportunity and ran with it ... have I told you how proud I am of you, Isla Allaway?'

Her heart fluttered. 'Maybe once or twice ... And I appreciate everything you do for me and our boys. I love you.'

'I love you too.'

'I couldn't have done this without Gran and you ... good job you bought these old vans, hey?'

Drew laughed, 'I knew there was a reason!'

'I had my doubts when Gran turned up, but ...' Isla felt tearful, everyone had worked so hard to pull this together so quickly.

'What we need is a grand opening!'

'We are meant to be making money, not frittering it away before we've made any! This is my grand opening now ... just me and you.' Isla planted a soft kiss on Drew's lips. 'I can't believe you've done all this for me,' she said, feeling the happiest girl on the planet.

'You're worth it,' said Drew, kissing Isla again.

'How long until food? I'm starving,' she asked, slowly pulling away and taking a sip of her wine.

Drew opened the oven door and looked panic stricken.

'What's the matter?'

'I've forgotten to turn the oven on ... it's stone cold.'

Isla laughed, leaning forward she turned the dial. 'So, what are we going to do for the next thirty minutes?'

'Mmm,' said Drew with a wicked twinkle in his eye. He tilted her face upwards then kissed her tenderly, sending shivers down her spine.

'Not sure how this is going to pan out with a cast on your leg!' She pulled away gently, tapping him on the tip of his nose and raising her eyebrows.

He gave her a lopsided grin, 'Me neither, but I'm willing to give it a go.'

His eyes sparkled as he tugged at her sleeve. Feeling like a teenager, she giggled as he shut the bedroom door behind them.

Isla's heart was bursting with happiness.

Chapter 32

The next day the heavens opened once more. 'I won't be long,' Isla shouted up the stairs to Drew. 'I need to check on the pregnant alpaca in the stable, the rain's coming down hard and the wind's up again, apparently Fergus reckons she's settling.'

'Wait there, I'll come with you,' said Drew, hobbling to the top of the stairs.

'You will not!' exclaimed Isla, giving him a stern look. 'It's lashing down and how are you going to do that on crutches? The fields are muddy and you'll end up on your backside, let's try and look after the good leg. Sit there until I get back,' said Isla, being forceful.

Drew sighed and manoeuvred his way to the chair.

'It won't be long until you are back out there,' she reassured him, knowing how frustrated he felt. 'Kit bag, I need the kit bag.'

'It's all prepared, plastic gloves – short and full-arm length. There's a bottle of water-based sterile lubrication, iodine, umbilical cord clamp, pocket knife. And there's a pile of old towels if the crias need to be kept warm and rubbed dry ...

you should have everything there.' Drew listed off the entire kit bag.

'Thanks … here goes …' she said, balancing the towels on top of the kit bag.

'You look sexy in those overalls,' grinned Drew, as she made her way to the door.

Looking down at her overalls, Isla knew there wasn't a cat in hell's chance she carried this look off well. She looked frumpy and felt frumpy as she plunged her feet into her wellington boots and pulled down a bobble hat over her ears.

'It may be best to give Rory a call if she's in labour, in case we need him,' she bellowed back towards Drew before closing the door behind her. Nate was waiting outside, leaning against the wall and tapping away on his mobile. The second he saw Isla he slipped it into his pocket, he seemed to have a habit of doing that.

'Hey,' Isla said.

'Here, let me take those,' offered Nate, taking the kit bag and towels from her. 'I think the birth is imminent, she's moved away from the main herd.'

'I thought she was already in the stable?' questioned Isla.

'Yesterday, Fergus let her out into the field because of the glorious sunshine, and now look at the weather.'

'I hope she's not too stressed.'

'We need both those alpacas to be born.'

'We?' asked Isla, feeling puzzled about his comment.

'Just a figure of speech. Come on, and watch your step – the field is lethal with all the rain. We could drive over in the tractor, but we don't want to frighten her.'

They began to hurry towards the orchard and Isla swung open the gate. Her boots sucked into the mud and squelched. 'Roll on summer. I suppose the weather in Ireland isn't as temperamental as Scotland?' she probed.

But before Nate could answer she let out a squeal. Her wellington boot was stuck in the mud and she'd landed on her chest with a bump, face down on the ground.

'Ouch!' she said, pushing herself up to see Nate's wellingtons standing in front of her.

He threw his head back and laughed, and even though Isla felt embarrassed she joined in.

'I'm so sorry,' he said, tucking the kitbag and towels under his arm and extending his hand to pull Isla up. 'I shouldn't laugh. I told you it was muddy.'

'No, you shouldn't laugh,' she said, spitting out the slop of dirt that had smeared over her face.

'You do pull the country look off well.' His eyes sparkled playfully.

'Urghh Nate, it's not mud, it's fresh cow manure.' Isla heaved.

'Yep, you hum,' he grinned. 'But that's the farmer's life for you.'

Isla steadied herself on his arm as she slipped her muddy foot back into the boot and wiped her hands on the back of her overalls.

Nate was still smiling at her.

'Stop smiling, I feel an idiot as it is.'

'Okay, I'll stop,' he said, not taking the broad grin off his face.

'In fact, I'll nip to the stable, there's a tap there. I'll quickly wash my hands.'

Nate wasn't listening, suddenly the grin had dropped and his gaze was fixed towards the field.

'There's no time for that.'

Nate's lightning reaction powered his legs across the field. Isla was lagging behind, her feet stumbling across the uneven ground of the field.

Despite the shelter of the barn and stables, the alpacas had become isolated due to a tree that had been crashed into the gate by the fierce wind.

'Where is she?' bellowed Isla, scanning the herd, but she couldn't see the pregnant alpaca.

Nate had already spotted her lying on the ground, a strewn branch lying across her stomach. He reached her first and placed the kit bag down and balanced the towels on top.

The rain was lashing down, and he raked his wet hair out of his eyes, quickly tossing the branch away.

With an awful slow-motion feeling Isla stood behind Nate and watched in horror as he placed a hand on the alpaca's stomach. The animal lay motionless, stretched out on the muddy ground. Isla knelt down next to Nate and saw the rise and fall of the alpaca's chest slowing. Isla was too scared to touch her.

'I'm hoping we've reached her in time,' his eyes full of worry. Isla helplessly looked on, feeling useless. She reached out a shaky hand and touched Nate's shoulder.

'I'll ring Rory. She can't lose her babies.'

Nate nodded and wrapped his arms around the alpaca, picking her up effortlessly.

'I'll carry her to the barn.'

Isla scrolled through her phone and hit Rory's number.

'Come on ... come on ... answer,' she was muttering under her breath.

Finally, Rory answered. 'Rory, it's Isla. Drew might have already phoned you, but we need you now. The alpaca is in trouble,' she said, her voice shaky.

'I'm on my way, Isla,' he said, and she imagined him grabbing his bag and coat and leaving the surgery at top speed.

Isla hung up the phone and caught up with Nate. 'The towels are wet,' she exclaimed, panting. 'We'll need some more. There should be some in the cupboard in the stable block.' Her voice was carrying in the wind as she ran behind Nate.

Nate kicked open the stable door and gently laid the alpaca down on the hay. It was more than likely the alpaca had already been in labour for a few hours. The animal's breathing was shallow and her fleece was drenched from the rain.

'Here,' said Isla, pressing clean dry towels into Nate's hands as she turned on the heat lamp in the corner of the stable. Nate began to gently rub the alpaca's fleece and Isla watched how gentle he was with the animal.

'Do you think she's going to make it?' Isla's voice was low.

'I think she's in shock, stressed probably from the branch hitting her, but I've checked her over and there are no obvious cuts.'

'I grabbed this too,' Isla passed Nate a stethoscope and he immediately began to listen to her heartbeat.

'Isla, where are you?'

Isla stepped out of the stable and was relieved to see Rory, 'In here.'

Nate quickly moved to the side to let Rory examine the alpaca.

'What happened?' he asked, running his hand over her stomach.

'This weather is what happened. The wind blew down part of the tree and she's been hit by a branch.'

'I need to wrap her tail to keep it out of the way, it's easier to keep the area clean then too.' Rory looked up towards Isla, 'The honest truth is, I've no idea whether the crias will make it, but these babies need to be delivered, and fast.'

Isla's eyes welled up with tears, there was nothing more they could do now except hope.

Nate stood by her side and they both looked over Rory's shoulder as he began to clean the perineal area with mild soap and water.

'The pelvic size is good,' stated Rory without turning around towards them, 'but the heart rate is high,' he said, hooking the alpaca up to a small portable machine from his bag. 'It's above 120bpm.'

'What can we do?'

'Absolutely nothing. If she was in the theatre we would probably perform a caesarean section but we can't move her now.'

After a closer examination, Rory took off his gloves and grabbed a clean pair from his bag. 'One of the babies is in the birthing canal.'

The atmosphere inside the stable was tense. Isla had no idea what was going to happen. She didn't like to see any animal in distress and she had her fingers firmly crossed behind her back that they would all make it through safely.

'Heart rate is decreasing,' stated Rory.

'What does that mean?' asked a tearful Isla.

Nate slipped his arm around her shoulder and gave her a quick squeeze.

'That's good sign, even though she's in labour she's feeling more settled, more relaxed, and she's warm under the lamps.'

'What's that?' Isla's eyes were wide.

At the vaginal opening a blackish baseball-sized mass was visible.

Rory looked over his shoulder and smiled. 'That's the birthing sack,' he said, calmly tearing the sack in front of their eyes as the water spilled out, allowing the baby to receive oxygen.

'Oh my God, is that what I think it is?' asked Isla, clutching on to Nate's arm. Her heart was thumping fast.

'Yes, that's the cria's nose. The mother is resting now. We need to keep an eye on the time. She needs to make progress within fifteen minutes but she's doing well, all things considered.'

They watched as Rory lightly cleared away the mucus from the nose and mouth to allow breathing to become easier.

'What's she doing now?'

The alpaca had lifted her head.

'She's munching on the hay, which is a very good sign … it's progression.'

'I don't know whether to laugh or cry,' admitted Isla, fanning a hand in front of her teary eyes.

They all watched patiently and in silence. The baby alpaca looked like a contortionist as one leg appeared over the head and another under the chin. The head was fully visible and the baby gasped and began to shake its head.

'It's here, it's here,' Isla's voice was filled with relief.

'It sure is, but we need to keep calm and quiet. If this cria is healthy she will be sitting up within ten minutes and standing within a few hours.'

'Oh my God, it's gorgeous, look at the colour of the fleece, how do we know if it's a boy or a girl?'

'Give me a second and I'll check.'

'Where is everyone?' Fergus's voice bellowed through the stable block.

'Shhh, in here,' Isla waved him towards the stable. 'We have a new arrival.'

Fergus was followed by Drew and they huddled round to watch. 'Oh my, look at that ... boy or girl?' asked Drew.

'It's a girl,' confirmed Rory who'd just finished examining her. 'And a great weight too.'

'I feel like a proud parent standing here, she's absolutely beautiful.' Isla couldn't take the beam off her face.

'She is,' admired Drew, slipping his arm around Isla's shoulder.

'What happens now? What about the second baby?' asked Isla.

'All we can do is wait.'

Rory carefully dried off the cria and placed it near the mother and then stood beside the others.

'You did well to carry the alpaca in here,' said Rory, turning towards Nate. 'She must have weighed a ton.'

'She definitely felt like it, but there was no choice.'

'Thanks Nate,' said Isla.

Drew extended his hand towards Nate, 'Yes, thank you.'

Isla gave Drew a smile. She was proud of him and he'd come a long way in the last twenty-four hours. Quickly pressing a kiss to his cheek, she turned back towards the alpaca.

'They'll keep warm under the lamp, it looks like they're both doing well,' announced Rory, who'd changed his gloves and bent down beside the alpaca. After a close inspection he spoke, 'This is it, the second one is on its way.'

'What are the chances of survival?' asked Isla tentatively.

'It's extremely rare, believe me, but we'll know very soon. Here's the second sack now.'

Trepidation was mounting in the stable and no-one spoke. Isla swallowed down a lump in her throat, emotion surged through her body as she waited, holding on to Drew tightly.

What seemed like hours waiting for the next birth was only a matter of minutes.

Isla could tell by the way Rory went to work – focused, not saying a word – that there was something wrong.

There was silence.

'I'm sorry,' Rory looked up over his shoulder. 'There's nothing I can do.'

Overcome with emotion, the tears burst from Isla's eyes like water from a dam, drenching her cheeks. Her chin wobbled and she stood outside the stable with her trembling hands pressed against the wall to catch her breath. It wasn't just losing the animal but a build-up of everything over the last twenty-four hours.

Life was so unfair.

She could hear the others talking quietly, as Fergus set to

work prepping clean hay, while Nate disposed of the old. Drew turned Isla towards him. 'Come here,' he said as she buried her face in his shoulder.

Her emotion came in waves, seconds of sobbing then short breaths to recover. Losing animals was always difficult. Over the years you'd have thought she'd got used to it, but she never did.

Isla watched broken-hearted as Rory carried the wrapped body to his van.

'Look,' said Drew, 'open your eyes.' Isla looked up then and smiled through her tears. The adorable survivor with her chocolate fleecy coat was standing on her feet.

'You need to think of a name.'

Isla nodded. 'She's gorgeous, I think I'll leave that to Finn. He's going to love her.'

'I'm sorry you lost one.' Rory appeared back by their side. 'Nature can be so cruel sometimes.'

'She's so special, the first baby alpaca to be born at Foxglove Farm,' admired Isla. 'I just hope we get to keep her. I couldn't bear to lose her to those wretched Kerr brothers.'

'Right, my job here is done. Leave them to bond, but check on them throughout the night to make sure the cria is suckling.'

'I will, and thank you, Rory.'

He hugged Isla, 'And I suggest you go and get a shower.'

She grinned, 'I slipped in the dung.'

Just as he was about to leave, Rory turned back round. 'And before I forget, leave the light on in the stable and the heat lamp. You need to create a daytime situation for nursing.

Baby alpacas look for milk in the darkest spot, which is usually in a paddock under their mum. In an unlit stable the darkest part is the corner, and she will keep head-butting the wall.'

'I will, and thanks again, Rory.'

They all admired them both before Fergus slapped Nate on the back. 'It's like *Call the Midwife* here today, one born every second. We best go and check on the lambs.'

They walked out of the stable block, leaving Isla and Drew folding their arms and resting them on the stable door.

What a day it had been. 'I don't know about you, but I could stand here and watch her all afternoon ... just look at that funny-looking face and those quirky little struts. I can't wait to have a cuddle.' Isla felt protective towards the cria and couldn't take her eyes off the new arrival.

'She really is something,' said Drew, watching over Isla's shoulder.

'I just wish ... I just wish.' Isla's lashes were heavy with tears again.

'Some things are not meant to be. We could have lost them all, but look at what we've got.'

Drew smiled at his wife warmly and squeezed her hand, and she squeezed his back.

'I've always been a sucker for animals,' she said. 'I prefer them to humans most of the time.'

'I hope that doesn't mean me.'

'Of course not,' she said, slipping her arms around his waist.

They watched the mother and baby nestle together. 'It's a

shame we don't know for certain that no-one's coming to claim them,' he said. 'We could have doubled our money.'

'What do you mean, doubled our money?' Isla took a step back and stared at Drew.

'The money crias bring in is astronomical.'

'You aren't seriously thinking of selling her!' Isla couldn't believe what she was hearing.

'Of course, it's an animal, we are farmers ... that's what we do. Rory has a buyer lined up.'

Isla spun round, her eyes bulging and her heart thumping.

'No. She's not for sale at ANY cost. That poor mother has just lost one of her babies, there's no way you're taking another from her,' Isla said, losing her patience, digging her hands deep into the pockets of her overalls. She was met with the same stare of defiance from Drew.

'We have bills to pay. Think logically ... you can't be ruled by your heart.'

Isla could feel the anger rising inside her. She was already distressed at the thought of losing the baby. 'Drew! That cria is part of the farm, the first-born. Please, we can't sell her ... At least say you'll think about it,' pleaded Isla, feeling distraught.

Drew was silent, looking at the alpaca, but before he could answer Isla had walked off in a huff. She couldn't take any more.

Chapter 33

Isla was showered and wrapped up warmly as she left the farmhouse thirty minutes early to pick up Finn from school. She pushed Angus in his pram down Love Heart Lane towards the River Heart. Isla was upset that Drew could even contemplate selling the baby alpaca.

Drew had followed her back to the farmhouse and tried to reason with her, but Isla wouldn't budge. She was determined that she wasn't going to part with the baby alpaca, even if it meant paying the Kerr brothers again to keep her.

She'd been researching petting farms on the internet, and alpacas were the ideal animal to bond with children. They were gentle and docile and Isla thought it would be an added extra for the camping business. They could even charge a fee.

She'd met Felicity at the school gate. 'Fergus has texted, he says the baby alpaca is gorgeous.'

'She is.'

'You don't seem too enthusiastic about it.' Felicity noticed the pained expression on her face. Isla filled Felicity in about Drew's suggestion to sell the baby and how she was determined to keep her on the farm. Finn and Esme, oblivious to Isla's predicament, splashed through the puddles and ran all the way home from school to the farmhouse. They couldn't wait to see the baby alpaca.

Finn burst through the farmhouse door and kicked off his shoes. 'Daddy ...' he shouted. 'Where are you?'

'I'm here,' said Drew, appearing in the kitchen.

Finn's eyes were wide with excitement, Esme was standing right behind him.

'Come on, we're going to see the baby alpaca,' said Finn, pulling on his wellies and taking off at top speed towards the stable.

Inside the stable Finn clutched his sides and pointed, letting his laughter out. 'That's the funniest thing I've ever seen, look at the mop on top of her head. She's very tiny. Can we have a cuddle?'

'Not today, she's only a few hours old. Let's wait until the morning, then I'm sure you can,' said Drew. Finn tugged on Isla's coat, 'Mummy, I've got an idea.'

'What is it Finn?'

'We can take her to Heartcross Show,' Finn was full of enthusiasm. 'We googled them, didn't we Esme?'

Esme nodded enthusiastically.

'They are easier to train than a dog, we could put on the Shetland's halter and teach her to follow on a lead.'

'That would be so cool,' joined in Esme, not able to hide the excitement in her voice. 'Do you think Daddy would let us have one?' Esme looked up hopefully towards Felicity.

'Did I hear my name?' Fergus had crept up on his daughter and tickled her tummy, causing her to let out a peal of laughter.

'Daddy, can we have a baby alpaca like Finn?'

'I can't see an alpaca hanging out outside the teashop, can you Flick? And I'm not sure Grandma Aggie could be persuaded either. How about you share this one with Finn?'

'Can I ... can I, please?'

Isla shot Drew a warning look, he was letting the children run away with the idea that they could keep the alpaca, when he had every intention of selling it.

'Please Dad, Esme and me, we can train her to walk through obstacles, jump over small hurdles. She will be so much fun. PLEEEEEAAAASSSEE.'

'You are being so unfair, how can you resist that face? Just look at them,' Isla whispered to Drew.

Felicity gave Isla a secret smile, if anyone could persuade Drew to keep the baby alpaca, it was Finn.

'Alpacas are a very good attraction,' chipped in Fergus. 'Imagine in the summer, the hikers renting out the vans with their children. They'll love them.'

'Please Daddy, I promise I'll do my homework and help you muck out the stables at the weekend.'

Drew threw his hands up in the air, 'Okay, you've all got me. She can stay and you and Esme can share her.'

Finn and Esme let out a squeal.

Feeling relieved, Isla's heart lifted as she planted a kiss on Drew's lips, taking him by surprise. 'Why the change of heart?'

'Because I love you, and how can I resist that face?' Drew nodded towards Finn who was delighted at the new arrival.

'Thank you, but what if they come for the alpacas?'

'It's not happening on my watch. I've rung the solicitors

over in Glensheil, we've got an appointment on Monday afternoon. As far as I'm concerned, those animals were bought in good faith, and they are going nowhere. Let's get some proper advice.'

Isla flung her arms around Drew's neck. 'Thank you ... thank you.'

'What is she called?' asked Finn, climbing up on the stable door as it swung open.

'She hasn't got a name, any suggestions?' asked Isla.

'Mop,' said Finn, adamant about his choice. 'Because of the hair on her head – it looks like a big curly mop.'

Everyone laughed.

'When you leave a kid to come up with a name, they come up with a ridiculous suggestion,' whispered Isla to Drew.

'I actually think it suits her ... Mop it is.'

'Am I late to the party? What's going on?' Nate appeared, pushing a wheelbarrow of dung.

Finn wafted his hand in front of his nose and Esme copied. 'That stinks!'

'It sure does, it'll help the vegetables grow, this will. Shall I put some in your shoes to see whether it'll help you grow?' Nate kept a serious face.

'No! Dad, tell him,' squealed Finn as Nate pretended to chase him with the barrow as Finn ran up the stable block.

'Before I forget, Pete has texted, he's coming on Friday now to shear the alpacas. He's got something on at the weekend.'

'Friday, did you say?' Nate cut into the conversation. 'A day earlier than expected?'

Drew nodded, 'Yes, he'll be here by lunchtime at the latest.

Fergus slapped Drew on the back, 'We'll be ready for them, boss.'

'Right come on, let's leave Mop to it,' Isla rolled her eyes. 'What a name! Anyone for hot chocolate?'

'Me!' Both Finn and Esme thrust their arms in the air before running off towards the farmhouse.

'Take off your muddy wellies before you go into the kitchen,' Isla bellowed after them.

As Isla and Felicity walked back towards the house, Isla watched Nate walking towards the barn. He stopped and placed the wheelbarrow on the ground before reaching inside his pocket and pulling out his mobile phone. Isla couldn't help but notice that he looked agitated again and he seemed to be having yet another heated discussion.

His voice carried in the wind, 'The plan needs to change. It's not my fault.' His hand was flailing in the air, then he shuffled from foot to foot before spinning round. Immediately he spotted Isla watching him and within seconds he hung up his call and turned back towards the barrow. Isla observed him until he was out of sight.

'What do you think of Nate?' asked Isla, looking towards Felicity as she held the door to the boot room open.

'Very easy on the eye,' she smiled. 'Which always helps ... why?'

'Because I'm beginning to get a feeling he's not what he seems,' Isla answered, kicking off her shoes. She took one last glance across the courtyard, but Nate was gone.

Chapter 34

S lumped on the settee in her faithful old trackies and sloppy
sweater, Isla was flicking between the TV channels. She
sighed, so many channels and still nothing decent to watch.
Drew had long gone to bed, but she'd stayed up creating her
business Facebook page, and Foxglove Camping was now
official. Martha was out with Aggie and the children were
tucked up fast asleep.

In the morning Pete was arriving to shear the alpacas' fleeces
and they were to be transported to the fashion-house buyer
first thing on Monday. Receiving payment couldn't come quick
enough; the second the money landed in their account the
mortgage arrears could be paid, along with the loan repayments, and the weight would be lifted off their shoulders.

Drew was adamant he would be in the fields tomorrow to
oversee the shearing operation and Fergus had promised Isla
he would keep an eye on him and pack him back to the
farmhouse if he overdid it.

Isla switched off the TV and pulled on her coat. She wanted
to check on the baby alpaca one last time before heading off
to bed.

As she padded towards the stable the security light lit up the courtyard. She could hear an owl hooting in the distance and the whistle of the wind through the trees. Pushing open the old creaky door to the stable block, she walked towards the alpacas. The heat lamp was still on only as a precaution and the stable was lit. She smiled and rested her arms on the stable door. It was a picture-card moment, Gemma was outstretched on the hay with Mop nestled close to her chest. Isla couldn't wait to get them both back out into the meadow. Mop was all legs and curls and Isla wanted to sneak into the stable and pick her up and give her a squeeze. Her heart swelled with happiness, Mop was so utterly gorgeous.

In the village nothing more had been mentioned about the Kerr brothers. They hadn't even turned up for their father's funeral and Isla was feeling more positive that they wouldn't be coming back to reclaim the alpacas. Things were finally beginning to settle down, and if the shower block was improved as per the councillor's bullet points, there was a good chance Alfie could push the licence through for the summer trade, meaning she could open up even more vans and really make a go of her new business venture. Everything was finally coming good.

Isla whispered goodnight to the sleeping alpacas and checked the water trough was fresh and full and the hay was clean. Rory was coming to check on them both during his rounds in the morning, and Isla took one last look over her shoulder towards the sleeping alpacas and tiptoed back towards the door.

'No, it's tonight, it's all systems go.' Isla stopped dead in her tracks and put her back to the wall. It was a voice she recognised ... Nate's voice.

With her heart thumping against her ribcage, she held her breath and slowly peered around the corner and prayed with all her might she wouldn't be seen.

Luckily, Nate had his back to her and was talking into his mobile.

'They've no clue. Now, don't contact me again on this phone, do you hear me?' His voice meant business. Not the nice kind Nate she knew, now his presence and the sound of his voice unnerved Isla.

She watched in silence as he hung up. She followed him and he quickly disappeared down the driveway towards Love Heart Lane. Her mind was a whirl and her gut feeling swirling in the pit of her stomach was telling her that something was not quite right.

As soon as he was out of sight she hurried back towards the farmhouse and, taking herself by surprise, she swiftly locked the door behind her. Isla couldn't actually remember the last time she'd ever locked the door. The crime rate in Heartcross was virtually non-existent. Hanging her coat on the peg in the boot room, her heart was beating fast, the conversation playing over in her mind. She'd no idea who Nate was talking to or what the conversation was about, but the tone in his voice hadn't been pleasant.

Switching off the lights downstairs, she climbed the stairs and hovered outside Martha's room. Lightly rapping on the door, there was no answer, but the door was ajar and Isla peered around it. Martha was tucked up in bed already fast asleep after her night out.

Damn, she wanted to talk to her.

Nate's conversation played over and over in her mind and before she could think about it anymore, she found herself shaking Drew.

'Drew ... Drew, wake up.' Isla shook him lightly then noticed the sleeping tablets at the side of the bed. He'd been taking them due to the discomfort of his leg. 'Drew!'

But still nothing. He was out for the count.

Double damn.

'For God's sake, Isla ... what is wrong with you?' she muttered crossly to herself. 'Everything in life isn't a drama.' For all she knew, Nate was probably arguing with an old girlfriend and wanted some privacy. Who knew? Granted, she hadn't liked the tone of his voice, and she wasn't sure what he was doing in the yard late at night, but maybe he'd been to check on the lambs and the alpacas ... there could be a perfectly reasonable explanation.

Isla was thankful Drew hadn't woken up, she was being ridiculous, and after quickly getting changed and brushing her teeth she climbed into bed and snuggled under the duvet. Isla tossed and turned for nearly forty-five minutes, but found it difficult to fall asleep. She willed herself to sleep, but it was no use; her eyes just wouldn't close.

The house was in silence as she crept downstairs and made herself a cup of tea. Sipping from the mug, she stared out over the yard while grabbing a chocolate biscuit from the barrel on the side. And that's when she saw a shadow in the yard. Isla froze.

Drew was out for the count and she didn't want to put Martha or the boys in any danger, but she didn't have a good feeling about this. Her heart was beating fast as she pressed Fergus's number on her phone and willed him to pick up.

His half-asleep and confused voice answered after three rings.

'Fergus, it's me.'

'Flick?'

'No, Isla.'

'Isla ... is everything okay?'

'No, I think there are trespassers in the field.'

'Okay, where's Drew?'

'Asleep, I can't wake him, he's taken sleeping tablets.'

'Okay, I'm on my way. Ring the police, better to be safe than sorry,' he ordered and hung up.

Immediately Isla called the police. She knew she should attempt to wake Drew again, but she was glued to the spot watching out of the window.

As she heard a rap on the back door, Isla's heart nearly burst from her chest.

'Isla it's me, Fergus,' came the muffled whisper.

'Thank God,' Isla exhaled, quickly opening the door, relieved to see Fergus's face.

'You're right, there's something going on in the field. It might just be youths messing about.'

'We know all the youths in Heartcross ... Fergus, I've got an uneasy feeling about this.'

'Try not to worry. I've rung Rory and Alfie and they are on their way over, just in case we need them. Did you phone the police?'

Isla nodded, feeling sick to her stomach.

'Fergus, I think this has got something to do with Nate.'

'Nate ... why?' he asked, keeping a watchful eye out of the window.

Isla told Fergus about the short conversation she'd overheard on the phone when she had been checking on the alpacas.

'That could mean anything. Probably an old girlfriend.'

'What are you pair doing?'

Isla and Fergus spun round to see a bleary-eyed Martha tugging tightly at her dressing-gown belt as she stood in the doorway.

'Christ on a bike, what are you doing sneaking around at this time of night?' Isla said, holding her hand up to her thumping chest. 'You nearly gave me a heart attack!'

'I nearly gave you a heart attack? What are you doing? I just got up to go to the toilet and could hear whispering. Well?'

'Something isn't right Gran,' said Isla in a hushed whisper. 'There's movement in the field and we can see torch lights,' her voice faltered.

'It might be something or nothing,' added Fergus, making a vain attempt to keep everything calm. 'Rory and Alfie are on their way over. I've told them to cut round the back, through Heartwood Cottage instead of up the main drive.'

Martha stared at Fergus. 'You are thinking it's more something than nothing if you've called for back-up. Shouldn't we be calling the police?'

'The police have been called.'

'So, it is something more than nothing. I'll put the kettle on,' said Martha, switching the light on.

'Gran! Turn the light off now. We don't want to draw attention to the fact we're up,' insisted Isla in a frantic whisper before launching herself towards the switch faster than Usain Bolt sprinting the hundred metres.

Martha put her hands up and mouthed 'Sorry.' Then she asked, 'What do you think they are after?'

'The alpacas,' said Isla and Fergus in unison.

Martha's eyes widened as their words registered, but before she could reply Fergus's phone vibrated.

'It's Rory, they're here.'

The door opened and Rory and Alfie sidled through the door like a couple of burglars.

'Where's Nate?' asked Isla, her eyes wide.

Rory and Alfie exchanged a glance, 'He's gone, there's no trace of him in the house.'

'So, all this has something to do with him,' exclaimed Isla, feeling foolish that she'd given him a job on the farm.

'Surely not. He seemed a decent young man,' added Martha in utter amazement.

Something caught Fergus's eye, and he put his finger to his lips to hush everyone, then forcefully pulled Isla to the floor where she landed on her bum. She stifled her urge to yell. The others crouched too and waited.

Through the kitchen window flashed a torch light. Isla

prayed with all her might that they didn't try the farmhouse door and screwed her eyes up tight as she forced herself to breathe. All she could think about was keeping her sleeping boys safe.

Two silhouettes were lingering outside the window. Isla's heart was racing. Fergus was watching from the corner of the window. 'They are moving away.'

'What's that noise?' Isla asked, as a slow rumbling started up. Everyone strained to hear.

Rory edged his way next to Fergus and carefully glanced out. 'It's a van, there's a bloody van coming up the drive, but the lights are switched off.'

'Is it safe to look?' asked Isla.

'I think so,' answered Rory as the others joined him.

'We need to move quickly. Where are the damn police? Ring them back and go and wake Drew. Isla ... Martha ... you stay here,' instructed Rory with authority.

'I'm not staying here, I'm coming with you,' insisted Isla.

'This really isn't the time for an argument, Isla.'

'So don't argue with me.'

Martha had already picked up the phone and was telephoning the police. She put her hand over the receiver, 'I'll wake Drew.'

Fergus nodded as they moved quickly towards the door. He lowered his voice, 'We'll head down to the field behind the barn.'

They all nodded and followed Fergus in single file in complete silence. Isla was right behind him with Rory and Alfie bringing up the rear.

They walked swiftly, gathering behind the ponies' shelter at the far end of the field.

'Look,' pointed Alfie. 'There's someone over there.'

Fergus squinted, 'It looks like there are at least four of them.'

'And there's someone sat behind the wheel of the van.'

The driver's door was open and the guy lit up a cigarette and threw the match on to the ground.

'I think you should go back, Isla,' said Fergus, clearly concerned for her safety.

'I'm staying put,' Isla replied, feeling fury, her voice defiant, even though she was terrified.

'They're herding up the alpacas,' whispered Alfie.

The torch lights were bouncing up and down the field and the sound of the men's voices was muffled.

Blinking through the darkness, Fergus tapped Isla's arm, 'Look.'

'Nate,' Isla breathed, not wanting to believe it.

There he was, standing in the middle of the field, waving to the rest of the gang to lead the alpacas into the back of the van.

Isla repositioned herself, her eyes had refocused in the darkness and she could see him clearly now. 'I'm going to bloody kill him. How dare he?' Rage enveloped her whole body.

Fergus lunged forward but it was too late, Isla was already sprinting towards the gang.

'Isla, stop!' instructed Rory through gritted teeth.

Isla heard footsteps behind her as Fergus rugby tackled her, bringing her to the ground with a bump. She yelped.

For a second, the torch lights swung round in their direction.

'Do not move,' said Rory in a hushed whisper. With bated breath, they waited, their hearts hammering against their chests.

They could hear the men talking and the driver was on his mobile. Even though they couldn't hear the conversation they could tell the man was irate, as he kept throwing his hand up into the air.

'Now what?' asked Rory as Fergus led Isla back to them.

'The police should be here by now.' A knot of anxiety clutched Isla's stomach. 'We can't just stand here and watch them load the alpacas into the van. We need to do something.' She looked exasperated.

'Nate's moving,' whispered Alfie. 'Look, where's he going?'

'Towards the stable, he's taking the baby ... Nate knows the baby's worth.' Isla was distraught. 'Please do something ... he can't take her.'

'Fergus, you head towards the main entrance with Isla and shut the gates, that'll slow them down. Alfie, you come with me to the stable,' instructed Rory. 'And stay low.'

'I'm staying put,' insisted Isla, already heading towards the stable block in the pitch black, quickly followed by Rory and Alfie.

They peered round the side of the barn and watched in silence as Nate disappeared inside. They followed him. Nate unhooked two pony harnesses from the tack area and headed straight towards the mother alpaca and her baby.

'He's got a damn cheek,' said Isla, taking a furtive glance from behind the wall.

Despite knowing they should wait for the police, Isla's instincts kicked in. 'There's three of us ... you stay back.'

Before the boys could object, Isla stepped out of the darkness. 'Hi Nate,' she said, sounding as friendly as she could under the circumstances.

Nate spun round, looking alarmed.

'Sorry if I startled you. I'm just here to check on mother and baby. Earlier she seemed a bit under the weather.' Isla swallowed hard and tried to act as normal as possible. Her hands were sweaty and she could feel her pulse throbbing in the side of her head as she tried to keep her breathing steady.

Nate look like a startled rabbit caught in headlights.

'What are you doing here this time of night? What's with the harnesses?' Isla nodded towards his hand.

They locked eyes. Nate was silent.

Suddenly, the stable door burst open and sirens could be heard in the background. Drew was standing in the doorway. 'The police are on their way.'

Nate lunged forward and Rory stepped out of the wings. Nate threw a punch at Rory, knocking him off balance. Stumbling, Rory tried to throw a punch back but landed with a bump on the ground. Alfie stepped out into the gangway and Nate looked startled, picking up a shovel resting against the stable door. Alfie put his hands in the air. 'Don't do anything daft, mate.'

Nate stared at him with a look of anger and took a slow

step towards Alfie just as Isla ran at him from behind and pushed him with all her might. 'You bastard!' she screamed. Nate lost his grip on the shovel and swung round.

'You step away from Isla,' ordered Rory, dodging a blow from Nate as Alfie grabbed the shovel and Nate made a run for it. Drew tried to swipe him with his crutch as Nate stormed past, but it didn't hinder him. He disappeared into the darkness.

'Scum,' bellowed Rory after him as Alfie held him back.

The blue flashing lights reflected off the farmhouse windows, and shouting could be heard in the field.

'Let the police take care of it now,' said Alfie, letting go of Rory's coat.

Isla ran straight into the arms of Drew, she was shaking. Tears stung her eyes. 'He nearly took them.'

Drew hugged his wife, 'And what are you doing tackling him? He's dangerous ... and where is Fergus?' asked Drew, looking around.

Just at that second, they heard the sound of screeching tyres and they all hurried out into the courtyard.

They saw three police cars surrounding the field, the headlights shining directly at the rustlers.

'Look,' Alfie pointed. Three men were sitting in the front of the van, its engine revving.

Drew snagged a look around the field, 'Where's Nate?' he asked.

'No idea,' answered Rory.

The commotion from the field carried in the wind.

'Can anyone see Fergus?' asked Drew.

'I'm here, mate,' Fergus tapped Drew on his back.

'Thank God.'

'They were definitely after the alpacas. Is the baby safe?' asked Fergus.

'Yes, mother and baby are safe ... but Nate is AWOL ...'

They watched in silence as the police officers gathered at the side of the field. One was talking into his radio and another began walking towards them.

'Drew Allaway?'

'That's me?'

'Is there another way out of this field?'

'Only if you want to swim the river.'

The officer nodded his understanding and returned to his colleagues.

All of them watched on helplessly as the officers shouted instructions between themselves.

'Are the alpacas in the back of the van?' asked Isla, taking an uncertain look and feeling sick to her stomach.

'I'm afraid so,' Drew couldn't hide the worry in his voice.

Isla buried her face into Drew's shoulder.

'Oh my God ... the van is moving ... they are going to drive through the fence,' Drew's voice was manic.

Isla looked up and they watched in horror as the van's wheels spun and kicked up mud. It began hurtling towards the fence, slipping and sliding. The men inside were being tossed around. Within seconds the van crashed through the fence, only slowing for a second, splintered wood resting on the bonnet, before it began to pick up speed again, skidding on the gravel of the drive.

'They're going to escape,' stated Alfie.

All eyes were fixed on the van.

'Please stop them ... please stop them,' frantically muttered Isla, jumping out of her skin as a horrific sound echoed all around, the grating of metal. The van had been brought to a halt by a stinger, a spiked metal ribbon placed across the drive by the police. The van tyres were punctured, and the van came to an abrupt halt.

The doors were flung open and the men took their chance in running. But the police took chase and the criminals were soon pulled to the ground, all were handcuffed and escorted to the police car.

'Nate's still out there somewhere,' said Isla. 'Where is he?'

Fergus hurried towards the officers, 'There's still one out there ... somewhere.'

One policeman began to talk into his radio whilst another addressed Drew. 'Are we able to go inside?'

Drew nodded, and they made their way back towards the farmhouse where Martha was waiting anxiously.

'Is anyone hurt?' she asked, the second the door opened.

'We are all fine, don't worry Martha,' reassured Drew. 'Rory and Alfie are just coming.'

Right on cue, they walked through the door.

'Oh my, your face is cut,' said Martha, looking alarmed. 'I'll get you something to put on it.'

'Honestly, I'm fine,' said Rory, not wanting any fuss.

'I watched it all through the window – it was like something off the TV. I'll put the kettle on, tea is always good in a crisis.' Martha busied herself while the policeman positioned himself at the kitchen table. Everyone else pulled out a chair.

There was a knock on the back door, and everyone looked up as another policeman popped his head around the door. 'The alpacas can be released from the van.'

Rory stood up, 'Hold my tea Martha, I'll go and check them over.'

Drew gave Rory a grateful nod. 'Thanks, mate.'

Martha hurried over with a pot of tea and placed it on the table, followed by a plate of chocolate biscuits.

'I'm Constable Williams from the rural crime team. What a night,' he looked around the table at all the worn-out, stressed-out faces.

'There's still a man out there,' Drew was irate and pointed towards the door.

'My men are looking for him now. He can't get far. There's only one way in and one way out of Heartcross, unless he fancies taking his chances over the mountain pass. And we are doing everything to make sure the man is caught and arrested, Mr Allaway,' reassured Constable Williams. 'These rustlers are professionals. They know what they are looking for and the value of your stock.'

'That man turned up out of nowhere and tried to make himself indispensable in our lives,' Isla felt maddened.

'Have you got a name?' asked the officer, poising his pen on his open notebook.

'Nate ...'

'Does this Nate have a surname?'

Isla shrugged and looked towards the others. No-one answered.

'How could I have been so stupid,' Isla exhaled and rubbed her face in her hands. Martha squeezed her shoulder.

Constable Williams looked around the table. 'Don't beat yourself up about it. Like I said, these type of men know what they are doing. They use their charm and prey on innocent people. You're decent people. Why wouldn't you see the good in someone?'

Isla's statement to the police took forty-five minutes and she felt battered by the end of it. Drew reached over and pulled her in for a hug. 'We have the herd and Rory will make sure they aren't traumatised, and mother and baby are both safe in the stable.'

Isla nodded.

'In the last few months rustling has been on the increase again. One hundred and fifty sheep were stolen just under a week ago from Young's Farm, over in Glensheil,' informed Constable Williams.

'We know it,' said Drew.

'White-faced Lleyn and black-faced North of England Mules. It's on the increase ... animals snatched by thieves during the last year was a huge cost to farmers ... 6.6 million pounds. It's a lucrative steal if you get away with it.'

Fergus let out a low whistle.

'But I have to admit, alpacas are a new one on us,' said Constable Williams.

'That prize-winning herd out there is worth more than any ewes,' chipped in Drew.

'From what you've told me, Isla, they've targeted you and Foxglove Farm for a reason. They knew the alpacas were here.'

'We think the alpacas are the stolen herd from Clover Farm,' blurted Isla.

'You've lost me now,' said the constable. 'Are you saying the herd out there is the herd from ...' He flicked back through his notebook.

'James Kerr's farm. I handed over cash to a man who called in the teashop trying to sell them.' As soon as the words came out of her mouth, she shook her head in disbelief, it sounded so far-fetched. No wonder Drew had been mad at her. She hadn't thought it through at all.

'Is that the usual practice for purchasing livestock, Mrs Allaway?'

Isla shamefully shook her head, 'No, I just didn't think. Oh my God, it makes sense now.' Her eyes widened, and she tapped Drew's arm.

Everyone looked towards Isla.

'Nate looking irate on his phone. The alpacas were being sheared tomorrow.'

Drew looked puzzled, 'And?'

'Nate needed to steal the alpacas tonight. Whether he ended up working here by accident or whether he was planted here, my guess is, he knew the bloke that sold them to me. I hand the money over, they steal them back and no doubt do it all over again with another farmer. But if those alpacas were sheared tomorrow, just think of all the money they would have lost from the fleeces. They needed to move quickly.'

'And Nate knew that he needed to steal the alpacas tonight, because he heard us say Pete had changed the time. If the alpacas had lost their coats, that would have been thousands lost.' Drew shook his head in disbelief.

'Do you know where this ...' Constable Williams looked towards his notepad. 'Nate ... any clue to where he's from?'

Isla shrugged, 'Your guess is as good as ours. For all we know it might not even be his real name, and he spoke with an Irish accent ... maybe he put that on too.'

Drew rubbed his face with his hands and sighed.

Constable Williams' radio began to crackle, and everyone looked up. He pressed down the button, 'Go ahead.'

'We've picked up the suspect on the bridge heading towards Glensheil, carrying a black holdall.'

Everyone let out a cheer.

'We are taking him to the station now.'

Constable Williams was still talking into his radio as Isla hugged Drew again. 'Thank God,' she said, feeling relieved.

The door opened and Rory walked in, 'What's going on?'

'Nate's been caught on the bridge.'

Rory exhaled, 'I hope they throw the book at him.'

'Let's hope so,' said Martha, handing Rory a steaming mug of tea which he gratefully accepted.

'And in other news,' continued Rory, 'the alpacas are all safe and well. I've let them out in the far field, where all fences seem to be intact.'

'Thanks Rory, you're a superstar,' said Isla.

Constable Williams cut in the conversation, 'I've everything I need for now. I'll be back over in the morning with an update but for now ...' he glanced at his watch. 'I suggest you all try and get some sleep.'

He stood up and slipped his notepad in his pocket and headed outside.

'Come on, let's go home,' said Fergus, tapping Alfie on the back before glancing up at the clock. 'I'll be back milking the cows in less than three hours,' he joked.

'Honestly, we can't thank you enough for everything that you've all done for us tonight,' Isla said, with tears in her eyes. They really were so lucky to have friends like this, and a community that looked out for each other.

'What are friends for?' smiled Fergus, slipping his arms into his coat.

'What a night,' exclaimed Isla, once the door had closed behind them.

'What a night indeed,' added Martha, placing the empty mugs in the sink. 'I'll wash these up in the morning. I'm off to bed, I suggest you pair do the same.'

'Night, Gran.'

Martha popped a kiss on top of her granddaughter's head. 'And can we try and keep drama to a minimum in the future, I'm getting too old for all this malarkey.'

'I second that,' laughed Isla.

'And I third it,' chipped in Drew.

Isla and Drew sat in silence, reflecting on the night.

'I'm sorry,' said Isla, taking Drew by the hand. 'I'm sorry about buying the alpacas, letting a stranger into our lives.'

'I think we lost our way for a wee while but tonight has taught me one thing,' Drew paused and locked eyes with Isla.

'Our boys, you and Martha are the most important things in my life and without any of you ...' Drew swallowed down the lump in his throat as he blinked away his tears. 'From now on, we have to promise each other ... we share everything, otherwise this team isn't a team.'

Isla agreed, stroking away the tears from his cheeks with her thumb.

'And another thing I've learnt, as a man – it's okay not to be okay. It's okay to cry ... it's okay to ask for help,' Drew said.

'We need more quality time together ... Drew-and-Isla time.'

'Agreed,' said Drew.

Isla's heart lifted, the connection between them had been mended, they'd found each other again.

'Now come on, let's get to bed, Pete will be here tomorrow.'

'Today,' corrected Isla with a chuckle.

'Today,' smiled Drew. 'The alpacas will be sheared, the fleeces sold, and the mortgage paid ... fresh start.'

'Fresh start,' Isla wholeheartedly agreed.

'I love you, Isla Allaway.'

Feeling the warmth of love rush through her body, Isla planted a kiss on his perfect lips. 'I love you too,' she said.

Chapter 35

The next morning Isla sneaked back into bed after milking the cows, and fell straight back to sleep. She was woken a couple of hours later by Drew kissing her softly on the lips.

'Are you awake?' he whispered.

'I am now ...' she said, grinning, turning and snuggling deeply into his chest.

'Last night I had the strangest dream. Someone was trying to steal the alpacas,' Drew said.

Isla swiped his chest playfully. 'We best get up, you know. Constable Williams could be round at any time.'

'Do you smell that?' asked Drew, sniffing the air. 'Your gran is worth her weight in gold.'

'I couldn't have managed without her in the last few weeks. Family is all that matters ...'

'And our best friends,' added Drew.

'We live in the best village with the best people.'

'And I have the best wife.'

'And don't you forget it!'

Isla threw back the duvet and pulled on Drew's old sloppy sweater over her head. 'Come on, get up.'

'I'm coming,' he said reluctantly, wishing he could stay in the warmth of his bed for at least another hour. 'It's not that easy with a broken leg.'

As they padded down the stairs, they were greeted by the aroma of sizzling sausages and bacon. Finn was helping Martha place the glasses on the table while Angus was strapped into his high chair.

'Good morning,' said Isla, breezing into the kitchen.

'Martha, you are just a superstar,' Drew said, balancing on his crutches. He puckered up his lips and kissed her on her cheek. 'I could get used to this.'

Martha smiled, 'Could you now. I was hoping you pair would look after me in my old age.'

'Old ... you will outlive us all.'

'Daddy, Great-granny has been telling us about the rustling alpacas.' Finn's eyes were wide and everyone laughed.

'Alpaca rustlers,' corrected Drew, smiling at his son. 'But they are all safe now.'

'Pete's already here,' said Martha, nodding towards the window.

'You're joking? I best get out there,' said Drew.

'You sit down, Fergus is already here too. Have some food first.'

Drew saluted, his stomach was rumbling and Martha did always cook up a good breakfast.

'How you both feeling?' she asked.

'Tired,' Isla and Drew replied in harmony, then laughed.

The last couple of weeks had been bedlam, but as Isla pulled out a chair and sat down at the table, she looked around at her gorgeous family and her heart swelled with contentment.

'This farm is going to go from strength to strength,' announced Isla from nowhere.

'You better believe it,' said Drew, kissing his wife on her cheek.

'Eww,' burst Finn, covering his face up with his hands, then peeping through his fingers, causing Angus to giggle.

'I love you lot, just for the record,' announced Isla, placing a noisy raspberry on Finn's cheek.

Martha took the plates out of the Aga and placed them on the table. They all began tucking into a hearty breakfast when Fergus appeared at the back door.

'Morning mate, grab some food,' said Drew, nodding towards the spare chair at the table.

'Thanks, but I'm in the middle of helping Pete ...'

'What is it?' asked Isla, noticing the wide-eye look of worry on Fergus's face. 'Those scumbags haven't been released without charge, have they?'

'You have a visitor.'

Isla and Drew noticed there was a figure standing behind Fergus.

'Who is it?' asked Drew.

Fergus moved out of the way to reveal Gracie Maxwell standing behind him.

Surprised, Isla dropped her cutlery onto her plate. 'Gracie, I thought you'd be in the South of France by now, enjoying your retirement.' Isla noticed the exchange of worried glances between Drew and Martha.

'Isla, Drew, Martha ...' Gracie acknowledged them all before turning back towards Isla. 'Something came up, I bet you didn't expect to see me again so soon.'

Isla's heart was thumping fast as she tried to keep her cool. 'What can we do for you?'

'I believe you had a bit of trouble last night.'

'How do you know?' asked Drew.

'News travels fast between farmers.'

'Gracie is married to a farmer,' chipped in Isla, hoping this conversation wasn't going where she thought it was going.

'Cup of tea?' asked Martha, pulling out a chair for Gracie and sliding a mug in front of her. She clasped her hands together and rested them on the table. Immediately the good mood in the kitchen had evaporated and the atmosphere was tense. If Gracie was here to claim the alpacas back, the farm was in danger of losing its financial security once more.

'I'll take the children into the living room,' said Martha, scooping Angus out of his high chair and grasping Finn's hand.

Gracie eyed Isla. To say that Isla was a nervous wreck was an understatement.

'My guess is, you've been looking after something that belongs to my boys.'

Isla quietly inhaled and grabbed Drew's hand under the table.

'How about you tell me all about it, as I'm surprised that you didn't divulge that Foxglove Farm has suddenly become an alpaca farm when you saw me outside Clover Cottage.'

Uncomfortable silence hung in the air.

Isla looked towards Drew who cleared his throat and took control of the situation.

'James Kerr was your former husband. I'm assuming you have no claims to his estate. Your boys were in jail.' Drew stated the facts.

Gracie unhooked her bony fingers and narrowed her eyes and pointed at them, 'You stole from my boys.'

'We didn't steal anything from your boys. We bought those alpacas in good faith.' Drew was thankful his voice was calm.

'And I bet you were rubbing her hands together, prize alpacas ... thousands landing at your feet, not to mention a contract with a fashion house. I bet you thought you'd won the lottery.' Gracie didn't take her eyes off the pair of them.

'Well, where are your boys, Gracie?' spluttered Isla, beginning to lose her cool. 'When they were released, they didn't even contact you, you said so yourself.'

'Those alpacas are not your property.'

'They aren't yours either, Gracie Maxwell.'

Everyone looked towards the door, where Constable Williams was standing in the doorway with another police officer standing behind him.

Gracie scraped her chair back but there was nowhere to run.

The police officer stepped forward, 'Gracie Maxwell ... you are under arrest on suspicion of sheep and alpaca rustling. You do not have to say anything, but it may harm your defence if you do not mention, when questioned, something which you later rely on in court. Anything you do say may be given in evidence. Do you understand?' asked Constable Williams.

A hollow laugh escaped from Gracie's mouth as the police officer led her outside to an awaiting car.

'What's going on? What's this got to do with Gracie Maxwell?' asked Drew, perplexed, watching the kerfuffle as she was led away.

Constable Williams pulled out a chair and Isla poured him a mug of tea.

'Mrs Maxwell and her husband have been under surveillance for the last six months. They've mainly been operating in the Lake District, running a lucrative criminal enterprise – livestock rustling – along with her nephew Nathan Kerr ... Nate.'

Drew blew out a breath, 'Nate was a Kerr?'

'Afraid so, and wanted by the police for numerous crimes.'

'The apple doesn't fall far from the tree,' stated Isla, feeling a fool. 'I suppose he wasn't even Irish?'

'Most certainly not Irish. He had no steady job, his criminal record was growing and when James Kerr passed away, they thought they'd try their luck at claiming the farmhouse, with Nathan Kerr posing as one of his sons. But unbeknown to them, James Kerr had made a will, and the farm and Clover Cottage was not left to either of his errant sons.'

Isla blew out a breath, 'I bet they were gutted. Where are the Kerr brothers now?'

'From what we know, they haven't headed back to these parts. The guy who sold you the alpacas was Gracie's husband. The plan was, whoever they sold them to, they would fleece them of a lump sum, then steal the alpacas back and do it all again. Gracie still had acquaintances over in Glensheil who'd told her that James's health was deteriorating and mentioned the prize-winning herd, and that's when they moved from sheep and upped their game with the alpacas. Nate pretends he's looking for work, susses out the place and masterminds the plan of when to steal them back.'

'And when I broke my leg, I bet he thought all his Christmases had come at once,' added Drew, amazed at the nerve of the guy.

Martha popped her head around the door, 'There's a police car outside ... oh sorry,' she said, clocking Constable Williams sitting at the table. 'Where's Gracie gone?'

'Gracie's been arrested,' spilled Isla. 'The whole thing was masterminded by her. Nate is her nephew.'

Martha blew out a breath, 'You're kidding me.'

Isla shook her head, 'No, it's all true.'

'Well I never.'

'I'm not sure I want to know the answer to this,' said Isla, looking between Drew and Constable Williams. 'But what happens to the alpacas now? You mentioned a will?'

Knowing the alpacas were being sheared right at this very second and that there was a policeman sitting in their kitchen, Drew knew the outcome was more than likely bleak.

They all waited in anticipation as Constable Williams flipped open his notepad. 'James Kerr's will states that he left the alpacas in the care of ...' he scanned his notes.

Isla closed her eyes and willed him to hurry up.

'... Stuart Scott, the local vet practice. Apparently James held Stuart in high regard.'

Drew slumped back in his chair, Stuart was a family friend. 'That's that, then. We can't sell the fleeces.'

Isla knew what this meant for the farm, the initial injection of cash was lost. The mortgage arrears and loan could not be paid without that income.

Before they had time to ask any more questions, the back door was flung open. 'Morning!' said Rory, beaming from ear to ear. 'I've come with news.'

'I think Constable Williams has just beaten you to that snippet of information,' said Isla. 'We've just heard, your father is the proud owner of our prize-winning herd of alpacas.'

'Well, there's more.'

'I'm not sure I can take any more,' admitted Isla, her emotions were all over the place.

Rory pulled out a chair, 'Believe me, you really want to hear this! Drew, according to my father, many moons ago, your father, Mr Allaway Senior, loaned my father the money to buy his practice. The money was paid back, but if it wasn't for your father taking a chance on my father's dream, he would never have been able to build up his business. He was always grateful. He knows the financial difficulty you are in and wants to help. He's decided he's too old to run an alpaca farm, so ...'

'So?' asked Isla, her heart thumping against her ribcage, hoping this was good news.

'So, my father thinks they are already in the best hands. They are all yours!'

'Are you kidding us?' asked Isla, astonished.

'I'm definitely not kidding you. They are yours ... all yours.'

Isla let out a scream and jumped on Drew, hugging him tight.

'Mind the leg,' he said, laughing, as he hugged her back before outstretching his hand towards Rory.

'I ... we can't tell you how much this means to us.'

'We've been friends from the year dot and that's what friends do. You are the good guys and good guys always win.'

With a heartfelt thanks, Isla couldn't stop the happy tears from flowing down her face as she hugged Rory. 'I'm absolutely speechless, absolutely speechless.'

'That makes a change,' joked Drew.

'There's nothing more to worry about and I think you should release the mother and baby out into the paddock. Mop is strong enough now and she's an absolute beauty.' Rory turned to leave, happy that after their ordeal things were finally working out for Isla and Drew.

'I'll be off too,' said Constable Williams, standing up and shaking everyone's hand. 'I'll have great pleasure putting Gracie Maxwell away in a cell. It's been a long time coming.'

Drew beamed at Isla and flung his arms open. 'Come on, you two ... group hug,' he said, gesturing for Martha to join in.

'I told you I couldn't stand any more drama,' laughed Martha.

'We promise life will be plain sailing from now on! No more dramas!' confirmed Isla.

'Mum, Mum,' everyone turned around to find Finn standing in the doorway, wafting his nose. 'Angus stinks.'

'Now that's a drama I can deal with,' chuckled Martha.

'My turn,' insisted Isla. 'My turn.'

Chapter 36

Six weeks later

The letter box clanged, and Isla bent down to pick up the envelopes, junk ... junk ... junk ... then she saw the writing on the next envelope, 'Highlands Planning Department'. Her stomach lurched.

'Drew ... Drew!' she shouted at the top of her voice.

He was sat in the passenger seat of the truck, his leg was still in plaster, but he was due back in hospital on Monday to have the cast removed. It couldn't come quick enough for either of them.

Fergus was behind the wheel, they were on their way to the Saturday Farmers' market over in Glensheil. Fergus was just about to start the engine when he noticed in the mirror Isla running toward the truck, waving something in the air.

Drew wound down his window, 'Where's the fire?'

'That's not even funny, after recent events.'

He grinned, 'I'm only joking ... what's up?'

She waved the envelope in front of him. 'It's here ... it's from the Highlands Planning Agency.'

327

'Is this what I think it is?'

She nodded.

'Well, open it then.'

'I daren't ... what if?'

Drew shook his head in despair, 'Get it open, we won't know until you do.'

Isla slipped her finger under the edge of the envelope and tore it open. She held her breath as her eyes scanned the words as quickly as possible. There it was, the decision in black and white. Foxglove Camping was now official. The licence had been granted, which meant all the other caravans could be moved to the field and she could really put her new business on the map.

'We did it ... we did it!'

To Drew and Fergus's amusement, Isla began jumping up and down on the spot. 'Foxglove Camping has arrived!' she shouted happily, waving the envelope in the air.

Drew clambered out of the car and kissed his wife. 'I'm so proud of you.'

'I'm proud of me too,' she said, 'but I couldn't have done this without everyone's help and support ... and especially yours,' she said, kissing him.

For the last few weeks Drew, with the help of Fergus, had modernised the shower block and Isla had spent those weeks cleaning and scrubbing the other vans, while Martha had kitted them out with more home furnishings. Life was certainly good.

'And don't forget, you both need to be back by two o'clock, showered and ready,' Isla said, turning to Fergus.

'We'll do our best.'

'You need to do more than your best,' insisted Isla, giving Drew the look that meant, *Don't even think about being late.*

'As if I dare!'

'Eek, it's so exciting. Everything's coming together.'

Drew climbed back in the truck and Fergus started the engine. Fergus tooted the horn as he turned on to Love Heart Lane, leaving Isla waving and smiling like a Cheshire cat.

Before walking back to the farmhouse, Isla hung back and watched Finn and Esme in the field. They were laughing and leading Mop by her lead and harness over makeshift jumps they'd created from old crates. They were convinced they were going to win the 'Best in Show' prize at the Heartcross village fair, but Isla didn't want to burst their bubble, as she wasn't sure the baby alpaca would pass for a miniature pony.

Isla pulled her phone out of her pocket, she knew the teashop would be busy on a Saturday morning, but she was bursting to tell Flick her news.

'Flick, it's me, guess what!'

'Tell me ...' said Flick, hearing the excitement in Isla's voice.

'I've got the licence ... Foxglove Camping is official.'

'Isla, that's wonderful news! And what a day for it to land on your doorstep. Are you excited? What time do the first guests arrive?'

'Checking-in time is 3 p.m. onwards,' said Isla, sounding all official.

'Which gives us plenty of time for the grand opening. We'll bring the buffet over around 1.30 p.m., and Allie is bringing the bar!'

'I have friends working in all the best places!'

'Oh, and Alfie's got the local press involved too, so get yourself spruced up, we want lots of photos of you!'

'I best get my skates on,' said Isla, hanging up the phone.

'Gran, where are you?' There was no answer. 'Come on, little man,' she said, scooping up Angus. 'Let's go and find Great-granny. She can't have gone far.'

Kicking his legs, Angus gurgled.

'Are you chatting to me?' she said, smiling. 'You are chatting to me. You're growing up so fast.'

Isla stepped out into the courtyard. 'OMG!' She spun round as she took in the sight around her. There was bunting draped from the entrance of Foxglove Farm over every fence leading to the courtyard.

'Ta-dah!' said Martha, appearing from behind the tractor.

'Did you do this?'

'I might have had something to do with it,' she grinned.

'You are like Super Gran. It looks amazing!'

'How you feeling?' asked Martha, tapping Angus lightly on the nose.

'Excited! I can't wait for the first guests to arrive, and then we are booked solid for five weeks so far.'

'I knew you'd make this work. Good on you!'

'And what's in there?' asked Isla, noticing an oversized marquee just left of the orchard.

'Come and have a look.'

Inside the marquee, floral bunting criss-crossed the ceiling and tables were draped with beautiful polka-dot tablecloths, with an impressive number of hay bales scattered around as seats. Allie had set up a drinks bar on a long trestle table covered in a crisp white tablecloth, and in the corner was a cluster of balloons.

At that very second, Finn and Esme walked into the marque followed by Mop on a lead.

Isla couldn't help but smile, it was one of the funniest sights she'd ever seen.

'Great-gran, here's the tickets!' said an excited Finn, thrusting them into Martha's hand.

'Marvellous,' she said, taking them from Finn and placing them next to a little cash box. 'You just make sure they give you the right money.'

'We will,' enthused Finn.

Isla narrowed her eyes, 'What are you all up to?'

'Walk with Mop for 50p ... have a selfie with her. All my school friends have already bought tickets!'

'A businessman in the making! You have it all worked out,' Isla said proudly, ruffling the mass of curls on the top of Mop's head.

'Great-gran, what time are the jugglers arriving?'

'Jugglers, surely not?' interrupted Isla.

'And stilt walkers and a bouncy castle,' added Esme, pleased she'd provided the extra information.

'What?! Who has arranged all this?'

'Drew, of course!'

Stunned and amazed, Isla felt like she was floating on air. 'He's a keeper, that one.'

Isla squeezed her eyes shut and smiled, she couldn't believe how happy she felt. In the last few weeks the world seemed quite different somehow. The alpacas' fleeces had been delivered to the fashion house and the transaction had gone through without a hitch, meaning they had been able to pay off the mortgage debt and loan, and leaving a little profit over.

'And I nearly forgot,' said Isla, handing her gran the letter. 'Today is a good day.'

Martha's face beamed as she read that Isla had got her licence. 'This is excellent news ... come here,' she said, wrapping her arms around her granddaughter and hugging her tight.

'I feel like I'm in this little happy bubble and I want to float around in it forever.'

'And you will! Come on, we need to get changed,' said Martha, taking Angus from Isla's arms.

They began to amble back towards the farmhouse, when Isla had to air something that had been on her mind for a short while. 'And what about you, Gran?'

'What do you mean, what about me?' Martha looked towards Isla.

'I've never known you stay in one place for very long. Will you be moving on again soon?' Isla hoped not, she knew she didn't want to be without her. Martha had become a huge part of their lives.

'I think at my age it's about time I settled down ... what do you think?'

Isla rolled her eyes, 'Thank God for that!' she said, relieved, as they both heartily laughed.

Isla watched nervously out of the farmhouse window, with Drew standing by her side. She felt happy and nervous. The idea for the camping had been born on impulse, but now it was very much reality.

'All those people are coming to support you,' said Drew, wrapping his arms around her waist and resting his chin on the top of her head. The villagers were sauntering up the long drive of Foxglove Farm with the sun beating down on their faces.

'Is that ... is that Alfie and Polly together?' asked Isla, narrowing her eyes. 'They are holding hands!'

'First date, apparently,' answered Drew.

'OMG, and is that Rona with ... what's his name? That guy from Tinder.'

'It looks that way,' said Drew, grinning. 'And before I forget,' he said, skimming his eyes over Isla's outfit, 'you look amazing ... I got this for you.' Drew reached inside his pocket and brought out a small burgundy box.

Immediately, Isla's heart fluttered.

'What is it?'

'Open it.'

Isla slowly lifted the lid and gasped. Inside was the most elegant delicate diamond ring she'd ever seen.

'Drew, it's beautiful, absolutely beautiful,' she said, goose pimples prickled her skin, her eyes welling with happy tears.

'It's an eternity ring. It's me and you forever, Isla.'

'Damn right, Drew Allaway.'

He took the ring out of the box and slipped it on Isla's finger. She held her hand up in front of her eyes, and the tears began to roll.

'You can't cry, your public awaits,' said Drew, quickly

rummaging in his pocket and dabbing Isla's cheeks with a tissue.

'It's just ...'

'It's just what?'

'It's just that I love you so much and it hurts ... in a good way.'

Drew beamed and kissed the tip of her nose, 'The boy did well ... come on,' he said, leading her by her hand. 'We need to go and greet everyone.'

As Isla stepped outside the farmhouse, Martha handed her a glass of fizz. 'I'll go and wait on the other side of the bridge and once you've cut the ribbon and people wander over to the vans, I'll be there handing out the champers! Enjoy your moment ... you deserve it ... you both deserve it.' Martha kissed them both on the cheek and made her way over to the orchard.

Isla couldn't believe the number of people that had gathered outside the orchard. She was beginning to feel a little anxious, but all her fears were eradicated the second she stepped in front of everyone and they all cheered. Isla felt like royalty standing there, all these people had turned up for her.

Drew thrust his crutch up into the air and hushed the crowd, 'Follow us!' Isla took Angus from Felicity's arms, who'd been minding him, and slipped her other arm around Drew's waist. 'I feel so happy,' she whispered.

As they led everyone towards the orchard, Isla stopped in her tracks. On either side of the bridge were beautiful bay trees dressed with sparkling fairy lights, and tied between the two was a vibrant pink ribbon tied in a bow.

'Speech ... speech ...' everyone began to chant.

'I'm so proud of you,' Drew whispered in her ear, then stepped to the side.

Feeling emotional, Isla clutched on to Angus, bit down on her lip and held on to her happy tears. Her heart thumped with excitement as she took in the view of the people in front of her.

But before she could speak, Finn interrupted her. 'Mummy ... Mummy, don't forget to mention it's only 50p to have your photo taken with our Mop.' Finn and Esme were standing next to the red ribbon with Mop on her lead.

As the crowd roared with laughter, Isla gave them both the thumbs up. 'I want ten pounds' worth of tickets.'

Finn and Esme locked their wide eyes, 'WOW! We are rich!'

All of Isla's friends were standing near the front, clapping and giving her encouraging smiles. The crowd fell silent and her body trembled. 'This is truly amazing, thank you all for coming,' she took a deep breath. 'Little did I know when Drew and Fergus decided to waste money ... I mean, invest in some old decrepit vans ... that they would become my future ... our future.' Isla pointed towards Drew and Fergus and shook her head in jest.

Drew gave her a gooey smile.

'We all know that in the last few months, Foxglove Farm has had its moments: fires, broken legs, alpaca rustling, but throughout it all we have stayed strong.' Isla took a teary look towards Drew. 'We are family and that's what we do, love each other, support each other and look after each other.' Isla swallowed down a lump in her throat, she couldn't bring herself to speak and looked helplessly towards Drew, who immediately came to her rescue.

'I'm super proud of my wife,' he cleared his throat. 'She saw an opportunity and ran with it.' He took a breath, 'And I wouldn't be without her or our beautiful children. And Martha, of course. We are family!'

'Daddy ... Daddy,' shouted Finn, 'remember to tell them it's only 50p for a ticket to have a selfie with Mop.'

The whole crowd laughed again as Finn managed to break the high emotion. 'I kind of get the feeling you are going to be quids in,' Drew winked at Finn. 'Drink, eat, be merry and have a selfie with our baby alpaca. It's a must because one, you will love it and two, this time next year Finn and Esme are going to be millionaires ... mark my words.' Drew took a swift look towards Isla who managed to compose herself. Drew handed her the scissors.

Isla took a deep breath and juggled and balanced Angus on her hip. 'My first guests check-in in ...' She looked at her watch. 'In one hour, so in the meantime, there's free booze and food in the marquee, and all I ask in return is that you tell your friends and family that Foxglove Camping is well and truly open!'

With one snip the ribbon fell to the ground with a resounding cheer from the gathered crowd.

Isla watched proudly as everyone trundled over the bridge towards the orchard and was greeted by Martha handing out glasses of fizz.

Isla stood back with Drew. 'Are you happy?'

'Happy? More than happy. We make the best team, and that

will never change, but I was just wondering ... How much to hire that van for the night?' Drew asked with a wicked glint in his eye.

'You don't get a discount ... I have a living to earn!'

'I love you, Isla.'

'I love you more!'

The End

Can't wait to get back to Heartcross? Don't miss the next book in the unmissable *Love Heart Lane* series ...

Clover Cottage

Order now

A Letter from Christie

Dear Readers,

Firstly, if you're reading this letter, thank you for choosing to read *Foxglove Farm*.

I sincerely hope you enjoyed reading this book. If you did, I would be grateful if you'd write a review. Your recommendations can always help other readers to discover my books.

I can't believe my ninth book is published; writing for a living is truly the best job in the world and I love spending my time in a fictional land.

I'm particularly proud of this novel and the storyline was inspired by my recent trip to Peru where I trekked the Inca Trail with a group of awesome individuals. The characters Isla and Drew have been a huge part of my life for the last twelve months and also appear in *Love Heart Lane* but the good news is there will be more books to come based around the little village of Heartcross in the Scottish Highlands.

Huge thanks and much love to everyone who has been involved in this project. I truly value each and every one of you and it's an absolute joy to hear from all my readers via Twitter and Facebook.

Please do keep in touch!

Warm wishes,

Christie x

Acknowledgements

I'm pinching myself! I really can't believe my ninth book has been published and there is a long list of truly fabulous folk I need to thank who have been instrumental in crafting this novel into one I'm truly proud of.

I owe huge gratitude to my four beautiful children Emily, Jack, Roo and Mop for their continuous love and patience when I'm locked away for hours in my writing cave. I couldn't do the job I love without the support of my awesome gang. I love you.

Woody (my mad cocker spaniel) and Nellie (my labradoodle puppy) you are both my writing partners in crime and always by my side ... and when you're not I know you're up to mischief!

Endless love goes to my best friend Anita Redfern, who without a doubt is generous with her time day or night. She is simply the best and always makes me a happier human.

Thank you to Team Impulse for their endless support. The gorgeous Charlotte Ledger who goes far beyond the call of duty to encourage, inspire and make the magic happen.

My utterly fabulous editor Emily Ruston, who in the most amazing way makes all my books the best they can be.

My agent Kate Nash, for your energy, vision and continuous support in me.

Big love to Rowan Coleman and Alison May who gave me hope when I thought all hope was lost. The RNA is a wonderful, supportive family to be part of. Thank you.

High fives to Bella Osborne, Jules Wake and Kiren Parmar … you rock!

Team Barlow! Huge love to my merry band of supporters and friends, Lucy Davey, Jenny Berry, Tammi Forbes-Owen, Louise Speight, Sarah Lees, Catherine Snook, Suzanne Toner, Sue Miller, Emma Cox, Bhasker Patel and Kathy Ford. I am truly grateful for your constant sharing of posts and your support for my writing is truly appreciated.

Thank you to all the readers and bloggers for getting behind all my books in such an overwhelming way. Sharon Hunt, Judy Corker, Jeanie Nic Fhionnlaigh, Rose Harding, Collette Ingham, Sam Peacock, Sue Perring, Lucy Siddorn, Colin Bell, Sian Elizabeth Thompson, Tina Hillan-McMahon, Virginia Cole, Cheryl Hamann-Goss, Sally Tolson, Sue Callcutt, Felicity Turner, Claire Wright, Debbie Lichfield, Lewis Barlow, Kyle Barlow, Hollie Barlow, Sarah Rothman, Nicola Clough, Elizabeth Buckley, Kim Feasey, Alma Stelfox and Rachel McAllister. I am eternally grateful. Writing can be a solitary profession but when your book flies into the big wide world it's a team effort and I have the most amazing team of merry supporters!

Finally, this book wouldn't have been written if it wasn't

for Lisa Hall, Natalie Emmerick, Charlotte Seddon, Louanne Martin, Kiersten Jerrett, Kieran Millward and Tina Valeriano. This awesome gang of people provided the little spark of inspiration for this story whilst trekking the Inca Trail in Peru. We are family!

Thank you so much for all your lovely messages, emails and tweets, please do keep them coming. They mean the world to me.

I have without a doubt really enjoyed writing *Foxglove Farm* and I really hope you enjoy hanging out with Isla and Drew. Please do let me know!

Warmest wishes,

Christie x